I0672745

The Shadow of Evil

A Kayne Sorenson Mystery

Thomas Paul Severino

The Shadow of Evil

A Kayne Sorenson Mystery

Thomas Paul Severino

Copyright 2020

Pollywog Pond Communications

tomseverino.com

tomseverino100@gmail.com

The names, places, and incidents in this work of fiction are either a product of the author's imagination or used fictitiously. Any resemblance to actual persons, living or dead (except for satirical purposes), is entirely coincidental.

Cover: *Kilauea*, Wikipedia Commons

ISBN: 978-1-7343753-4-3

Thomas Paul Severino

Also by Thomas Paul Severino

The Kayne Sorenson Mysteries: The Quartet of Blood

Seed Blood

Tribal Blood

Stage Blood

Ancient Blood

The Kayne Sorenson Mysteries: The Quartet of Evil

The Evil Genius

The Shadow of Evil

The Pearl of Great Evil

The Evil League

The Kayne Sorenson Mysteries: The New Adventures

The Crystal Orb

The Flower of Gold

The Amazing Adventures of Rebecca Quinto

The Frozen Diva

The Lost Museum

The Last Maya

Thomas Paul Severino

In memory of my Dad, Orlando

I'm just a little Hawai'ian and a homeside Island boy

I want to go back to my fish and poi

I want to go back to my little grass shack in Kealakekua, Hawai'i

Where the Humuhumu, Nukunuku a puaa goes swimming by...

"My Little Grass Shack In Kealakekua, Hawai'i"

Bill Cogswell, Johnny Noble, Tommy Harrison

Introduction: <u>Hawaii</u>

Nick Sechi's Journal

Book Title: <u>Hawaii</u>

Author: James A. Mitchner

Copyright: November 20, 1959

Report Date: October 17, 1994

Prepared for: Sr. Mary Margaret O'Dwyer, SC

By: Nicola Michael Sechi, Grade 7A, St. Raymond Elementary School, Bronx, New York

This book is a novel, and that means it is fiction. The story is based on real events and history, and natural things like how the islands came up from the bottom of the sea. They were formed by erupting volcanoes.

They started under the sea, and the lava came out into the water and cooled. Layers of hard rock were built up section by section. When they got tall enough, they were islands above the ocean, which was the Pacific Ocean. But this did not stop the hot lava from coming out more. It cooled and piled up. This made bigger and taller islands, like eight or nine in all.

The wind and water eroded the rock and made soil. Plants and animals came to the islands in a lot of ways. Some grasses and other plants came because the seeds came floating ashore on the islands or came in bird shit.

Sister, my mother said I cannot write that in a book report, especially for a nun, but that is how it happened. And anyway, that is what James A. Mitchner says.

People came to Hawaii by rowing there from other islands in the Pacific. They were oppressed by other people. These people were called Polynesians. They had dark skin and worshipped false gods.

White people came from New England and were missionaries, and some fell in love with the sailors and fishermen who were in Hawaii. The missionaries tried to convert the pagan Hawaiians to Christianity, but they were Protestants and not Catholics. The royal people of the Hawaiians were called *Ali'i* and were very important to the people. That is a Hawaiian word that means royal.

There was a part in the book about the Chinese people who came to the Hawaiian Islands to work as farmers and grow pineapples and sugar. One guy gets leprosy, which is a disease that makes your fingers and, nose, and feet rot off. They make a leper colony on one of the Islands, Molokai, and he has to go there because everybody thinks he is gross, but he is still a human.

The Japanese came also and created businesses, and then Japan bombs Pearl Harbor in World War II. So, they put the Japanese in camps. All the different groups marry each other and have kids, and so you get the Hawaiian people of today.

There are a lot of brave men in this book and brave girls too. The bad guys were pretty evil in everything they did to the people, making them suffer and die and stuff.

One part that was very interesting and sad in a way was how the American business guys overthrew Queen Lili'uokalani and took her kingdom of Hawaii. First, it became a US Territory, and now it is our 50th state. It was a lot like stealing.

Sister, I really liked this book, and I swear I read the whole thing, and I did not have my mom rent the movie or watch it on TV. It is 1162 pages long, but I read it a lot at home, on the train, and at school. I even read it when we had a break during soccer practice (though not at matches), even though the guys made fun of me and called me a geek. Except, I will never tell on them because I am trying to become a man like my Dad taught me.

Two things – I wish I could write like James A. Mitchner. He is real good. Oh, yeah, and I want to go there someday, to Hawaii, I mean.

Grade: B+

Nicola,

This is a very good book report. You followed the form we went over in class and provided a comprehensive summary of the plot. I also liked your personal comments. Writing is a noble and enjoyable profession. Let's see if we can sharpen your skills as you continue your schooling. I foretell you will get to Hawaii one day. I hope you go there with someone you truly love and write about this beautiful place where they say love is everywhere.

On a personal note: Both your father and mother are correct. A mature person never carries tails. In addition, a good Catholic boy does not think, speak, or write profanities. Please remember that as you grow older. In that regard, an accomplished writer who is a mature person finds another way of expressing what he or she intends.

Finally, when you write a book report, it is important to spell the author's name correctly — "Michener," not "Mitchner."

Aloha, and God bless you.

Sr. Mary Margaret, SC

The Shadow of Evil

Prologue: The Earth-Eating Woman

The Summit Caldera, Kilauea, Hawai'i

"Yeah, Sam. It is definitely a hiker. How the hell did he get by the Park Guards?"

The response came from a walky-talky. Cell phone service at 4,000 feet was non-existent.

"Mace, you know the park is still recovering from the 2018 eruption episodes. 'S what happens when the infrastructure gets buried in massive lava flows. Gets hard to tell who is in the Park and who is not."

"The vog is going down the southwestern slope. Our man is easily seen from here. Thinking it's a guy, anyway. What the fuck? The ground out there is impossible to walk on, literally hot as hell. How is he even moving around? Talking melted shoes for sure."

At the beginning of the Kilauea eruptions in the spring of 2018, Hawai'i Volcanoes National Park was closed to the public in the volcano's summit area. Explosions, earthquakes, and copious sulfur dioxide emissions or vog closed the park. Halema'uma'u, the pit crater within the summit caldera, collapsed, and the hole in the earth doubled in size that May. The Hawai'ian Volcano Observatory continued to monitor Hawai'i's four active volcanoes.

In the fall, as Kilauea's eruptions subsided, much of the park was reopened. Still, considerable damage was done to the Observatory and MIT's Thomas Jaggar Museum nearby. Consequently, besides the volcanologists and their staff at the Observatory and an occasional Park Ranger, there were few humans on Kilauea.

"Whoever he is, Tūtū Pele will devour him, stupid bastard."

The Ranger, Sam Kuahu'ula, referred to the Hawai'ian goddess of fire and volcanoes. She is the creator of the Hawai'ian Islands and was believed to live in the fiery pit of Halema'uma'u. She was the "earth-eating woman" and "she who shapes the sacred land." The Goddess could be counted on to reach out with her fire and deadly gases to those who intruded.

While the Observatory worked on repairs, some seismology monitoring was back online. The tower windows of the facility provided a sheltered view of Halemaʻumaʻu, the Kīlauea Caldera, and the lava flows. Without lowering his binoculars, Chief Operations Officer Mace Keōua said, "Sam, go get that idiot before shit happens."

Ranger Kuahuʻula took the gravel emergency access route at the end of the Chain of Craters Road and up to the caldera. Driving on the lava flows amounted to deliberately taunting Pele to melt the Jeep's tires and ignite the vehicle's gas tanks. Sam got as close as possible and then left the Jeep wearing his protective suit— metal-coated outerwear, gloves, helmet, and heat-proof boots. The Ranger carried no walking staff. He believed with his ancestors that lava was sacred and that piercing it would enrage the Goddess.

This is not going to end well. That fucker is far out there.

The vog was blowing the other way, but the intruder was weaving as if he had sucked up a lethal dose of the noxious gas. It was indeed a man, and as the Ranger got closer, he quickened his pace towards the edge of hell.

Sam slapped his large, heavy gloves together to gain the attention of the crazy man. He signed, waving his arms in great loops, signaling the man that he should retreat and come to safety. A cold realization began to form within the silver suit. No cameras or anything. This guy wants to die.

As the man on the rim of the abyss turned to face his would-be rescuer, he threw his arms wide and screamed to the sky. The caldera quaked – a noticeable earthshaking. Sam rocked back onto a crest of sharp lava rock. Fire reached up from the bowels of Halemaʻumaʻu.

Pele's embrace.

The man crouched and then snapped up and back, vaulting head over heels into the pit of fire.

Chapter One: Stirling

Stirling Range National Park, West Australia
Nick Sechi's Journal

The big red staggered out of the bush and fell on his face, eyes half-open.

The workers ran to get him into the net and dragged him to the van. The dart would wear off in about an hour, and the kangaroo needed to be treated and whisked away to a paddock on safer ground. His limp body strained at the netting. He was burned and badly bruised and looked to be about 90 kilograms or 198 pounds.

Vets shot him up with antibiotics and pain meds before lifting him into the van. One doctor attached an IV to the "roo" to help with dehydration. The big fella joined his mates in the vehicle.

Roustabouts on horseback herded the rest of the mob, adults with their joeys, up out of the canyon. The kangaroos had taken shelter there from the burning brush and trees. There was safer ground to the northeast beyond the surrounding agricultural fields, backburned by resourceful farmers. Earth movers at that end of the park created a firebreak, but the problem now was to get the animals through the gap and onto less dangerous lands.

As we worked on the eastern edge of the park, we witnessed the migration of the two First Nations tribes who lived in the area. The Qaaniyan people in the west were assisted by the Koreng community in the east, moving with as many belongings as they could transport to the northeast tribal lands.

Davion Katolawaymah, a fire captain for the region of Western Australia, gave me an update on the animal rescue efforts.

"Many of the birds seemed to get out on their own, the cockies and the mallleefowls. Reptiles like a few Gould's goanas and the swamp tortoises chose to head for the rocks and streams. We found a few of them hiding out there. There are some frogs that no one seems to have seen— white-bellied and yellow-bellied. They may have gone into the mud."

He continued, "Those mountains on the horizon are about two million years old. The soil around here is poor, creating a rare species habitat. Besides being a designated Important Bird Sanctuary, other endangered species make their home here."

Anna Jones-Wilson, a volunteer vet and recognized leader in the rescue effort, joined the conversation.

"Nick, we are so grateful to your family for their assistance in this effort. Right now, it's the mammals we are most concerned with. The park is home to twenty species of mammals."

Anna continued, "Your husband and a pack of ranchers found some Rock Wallabies trying to get through the fields to the north and gave 'em a boost. He is quite a horseman."

"Grew up on the ranch. Yeah, he gets the job done."

The wildlife medic checked her tablet.

"Afraid we lost a lot of Western Quolls, but we managed to get a number of them to a safe haven. Some of the habitats were unharmed … so if it ain't broken… It was a matter of getting the critters not to fear us and to let us get them out of the way of the blaze. Not easy."

I asked, "What happened with the kangaroo rats?"

"Ah, the Potoroos. Afraid we may lose 'em, mate. A shame. The world's rarest marsupial and one of Australia's most threatened mammals. No one has seen 'em."

"Nick, Anna, I know this park like the back of my hand. There is a major habitat up the Creevus Billabong not far from here."

I dashed to the truck and yelled to the two Australians. "Let's hit it. Davion, you are the co-pilot." We hopped in the Jeep and headed west into the park.

The wildfire was mainly under control in the Sterling National Park, but here and there, around and into the mountains, some of the critters were in trouble. The creeping wall of fire and dense clouds of smoke continued to threaten all it encompassed.

"Nick, watch the trees up ahead."

"See 'em, bud, there's a workaround there. Hold on."

It took a week for over 200 firefighters to contain a blaze in the Stirling Range National Park. After winds pushed flames eastwards across the ranges, crews dealt with a 150-kilometer fire perimeter. Close to where we were headed, most of the hiking trails, a Park Ranger's hut, and swathes of bushland were reduced to fire and ash. As we drove through the smoke, burning embers blew from the blaze onto the untouched areas of the bush and the adjoining fields.

The Park's Volunteer Bush Fire Brigade and local state MP called for a heavy-duty 4WD fire truck to be permanently stationed at the tourist hot spot. For many years, the park authorities and the surrounding farmers called for more firefighting equipment to be permanently based near the Stirling Ranges. With more resources, locals could respond quickly to fires and avert potential disasters.

Anna said, "The deal for us here is to get in and check on the animals and get out safely, possibly with some of the injured. We are so gonna get our arses kicked for going in here. It's like driving into bloody hell."

"There along the scree, the stream water will provide some shelter. Damn, are you sure the smoke eaters have this bitch under control?"

I swerved the Jeep along the pebbles and fallen trees beside the rockfall adjacent to the mountain ridge and a troubled stream.

Anna yelled, "Stop!"

I skidded right and braked, spinning the Jeep a bit. Anna jumped out of the back and grabbed a net. She made for some things rolling in the dirt and sand a few meters away. With us playing defense, Anna scooped up two numbats, rare insectivorous marsupials native to Western Australia, playing as the world around them burned.

Davion said, "These puppies are endangered and eat termites by the truckload." Anna lifted the pair up in the net and hustled to the back of the truck to put them in containers. Smoke and fire encroached. We were off.

"Just up there is a dale between the hills. Head for it."

I turned through an opening that was almost sealed off by fallen trees, mud, and rock. It was a box canyon, enclosed by sheer rock walls, parts still lush and green. Smoke was everywhere. But it seemed like the canyon refuge had a sign on it for the animals saying, "Get your Collective Arses In Here."

Davion pointed, "There, see 'em."

"We gotta hurry, man. If the fire gets through that narrow opening into this ravine, we are major fucked."

A family of rat kangaroos, Gilbert's Potoroos, was scratching at the rock for a holdfast, a hole, or a chance to burrow into the ground. Anna and Davion netted the group, one of which was severely burned. They put them in carriers and loaded them up.

"Get the rifle, Dav. Wallabies up ahead near the stream."

The three of us darted and carted five black-footed wallabies who made a fuss about "WTF? Who were these guys? We've got enough trouble. Ouch, I'm shot. Good night."

"Truck getting full, dudes."

That was when I looked up. Yep, you guessed it, folks, Koalas up in the Eucalyptus trees that lined the chasm. The little teddy bears were calmly eating their leaves and hugging their babies with one eye on the fire that was threatening to breach the firebreak. Fiery embers were blowing over and through the opening. In a flash, the first trees burst into flames.

A few of the critters we plucked from lower branches. Three, we had to dart and catch as they fell. A pair was in trouble and moved up higher in their tree, the wrong move. Right now, the eucalyptus trees were burning from the top down. Soon, it would be the other way. We put on our breathers and stowed the critters, tossing in some leafy branches in case they regained consciousness.

Davion said, "Let's hit it. We will be trapped in here soon, and this Jeep will explode if caught by the fire."

That's when I did one of my typical shit arse stupid things. I climbed the tree. Tough going with a tank on your back.

"Nick, it's too dangerous. Come down."

My athletic abilities and my gymnastic experience paid off. I got up the branches and extended my hand to the young male. Painfully, slowly, he reached for me and allowed me to pull him onto my back. His mate was somewhat more reticent.

"Come on, sweetie, let's go for a ride."

The highest branches began to burn. The smoke was thicker in the canyon by the minute.

I heard Anna say, "Gimmie, that chubby boy." She was right below me. The male was afraid but made the switch, and she started down. Below us, Davion pulled an extinguisher from behind the back seat. He was attacking the cinders and burning branches that surrounded the Jeep.

"Let's go, mates. This bloody mess is turning into our own personal barbie."

I stepped up higher and caught the female. That is when I saw the fuzzy kiddo clinging to mom's back.

"Gotcha. It's OK, babies, we're almost outta here."

I climbed down, dropping the last few feet and clutching my cargo, which gripped back. I raced for the Jeep.

"Strap in and hang the fuck on."

We spun in the dirt and sent it flying behind us. In the opening ahead, a bridge-like mess of burning branches and logs at the top of the pile started to descend. We were so fucked.

I floored it.

We blasted through like shit through a goose. The opening collapsed behind us as we cheered in unison at our unbelievable luck. Sitting next to me, Davion yelped and pulled a net bag from beneath his vest.

"Don't bite me, ya bloody rodents. I just saved your arses."

He handed the group of Woylies, slithering and fussing over one another in their confinement, over the seat to Anna. She put the group into a carrier on the place next to her. Another cage held a sleepy "Pops" Koala.

I backtracked as best I could. There was burnt shit everywhere. Above us, aircraft were dousing the new flare-up behind us with fire-retardant. There it was, the remains of an egress road that had not been blocked for a fire break. I right-turned, but the opening was a bit narrow. The jeep went up on two wheels before hitting the asphalt safely.

About a mile down the road, we came to a relief post where we would offload the animals for transport to the veterinary station in the northeast. I hopped out and came to a startling realization. Mom and baby Koala were still hanging around my neck.

As I tenderly reached for them, a tall-in-the-saddle, sexy-assed rancher covered with soot turned on his horse. His open work shirt revealed dirty but spectacular chest muscles. Rolled-up, long sleeves uncovered a filthy pair of forearms that you wanted to be wound around you at any time of the day or night. Under his Aussie slouch hat, his blue eyes twinkled above his handsome, lean face as he flashed a killer smile in the scorching afternoon sun.

Kayne's soft baritone, rich with notes of humor and sarcasm, teased.

"Well, my love, you make a very hot Doctor Doolittle."

Chapter Two: *Vita Dulcedo Spes*[1]

The University of Notre Dame, Notre Dame, Indiana
Nick Sechi's Journal

"Those were my digs, Nick. Second Floor, Saint Edward's Hall. I shared rooms with a senior man for the first two of my undergraduate years. I was the student assistant to the Hall Rector, Fr. Michael, in graduate school.

"Kick and Mitch were in Sorin Hall, and Eric was housed in Keenan-Stanford. Brothers were not usually assigned as roommates, so we were separated. However, Mitch and Kick were the exceptions. He convinced the Dean of Students that Kick needed to be his roomie. He served as a stabilizing influence."

"I understand Mitch labored under a spell of an obsession for the littlest triplet from an early age."

"Oh yes, my love. The 'Hot Mess,' as we called him, was quite a handful. Superb soccer player, but in the end, I believe the University Dons were happy to see us graduate."

"I understand the four of you were amazing athletes."

"Yes, truth be told-- The Archangels... started with Mitch. The priests call him 'Saint Michael the Warrior.' Three national championships in three years... By our third year, Mitch had graduated, and Eric had been expelled. That just left Kick and me. It seems like so long ago. It is incredible how one can channel conditions of a brain disorder into sports, but the three of us did so. Mitch was always just the stalwart, the anchor of the squad, calm, reliable, and in charge."

We walked from the main quad with its historic statue of the Sacred Heart to the prestigious dormitory designed in the French Gothic style, typical of the university's landmark buildings constructed back in the

---

[1] "Our life, our sweetness, our hope." This is a traditional Catholic prayer to the Blessed Virgin Mary. It's also the motto of the University of Notre Dame, The phrase appears on the university's crest and in the Salve Regina prayer.

1840s. Saint Edward's Hall still housed the cream of the Notre Dame students who passed us on the walkways, watched over by an effigy of St. Edward the Confessor.

"Where is our meeting, Boss?"

He pointed.

"In there."

From the portico of Saint Edward's Hall, we moved through the dappled Indiana sunshine to the Administration Building, a short walk through the connecting quad. Directly in front of the ubiquitous Golden-Domed Administration Building, but some distance further, was the large quad with the shaded statue of Father Sorin, the Founder of the University. He presided deep among the hedges and drooping sycamores. Directly in front of us, shining in the mid-fall sun, was the Basilica of the Sacred Heart. Morning Prayer was just letting out.

Climbing the stairs, we walked inside through wide-wainscotted corridors of the Administration Building and up to the second-floor offices of the dean to meet with Father Colin Grey, CSC. The administrator was a distinguished academic who had worked his way up through faculty positions to become the Dean of the University of Notre Dame's most illustrious School, the College of Arts and Sciences.

"Nick, in this building, Father Julius Nieuwland, a chemistry professor, invented synthetic rubber in the 1940s. Without it, the US would not have won the war. During the war, most of the rubber-producing lands were in the hands of the Japanese. Neoprene was born here."

"Rubber... rubber... humm, reminds me of a joke. These two priests..."

"Do not blaspheme in here, Nick. This is Our Lady's University, *The* Catholic University of America."

"Go, Irish!"

"Sorenson! You Aussie dog. I can't believe it's you! Man, what's with the long hair? How the heck are you?"

Even the dude in the wheelchair, rolling towards us, was watching his language in these hallowed precincts.

"John Hrynsyshyn, the only bloke I ever met with no vowels in his last name. Jack, so good to see you. It's been a long time."

Kayne's fellow alumnus introduced the woman who accompanied him.

"Gentlemen, this is my wife, Risë. Sweetheart, Kayne and I were teammates. We killed on the soccer field. I still remember the nationals in '05. Goddamn. I mean darn."

Jack looked around for the swearin' police and decided he was cool.

Risë was a dark-haired woman with a distinguished look, professional and friendly. She smiled easily, especially when it came to her little one.

"This is Jack, Jr."

The boy was blond like his dad but dark-eyed like his mom.

"I'm five."

He illustrated with a small hand stretching out as many fingers and a thumb.

I squatted and extended my hand.

"Hey, Bud. I'm Nick, and this is Kayne."

To my surprise, he fist-bumped me.

I chuckled and said, "Five and very cool."

Jack's Mom went down on one knee on the other side of the boy and said softly, "Give it a try, Spud."

The child pointed timidly, "Nick."

"Bingo, kiddo."

I pointed at myself.

"Nick."

"Whoa, you smart cookie. What kind cooook eee?" I was imitating the eponymous Muppet Monster, and the boy giggled as I growled out the blue puppet's favorite food.

"Cooook eeee!"

He jumped a little as he said, "Chocolate Chip."

We bumped again.

"Folks, this Cookie Monster is my husband, Nick Sechi."

We exchanged greetings.

Jack was obviously an athlete, and it appeared that either an accident or a medical condition had landed him in the wheelchair. He asked about the other Sorenson brothers, and Kayne gave him the family elevator speech— highlights only.

"Yeah, so imagine this Aussie blue blood in triplicate and with an adoptive brother who was also a force of nature. Incredible, Hon, coaches, deans, and instructors had their hands full. Just when they'd start brawling, someone would score a winning goal or get incredible scholastic honors. 'Member when Mitch took over for the lead in 'Miss Saigon', Kayne? That bastard could sing, and he sure as hell made the females go apeshit with the naked scene."

"Jack."

"Sorry, dear."

"I sense that we are holding you up from something. Would you guys be open to meeting for a drink later?"

"Rippa, mate. Shall we meet at the Morris Inn at, say, seven? We could have cocktails and dinner after."

The Hrynsyshyns were delighted and started to depart.

The little guy turned to wave bye-bye.

Chapter Three: The Bell and the Umbrella

The Main Administration Building, The University of Notre Dame, Notre Dame, Indiana

Nick Sechi's Journal

"Father, please allow me to introduce you to my husband, Nick. My love, this is Father Colin Grey of the Congregation of the Holy Cross, Dean of the College of Arts and Sciences."

I was being introduced all over campus, it seemed. I half expected a Catholic institution to be uncomfortable with two world-renowned gay guys, one who was an illustrious alumnus. I have to say, our reception among the University community was without even the slightest hint of an issue.

"It is a pleasure to meet you, Father."

The salt-and-pepper-haired cleric came up from his desk, where he had been working at his computer.

"Nick, so great to meet you. Kayne, I am so glad you came to Notre Dame for Alumni Week; it has been a while. How is your family?"

"The insanity we caused as adolescents here in South Bend seems to have taken on more significant proportions as we grew further into manhood. Regardless, we are all very well, indeed, Father. Thank you."

"But not the Warrior Angel, correct? Not Mitchell. He is still the stalwart. That much, I know."

The cleric, a small man in his sixties, pointed to the computer, turned back, and pressed his office intercom.

"Ms. Bodie, may I have that report on Sorenson that we spoke about? Thank you."

He turned back with a broad smile and sparkling eyes.

"Not to disparage you, my son. Your accomplishments in the world outside of Our Lady's University are a glowing testament to a *Summa Cum*

Laude-- crowned heads and leaders of state, heads of industry, all consulting for your expertise over some very distressing crimes."

The priest clapped Kayne on the shoulders and added. "And you're… why the two of you… championing social justice. You make us proud, Kayne."

He thumped the chest of his former student. Fr. Grey turned to me, saying, "I am impressed with your harrowing exploits, saving lives… your Jesuit masters at Fordham University are most likely deciding how they will honor your accomplishments, young man."

He saw the question in my expression. He smiled and pointed to the computer.

"I am keeping abreast of your adventures. Addicted to the blog, I am afraid. I am halfway through the e-book of <u>The Evil Genius</u>. I know all about your adventures. No, no need to blush, my boy. The lusty content drives the story. Nothing I haven't heard in the confessional.

"Sit down, please, gentlemen. May I get you something?"

We sat and explained that we did not require refreshments, but the Dean insisted. He poured two scotches and waters for Kayne and himself, and I took a Perrier.

Kayne shot his forelock and said, "Ah, yes, 'The Mysteries.' One of the things we disagree on, Father. I find all this attention to marketing and the ensuing notoriety a bit of the 'Mrs. Palmer and her five lovely daughters,' if you take my meaning, Reverend."

I did a spit take and grabbed a napkin to catch the slop. Kayne's expression was indiscernible except for a slight twinkle in his eyes.

"Ah ha-- the Aussie slang. I am at a loss."

I jumped in.

"Doctor Sorenson is just commenting that he finds my literary attempts an obstruction to our work. We disagree, you see, Father."

We were thankfully interrupted by the Dean's administrative assistant. Fortunately, I escaped translating Kayne's colorful phrase describing my embellishments of our cases as acts of useless masturbation.

Mrs. Brodie placed a stack of five hardbacks on the cocktail table before me.

She handed me a pen and said, "Mr. Sechi-Sorenson, if you would be so kind, for the Father Theodore Hesburgh Library."

I opened each of the four copies of the <u>Blood Quartet</u> Series and the newest Kayne Sorenson Mystery. My signature accompanied a message of dedication to the Notre Dame students. Kayne was beaming.

Father Grey handed Kayne the bound report.

"I sent this to your father, Kayne, with a note of thanks. It is a report on the Sorenson Endowed Scholarship for the Department of Physical Chemistry at Notre Dame. Because of the excellent performance of our investments this year, the University has been able to award five scholarships. I have included brief bios on each of the award recipients. We hope that Captain Sorenson will appreciate this."

"Thank you, Dean. Nick and I will be considering a similar gift soon. And I would be happy to speak to my brothers on behalf of the University."

"That would be excellent and most generous, thank you."

"Gentlemen, I do not want to keep you from the festivities, so I will get to the point. It seems we have had a theft of some concern here. Two important liturgical insignias have been stolen from the Basilica of the Sacred Heart."

"Please continue, Fr. Grey. Do I understand that you wish us to solve a crime?"

And therein, Kayne was instantly intrigued. Long periods of mental inactivity were the height of boredom for him.

"Gentlemen, let's take a walk. It is truly a grand day out there."

***

The Dean led us next door to the main portico of the University Church, the Basilica of Our Lady of the Sacred Heart. Above us, the bell tower rose 230 feet into the blue Indiana sky.

"In 1992, Pope John Paul II designated Sacred Heart a minor basilica, an honorific bestowing canonical status."

I said, "So this church gets a lot more visitors having the *gravitas* of the Pope– good marketing strategy."

I winked at Kayne, who pulled a face.

"Correct. There are three symbols of Vatican approbation for a church, the papal crest ...

Fr. Grey pointed upward to the frieze of the crossed keys and the papal tiara above the entrance to the church.

"... the *Umbraculum* and the *Tintinnabulum*." The Dean opened his phone as we stepped into the church."

Kayne said, "The umbrella and the bell."

The Dean showed us pictures of the ornate, red, and gold silk parasol and the golden bell mounted on a ceremonial pole.

"So, this bling tell everyone when da Pope is inda hause?"

The priest laughed and said, "An excellent way to put it. Yes, Nick."

We walked up the main aisle of the neo-gothic nave. Above us, amid starry skies, angels and saints looked down from the walls and ceiling bays. These adornments were done by the Roman fresco master and the University's artist-in-residence, Luigi Gregori, in the 1800s.

Upon entering the sanctuary, Fr. Grey introduced us to the assistant sacristan, Brother Generoso Cataldi, a mousey little man busy rearranging the sacred space. He explained that he was setting up for Evening Prayer and the usual Sunday evening organ concert.

Curiously, Kayne held and patted the brother's hand, turning it over in his hands before the little guy pulled it away. I gave the dude a millennial-style fist bump and a "Sup, bud?"

"Brother, can you please show us where the missing objects are usually placed here in the sanctuary?"

The little monk in a work cassock, jeans, and running shoes pointed to two places on the polished marble floor.

"I took the stands away so no one would trip on them. The bell thing was there, and that umbrella on the opposite side."

He took a handkerchief out of his sleeve and wiped his nose.

"Sorry, caught a cold."

So here's where the great consulting professor usually whips out his jeweler's loop and evidence envelopes and hits the deck, examining the crime scene like a bloodhound. I had the impression that Dean Colin Grey was expecting the same sort of detective action on the part of the eminent Doctor Sorenson. But, Nada.

Instead, Kayne said, "Brother Generoso, will you show me the sacristy, please. We may find a clue to this business there."

The assistant Sacristian gave a puzzled look, wiped his nose again, and nodded. As we began to leave the sanctuary, Kayne turned around and held up a single hand to the Dean and me.

Stay, boys. Be right back.

I looked at the priest and shrugged.

"Come, Nick. Let me show you some of our treasures. The tabernacle tower and the main altar were created for the 1876 Centennial Exposition in Philadelphia. Fr. Sorin purchased it for the University."

I got the grand tour, including an explanation of the French-made stained glass windows and the Bernini altar in the Lady Chapel. In the Chapel of the Holy Family, Kayne caught up to us next to Ivan Mestrovic's masterpiece, *The Descent from the Cross* or *Pieta*. I took a picture for my mother, a devout Catholic.

As Kayne began to speak, I noticed acolytes completing the sanctuary set-up without the supervision of the sacristan.

"Father Grey, the University Post Office opens tomorrow morning at 7 AM, am I correct?"

"What a curious question, Doctor Sorenson. Sister Jean Workmaster, the postmistress, is as regular as the sunrise."

"Capital. You will have the Umbraculum and the Tintinnabulum back in place in time for the 11:30 AM Eucharist."

Chapter Four: Of Saints and Sinners

The Theodore Hesburg Library, The University of Notre Dame
Nick Sechi's Journal

"Touchdown!"

I tackled and then wrestled Kayne to the lawn at the end of the reflecting pool in front of the University's Library. I was attempting to crack wise on the lawn in the shadow of the gigantic mural, *The Word of Life*, aka "Touchdown Jesus." The famous image filled the side of the building, covering 61 feet of the facade of the Library's southern exposure.

We tussled a bit and then settled into a sprawl, lying on the grass, my head on his shoulder.

"Grass stains, my love. Quite ungentlemanly."

"Whateva. Such a high-toned place. I am not much of a Catholic anymore, Kayne, but this place... It's like Catholicism on steroids. Vatican jingoism out the ass."

"I agree. Quite inspiring, all the history and the tradition. Men and women with an incredible vision of education and salvation. Sorry you left the fold, my little Bronx altar boy?"

I one-elbow propped and looked into his blue eyes, as blue as the Indiana afternoon sky.

"I didn't leave the Church, Boss. They left *me*. After being told over and over that you're not welcome at the party, it's time to haul ass."

I sat up and did a shoulder brush-off to illustrate my exit.

Kayne mused, "I remember, some years back, I attended a debate entitled 'Intelligence Squared' during the Ratzinger papacy. Participants argued whether the Catholic Church is a force for good in the world. The British actor, writer, and activist Stephen Fry made this point regarding his homosexuality:

"It's a little hard for me to know that I am 'disordered' or, again, to quote Ratzinger, 'that I am guilty of a moral evil' simply by fulfilling my sexual destiny as I see it. It's... It's hard for me to be told... to be told that I'm evil because I think of myself as someone who is filled with love, whose only purpose in life is to achieve love, and who feels love for so much of nature and the world and for everything else...."

Kayne ended his recitation but went on.

"I cannot say that I was ever an observant religious anything, although I attended Notre Dame and participated in services from time to time. I have reflected on my own spiritual heritage, my love, for quite a long time. I am profoundly engaged by the theology wherein the Catholic Church understands herself as the community of saints and sinners. I expect to some, we fall into the latter category, so deliciously sinful."

He laughed and bit me with passion on the neck.

"Doctor Sorenson, please keep your lustful nature in check." I pointed up at the image of the Resurrected Christ surrounded by scholars, scientists, and saints– the monumental mosaic, *The Word of Life.*

Kayne rolled back with his arms behind his head.

"When I was an undergraduate, I used to come here at night and sit and gaze at this beautiful facade. The stones are from sixteen countries, putting this illustration of the Church Triumphant in a diversity framework. It would seem that there is room for us all within the promise of divine grace. Oh, the naivete of my youth... and the utter beauty of some of my University mates... hearts and minds filled with the noblest aspirations, not to mention the physical... ahhh... intoxication."

"My gosh, Bossman, how many religious scholars and holy men did you do, and I mean *do*, not to mention your frisky brothers? Sorenson ass pirates? Community of sinners, indeed. Got some real religion in you, bud."

"Isn't religion all about bad sex anyway?"

"Gentlemen, the University strictly forbids makeout sessions in front of 'Touchdown Jesus.' I shall have to call the ND sex police."

"Tamara, thanks for meeting us. This is my husband, Nick."

The congenial woman was dressed in business casual, with hair extensions in gray and black. Her countenance was genuine-- a warm and caring smile. She wore a colorful Kente Cloth shawl over one shoulder.

"How great to meet you, Nick, although I feel I know you from the blog."

"Nice to meet you, also."

"Nick, Doctor Mutira is with Counseling Services here at the University. I asked her to meet us regarding the assistant sacristan."

The psychologist pulled at her ample skirts and sat cross-legged on the lawn with us.

"So you ended up with this one, eh Nick? Well, I know you have quite a handful with Kayne. We met when we were both finishing our graduate degrees in Europe. Amsterdam, 2014, wasn't it? Found we had Notre Dame in common. So many on his dance card in those days, including one very hot Hungarian Captain of the Royal Guard."

Tamara Mutira's bright eyes twinkled with memories.

"How is your friend, that lovely woman, Rebecca? The two of you were the toast of the continent."

"A woman of powerful abilities and importance– she is the CEO and President of the Ft. Lauderdale Fritcher Museum of Art."

"Please give her my best. I remember her fondly."

Dr. Mutira smiled again. It came naturally, it seemed.

"How may I help you, gentlemen?"

Kayne related the case of the Dean, the Sacristan, the Bell, and the Umbrella to the psychologist up to our seeming resolution, not 30 minutes ago.

"Brother Generoso needs help, my dear friend, and perhaps you will be kind enough to see that he gets the services he needs."

"Kayne, I am familiar with the Brother's struggles as he has come to us for assistance in the past. It is not uncommon for a person with a substance use disorder to need additional support. Often, we humans fall back on old crises and negative behavior patterns. I would be glad to see him."

"Thank you, my friend."

He jumped up.

"The game's afoot, my friends."

"Kayne, where are we going?"

"To see the Blessed Virgin, my love. After all, this is her University."

Chapter Five: Candlelight

The Grotto of Our Lady Of Lourdes, The University of Notre Dame, Notre Dame, Indiana
Nick Sechi's Journal

We walked back across campus to the Basilica and found the path that wound down to the Grotto.

Kayne conducted the tour.

"Father Sorin, the founder of Notre Dame, was French. On one of the trips to his homeland, he visited Lourdes, where it is believed the Virgin Mary appeared to Bernadette Soubirous, a poor French girl, on eighteen occasions in 1858."

As we stepped down into the hollow to the plaza behind the University Church, we could hear and see hundreds of the faithful reciting the rosary. Thousands of candles filled the rock grotto with golden light in the coming twilight. Behind an iron fence, statues of the Virgin and St. Bernadette reenacted the famous apparition. The folks knelt and prayed on the plaza side.

Dr. Mutira said, "A daily ritual every evening. Can't get near the place during football weekends. Students, faculty, and alums all love it. Many proposals and weddings happen here, too. Students especially like the solitude for meditation."

Kayne continued, "So, Father Sorin reproduced Lourdes on the campus of his new university. The stones and boulders from surrounding farms here in South Bend were used in its construction.

"Observe, Nick. A small piece of stone from the original cave in France is located on the right-hand side of the shrine, directly below the statue of Mary. "

I said, "Man, this is a special place. Pretty cool, all those candles and folks praying. So hypnotic– the light and the flickering. Think about it. Each one represents somebody's prayers, like making a plea for help or saying thanks, even after they leave and go back to where they came from. Pretty special mother devotion– warmth and light."

I returned from my reverie to find Kayne and Tamara Mutira staring at me, each with a sly smile.

"What?"

Our friend said, "You are quite religious, I suspect, Nick. Catholic?

"Yep, cradle Catholic. Elementary School through Fordham U."

"And an altar boy. A service role he has passed on to our nephew, Kris."

"Naw, Boss. The Kris is his own man."

Kayne waved a hand.

Tamara looked at Kayne and teased, "Still the doubter?"

"I find this– all of this, incredibly fascinating. And I mean no disrespect. But it is inconceivable that this cult of the Virgin is based on the ravings of a hysteric as most mystics prove to be upon critical examination."

Tamara challenged, "But the healings and the exhumation? Surely, Doctor Sorenson... more hysterics, psychosomatic healings by the thousands?"

Kayne pulled a face, and he pushed back his forelock, saying, "There you have me, Doctor. It simply defies explanation. The Lourdes water as curative... alas, I do not know."

I jumped in, "Wait, wait. Exhumation? Who? What's that all about?"

Dr. Mutira explained, "St. Bernadette. When they opened the casket forty years after her burial, she had not decayed. She is a member of that elite Catholic group known as The Incorruptibles. It is a sign of her sanctity."

"Get out."

"It is true, my love. Have a look-see."

He took my phone and Googled it. I looked and was amazed. Next, I glanced up at his face to get some sort of explanation.

34

Kayne shrugged.

"It is beyond science, and therefore, I have no way of understanding this."

We were interrupted by chanting, billowing fragrant smoke, and a gold and white procession winding down the steps from the Basilica above. In a richly embroidered cape and vestments, a priest held a gold sun disc thing aloft with a white center. The reliquary held the Eucharist to be adored by the faithful. We stepped back as the procession of ministers and the laity approached, made a right turn, and walked to the altar where the priest placed the monstrance. The dude with the "smoking purse" hit us big time with the incense as he passed– the high drag of Catholicism.

The folks sang the Eucharistic anthems and paid homage.

"*O Salutaris Hostia...*"

I couched and whispered, "That guy, Ole Smokey, so winked at me."

My companions laughed as Brother Generoso came forward at the end of the procession. He looked pale and drawn.

"OK, so I gotta get back up to the sacristy to put all of this away in a bit, but here goes."

Generoso was hell-bent on keeping this all under wraps for many reasons. He was talking fast and wiping his nose. Kayne moved us further back away from the crowd.

He instructed, "Two things are required now, Brother. You will meet me at the post office tomorrow as soon as it opens to retrieve the packages."

The skinny cleric nodded. He kept eyeing the ceremony and the crowd.

"Yes, I will be there, Doctor Sorenson. This goes no further, as you agreed, right?"

The assembly began to sing, "Holy God, We Praise Thy Name," as the service ended.

"That depends, Sir. You must report to Doctor Mutira immediately after that to resume your treatment."

Tamara said, "You will be required to spend some time away, Brother Generoso. I will speak to your superiors if you like."

"Yes, I cannot face them regarding this. I thought I had it licked the last time."

The psychologist took the hand of the devastated religious, "My dear, recidivism in cases of addiction is very common. As Catholics, we are great believers in second and third chances, am I right?"

The little monk nodded, dropped her hand, and said, "Tomorrow, then."

He was about to leave when I asked, "Dude, who...?"

"I do not know, Sir. I was offered a lot of money for the two holy items. He said he was acting as an intermediary."

Kayne confirmed, "The address on the cartons will no doubt prove to be a dead end."

As the service ended, the assembly at the Grotto sang loudly. "Infinite thy vast domain. Everlasting is thy reign."

"Doctor Sorenson, I need to tell you I am pretty sure these guys will come after me."

Chapter Six: Logo

Kilauea, The Big Island, Hawai'i

"There *is* no corpse. The volcano instantly vaporizes anything falling into that crater."

The Director of the Observatory of Volcanoes National Park, Marion Blakely, continued, "The internal temperature of Kilauea's caldera at this time is approximately 1,170 degrees Celsius or 2,140 degrees Fahrenheit. The lava tubes are about 100 degrees hotter. At those temperatures, solid rock melts.

Sam Kuahu'ula shook his head and said, "Suicide. Crazy-assed as they come. No way to tell if the guy was high or what."

"You were the last person to see the deceased, Ranger Kuahu'ula. Can you describe him?" The speaker was Sergeant Mark Suzuki of the Hawai'ian Police Department. His companion, Officer Amy Nguyễn, took notes.

"I was pretty far off, but the guy was definitely Polynesian. Five-eleven, gonna say one-sixty, one-seventy pounds. Had to have been a young man, Officer. The backflip was unbelievable. Only an athlete could have made that move so expertly.

"Another thing. Maybe it doesn't mean anything. As I tried to get near the guy, he was checking his pockets."

"What do you mean?"

"Like he was looking for keys or cigarettes or something."

"Probably wanted a last smoke."

"Standing on the edge of a volcano? Pretty weird."

"How was he dressed?"

"Dark pants and a red corporate shirt. Oh yeah, there was a logo, can't be sure."

"Why was your body cam off, Ranger?"

"Circuits on the main transmitter were fried when the Center was damaged last spring."

Director Blakely added, "Funding for the park's repairs and the observatory has been slow in coming."

"Can you describe the logo?"

"Some kind of triangle, but not really. You know, cut off at the top."

Officer Nguyễn handed the man her notepad.

"Can you draw it for me, please?"

"Can't believe you guys don't use iPads or something more high-tech during an interrogation."

The sergeant said, "Old ways are often the best."

The Park Ranger showed the police his sketch. Marion Blakely commented, "A bit like a volcano."

***

"Right, Sarge. We got a black 2014 Dodge Ram 1500 Express, off-road on the east side of the park, about a mile in from the service gate entrance on State Highway 11."

"Got a plate number?"

"DMV says it belongs to a family on Hoohana Street in Puakō here on the Big Island, off 19."

"What's in the truck?"

"Not much, Boss. Set of keys. Gym bag with the usual gear, gloves, towel, and water bottle. The guy was definitely into sensible eating—empty containers from Whole Foods. Bar code on the driver's window, running that down now. Taking prints where we got 'em."

"Let me know what you find."

"Strange…"

"What?"

"Couple of things-- looks like someone broke into the truck before we got to it. The passenger's side window is broken. Things scattered. Someone was looking for something."

"What else, Officer?"

"It's just that... well, religious folk usually think twice about suicide. All that about it being a mortal sin and can't be buried in holy ground stuff."

"He made sure that there was nothing to bury. Why did you bring religion up?"

"Dead guy has a cross dangling from his rearview."

***

The girl behind the rock outcrop saw the squad car pull away from the truck. Most likely, they would send a tow truck, she thought. She would high-tail it out of here before then.

Not being picked up by the police or whoever owned the dead guy's truck. Gotta get to a town or something. Sure is barren around here.

A couple of old sandwiches and an apple were all there was. Full water bottle-- that was good.

I wonder what's on this flash drive.

Chapter Seven: The Legacy of Dexter the Horse

The Morris Inn, The University of Notre Dame, Notre Dame, Indiana
Nick Sechi's Journal

As night settled over northern Indiana, we found ourselves ending our walk through the campus and heading down Notre Dame Boulevard to the Morris Inn. On the Wind Family Terrace, we settled into comfortable chairs. To the west, the last glimmers of the setting sun filtered through the sycamores and melted into the grays and deep blues of evening. Soft strains of organ music wafted over the campus from the Church as lamps came on in the many buildings and on the pathways of the University.

"Tamara Mutira and his Religious Order will make sure that the whereabouts of Brother Generoso remain a closely held secret once he reports for treatment. I will alert our friends at the FBI to make sure they are aware of this affair."

A server took our drink order and went back inside. The fire pit blazed with warmth and light as the summer evening came on. Risë and John joined us. She walked beside his rolling chair as he pulled up to the fire with his wife.

I asked, "No Little Jackie?"

Risë said, "A delightful University student came to our rescue. We hired her to be our sitter for the evening. She is majoring in Elementary School Education. Spud took to her, and we got to spend some time together. We just love the Morris Inn."

Jack said, "You know the story, right?"

Kayne nodded, smiled, and said, "A wonderful horse named Dexter...."

Our server brought our cocktails and took the order for the Hrynsyshyns.

He interrupted.

"Talking about the horse story."

"Yes, so, tell it, ahhh...." I leaned in to look at the young man's name tag.

"Stuart."

The kid smiled and began the tale. "So, a long time ago...."

Kayne said, "Nineteen-o-two, to be exact. Sorry, mate. Continue, please."

"This dude couldn't pay his tuition, so he goes to the University president and asks to be able to run a tab so he can stay at school. So, the priest agrees. Then, John Morris, that was the student's name, asks the Father to take care of his horse, too. "

"Again, I apologize, Master Stuart, from Boston, Mass. The President was Father John W. Cavanaugh, for whom Cavanaugh Hall is named. Not John but Ernest Morris, and the horse, glorified with the portrait in the lobby, was the famous Dexter."

"Hey, right. Man, you sure know a lot."

The young man snapped his fingers and leaned in to get a closer look at Kayne and me.

"Say, you're that detective guy everyone on campus is whispering about. Very cool. Yeah, and you could tell I'm from Boston by my accent, right? That's easy."

"Roslindale and a graduate of Catholic Memorial High School. How's the soccer team doing, lad? The University's first-string goal man would have a lot to say about that. "

I grinned-- the big show-off. Kayne loved doing this. John and Risë were open-mouthed and amazed.

The young jock dropped his empty tray with a clatter.

"Holy crap!"

He stood stock-still.

"Oh, sorry. But... but, that was amazing."

Kayne said with a sly smile, "The Irish lilt in the accent of your Boston neighborhood is quite unmistakable, as is your high school graduation ring."

He gestured to the sharp, shaved point of Stuart's buzz cut at the back of his neck.

"*De rigueur* for this season's Notre Dame soccer players-- very Spartan warrior for a Fighting Irisher. You are 'The Falcon' on the soccer pitch."

He gestured again to the lad's nametag and his surname, de Falconi.

"Now it gets a bit complicated, but still quite effortless. May I?"

He took the kid's left hand.

"A total giveaway-- please observe.

"It has been a hot and sunny summer. Soccer practice stretches through the summer months."

He traced the crescent on the back of Stuart's hand.

"Please notice the tan line on the back of the hand. Gloves with an opening on the back of the palm are a goalie's equipment. Furthermore, our champion here plays a great deal of the time, indicated by the contrasting shades of melanin-- *ergo*, first string. And you remove your ring during practice and matches. There is no change in the skin coloration beneath it.

"No soccer man is allowed to touch a ball in play except the goaltender– usually tall, agile, and highly coordinated, all evidence to the contrary notwithstanding."

Kayne reached forward and retrieved the dropped tray, handing it to the young jock.

"A series of simple observations, my lad. Please continue with your story."

"Ah shit, where was I?"

Stuart de Falconi, aka The Falcon, grimaced as he realized he had cussed again in front of customers.

Risë said, "Dexter."

"Oh yeah. Dude, you are amazing... so, anyway, the Father agreed, and the Morris guy graduated and created this huge investment firm. He gets super-rich and gives a chunk of it to the University. So, they named the Morris Inn after him."

The young man pulled himself up as if recalling the lines of a memorized marketing speech and sounding all concierge-like.

"When Ernest Morris was asked why he did so much in return, Morris said, 'I'll just never forget how kind Notre Dame was to my horse.' Welcome to the Living Room of the University. We now offer 150 guest rooms, including 18 spacious suites."

"Well, done, Master de Falconi."

Kayne placed some cash on the boy's tray. Stuart expressed his thanks and hurried away.

"Still amazing, Kayne." Jack continued, "He used to do this stuff all the time when we were undergrads. Loved when he would get into it with the profs or the cocky frat boys. Took down many a pompous asshole who did not really know the meaning of courtesy. I remember you shredding our Philosophy of Science instructor a few times."

"Father Simpson. It got so that he made it a point not to call on me in class. But it wasn't me who nicked his bookbag, Jack. You know that very well."

"Still remember that old don getting one of the footballers to shinny up the Vengence Tree and get it down."

We laughed and toasted glory days.

When our table was ready, we moved from the patio into the Inn's restaurant, Rohr's. We continued to get acquainted, sharing more stories of when Kayne and John were hot jocks on campus. This segued into our adventures in crime-fighting and their life together.

"How did the two of you meet?" I asked Risë.

"Good lord, I thought he was the biggest jerk on the planet. Talk about pompous."

"And for me, it was love at first sight."

I chucked, "Story of my life."

Risë said, "I don't understand."

I said, "Inside joke— hit by the thunderbolt. It happens all the time with me."

Risë smiled and said, "So, John was working for the district attorney, and I was this hotshot lawyer for a premier legal firm whose lead attorney on this murder case left the firm just before trial. We had the defense. I got the step-up to lead defense attorney."

Kayne said, "Risë Vance, J.D. The Feldenstine Case. Rosa Feldenstine was accused of murdering her husband and his lover. It was the scandal of the decade in Santa Barbara. And I remember you were the woman who cracked it."

"You have an excellent memory, Kayne. Yes, Mrs. Feldenstine was framed by one of the elders of her Church. That group was out for the family money. Alexander Feldenstine, a convert to that Pentecostal sect, had left the majority of his fortune to the church if he survived his wife."

Jack added, "If Rosa Feldenstine had been convicted of murder, the Fellowship of the Lord's Love would have gotten $150 million. The evidence pointed to a member of the church leadership team. She was apprehended and confessed. My dear wife made some enemies that day."

"They all seemed to leave town after it all came out. The Fellowship hightailed it into the shadows," Risë added. She looked away as she spoke. I saw Kayne take notice and do a slight eye flicker. He shot his forelock.

Strange. Something more is going on here.

Jack picked up the conversation fumble, "The DA's office looked pretty bad. I had egg on my face, big time. Got the cockiness knocked right out of me for a time anyway. Asked her to go for a drink, and our competitiveness seemed to fall away over martinis."

"I began to realize he was not so bad after all."

We took our after-dinner drinks to a private corner of the bar. As we settled in, Jack reached up and pulled Kayne's head closer to his. He grabbed his old bud's forelock.

"This fucker used to drive me crazy with this forelock when we were undergrads-- pushing it back, pushing it back. Risë, gimme a hair clip, please, or a pair of fuckin' scissors. Nick, how do you stand it?"

Kayne faked, "Ow, ya mug. Leggo. I swear I will smack you in the noggin, ya brogan."

I kissed Kayne behind the ear as he straightened up and said, "It's one of his endearing trademarks."

When the Aussie slang makes its appearance, my husband is feeling his liquor. He quaffed a bit more of his Hibiki on the rocks.

Risë got serious and said, "Gentlemen, after Jack and I met you in the Administration Building, we got to talking. We decided to ask for your help."

"Please continue."

"Kayne, it's my sister, actually her daughter, our niece. Nancy and her husband, Rolf, are big-time fundamentalist Christians. Cloë, their youngest, is fourteen. She decided to come out, and the family freaked. Everyone but us. I mean, who cares, right? Our niece needs supportive love and not judgment. Nancy and Rolf went ballistic."

Jack said, "We think that they are contemplating sending her away for a church program that claims to change kids' sexual orientation."

I remarked, "Conversation Therapy."

"Yes. Outlawed in California, so..."

Kayne interjected, "Many of these groups take their clients out of the State. The religious right is challenging laws that forbid conversion therapy. Many conservative federal lawmakers are rabid homophobes who will stop at nothing to legislate the hatred. The wealthier church groups are moving their youth programs offshore, outside the country. Others are simply re-formatting the old programs,"

Risë added, "We are worried about the girl. Things being so hostile at home, we offered to have her live with us, but Nancy and Rolf are not responding to our concerns."

"Their congregation is the Church of the Lord's Shadow, and its headquarters are on the big island of Hawai'i on the Kona coast, northwest shore. They have a retreat center for children who, in their words, have gone astray— gay kids."

"I am not familiar with this group. Can you tell me more, please?"

Risë began, "There is an account in the Acts of the Apostles where the crowds brought sick people out to the road and placed them on mats. It was hoped that Peter the Apostle would walk by and his shadow would fall on them and heal them. The church uses as its slogan the verse from Psalm 91 – 'He who dwells in the shelter of the Most High, will abide in the shadow of the Almighty.' It all makes sense somewhere— to them anyway."

Jack added, "This group is farther right than Focus on the Family, The Family Research Council, and many other arch-conservative groups. They claim to be the self-appointed conscience of the country. They take a position to criminalize homosexuality…."

I broke in, "Great, I so wanna party with these folks."

Jack continued, "Right? They see same-sex marriage as the central issue in the culture wars. They are crazy militarists. Their positions include policies that reflect ecological irresponsibility, an insensitivity to the poor, an antagonism to science, and all rational thought, for that matter. They also espouse gun ownership out the ass."

Kayne chuckled, "Yes, my favorite kind of humans."

"They are very young— established about eight years ago, though some critics say that they have been around much longer."

Risë did an aside. "Jack, you don't suppose that the …."

"Dunno, babe. That other group seems to have vanished. We seem to have bad luck with the Christians."

Jack looked down at his legs.

"Fancy a working vacation, my love?"

"I'll start waxing my surfboard when we get home, Boss."

"We will do our best to get to the heart of this business, my friends. We will begin with a trip to California to visit the…."

"My sister's married name is Alden, and they live in Bakersfield."

"… the Aldens. I always look forward to discussing family, politics, and religion with the zealous."

Chapter Eight: Holy Waters

The Lakes of the University of Notre Dame, Notre Dame, Indiana
Nick Sechi's Journal

I took his hand and brought it to my lips.

"No more history unless it is filled with pornography. I feel like my readers are getting a travelogue of Notre Dame. And anyway, I am feeling very, very energetic."

I annotated the last three words with a kiss to his neck, earlobe, and lips, each a little longer than the previous one. I moved my hands over his hard body, doing make-out maneuvers.

"My love, we are in the carport of the Morris Inn. Dexter would be scandalized. Come, please allow me to show you a favorite trysting place. However, many will deny its scandalous reputation, and among those, I cannot number my brothers and me, for we were frequent habitués. Satyrs and fauns on hot summer nights…"

He changed the subject as we began to walk across the quad.

"So the Falcon sings in our choir, Nick."

"Kayne, how could you possibly know that? And do not tell me the freakishly accurate Sorenson gaydar."

He chuckled, "Our sexy Fighting Irish jock boy has the Greek letter lambda tattooed on the inside of his right wrist. He is signaling that he is receptive in a sexual relationship."

I chuckled, "Our hot goal tender is a catcher."

"Makes sense. With his looks, I would say young Stuart from Massachusetts is quite popular."

"We should introduce him to The Kris. Our nephew and Stu boy have a lot in common, and much that would be compatible, it would appear."

Kayne chuckled, "In that regard, I will reserve my thoughts. Just when you think the Sorenson scion's sexual orientation is clear, some other 'opportunity,' shall we say, presents itself. I do not get Kristof's generational sexual fluidity-- make up your bloody minds!"

"Perhaps it is not that simple, Boss."

We strolled through the campus to the twin lakes, St. Mary and St. Joseph. They were both fringed with trees and thick tanglewood brush. A path meandered along the banks where, here and there, a street lamp cast a pale halo in the darkness. We were not the only couple with sins of the flesh on our minds. Shadows moved along the trails into intimate corners within sight of the towering statue of the Virgin atop the Golden Dome, lit up for all to see.

Kayne pointed out, "Eastern Arborvitae, *Thuja occidentalis;* Eastern Red Cedar, *Juniperus virginiana;* White Cedar, *Thuja occidentalis;* Hemlock, *Tsuga canadensis.* That tall one is a...."

"Whoa, Boss. Lemme re-set here. No life-science lesson. No forestry... botany..."

"Dendrology, my love, the study of trees."

"Yeah, whatever... as a matter of fact, the only biology shit I wanna hear in this ramble is the sounds of hot man sex. Your begging always gets me going."

I persisted in my friskiness. "And I am so sure I need no instruction on how to ravish this hot Aussie jock body. Are we clear?"

I backed him against a sturdy hardwood and proceeded to unbutton his shirt. The night was sultry, humid, and oppressive– excellent for savage and forbidden sexin'. Nature seemed to play up the outdoor setting of our forest of carnal desires. A bullfrog called out for possible mates. Crickets and cicadas punctuated the shadows and lakesides with their musical throbbings. Ducks and cranes softly chatted in the warm shallows. A mother raccoon took her time wandering by with three kits in tow. She sniffed at the entangled humans and continued in search of a midnight snack. No fear.

Kayne lip-locked me and pushed me away, his sexual excitement increasing by the moment. Something about high-powered academia, the naughty Catholics, the borderline savage jock culture– my man was revved. As usual, many details crowded into his consciousness. My response was to use my strength to physically focus him on the task at hand.

Kayne came in for a hearty kiss again and gripped the back of my neck with a steady hand, taking his mouth's pleasure with ardor. He pointed to a tree a bit further down the trail and pushed me ahead of him. We approached, and he traced the outline of some initials in a carved heart on the trunk.

"This is a tulip tree— straight, tall, and massive with a thick trunk. *Liriodendron Kayniis.*"

I came around and stood against him. I slowly peeled his shirt off from behind him. I mused, "*Kayniis?*"

"Yes, my love. This is my tree."

I stopped tasting him and looked at the carvings. There had to be at least 20 sets of initials, all connected by KJS— Kayne Jason Sorenson.

His blue eyes twinkled in the moonlight above a shit-eating grin.

"You were a complete man whore. 'Christina, bring me the ax!'"

"No judgment, my love. Play your cards right, and you can also get your monogram on the Kayne Tree."

I grabbed his right wrist and raised it above his head, pinning it against the tree. Then, I reached around with my free hand and proceeded to unbuckle his belt to...

We were caught in a bright, invading light.

"Is um... everything OK, gentlemen?"

Kayne grabbed his falling pants, shot his forelock, and addressed the security guard, who played the beam over each of us, beginning with our faces.

"Absolutely, officer. I was just showing my husband the flora and the fauna of these lakeshores. So much nature, as it were." He fumbled noticeably, saying, "Nick, one story has it that when Father Sorin came here in the winter of 1842, he did not realize there were two lakes hidden under the ice and snow. A bit of an error that brought about the slight misnomer-- the University of Our Lady of the Lake."

More Catholic tradition out the ass... I felt the rent-a-cop smile in the darkness as I stooped to retrieve Kayne's dress shirt.

"Well, carry on, gentlemen. Or don't. Or whatever." He chuckled as he left.

I waited a moment and nailed Kayne to his trysting tree. His expression changed suddenly, and he pushed me off with such force that I landed on my butt.

"Hey. What the fuck?"

He said nothing. Sprinting down the short trail, Kayne stopped to kick off his shoes and dove into the lake.

Chapter Nine: Ash

The Lakes of the University of Notre Dame, Notre Dame, Indiana
Nick Sechi's Journal

The return of the Sorenson... well, I'll be."

Both Kayne and I were dripping. The ambulance's back doors were open, awaiting the gurney with the body. The head of campus security, the County ME, and a local police captain joined us in a clearing just outside Moreau Seminary on the lake. Fr. Colin Grey was joined by the superior of the Brothers of the Holy Passion friary, Br. Martin Gartland. Members of law enforcement combed the area while campus security kept the University folks out of the Rambles.

"Yeah, I knew your brother Mitch. We were friends in our Notre Dame days. You guys were so crazy– all except the Archangel. He was a rock."

The speaker was the cop, Darren Hughes, chief of detectives.

I said, "Chief, Kayne saw the floater and went for it. The deceased was face up. I helped pull them both from the lake. No one else seemed to be around. We finally found a security guard after dialing 911 for the police."

"You're a good cop, Nick. I read all about you. They are fools to put you out to pasture." He clapped me on the back.

Kayne called the Medical Examiner, Alice Dunn, over to the stretcher, and we joined her. My husband was scintillating with the energy of a possible murder case. His ADHD was in overdrive. I know he regretted not being able to revive the dead man once we got him out of the water, but finding out who did the horrendous deed now occupied his entire intellect.

He addressed his words to the ME.

'You will agree that he did not drown but was dead when he was put into the water."

Officer Dunn was a bit perplexed.

"Well, Doctor Sorenson, I fear that that is a premature conclusion. While there is no external evidence of drowning, an autopsy will confirm whether or not there is water in the lungs. It appears that the body has been in the water for at least three hours."

I said, "Time of death approximately nine PM as a result of trauma to the head."

She said, "Dove in and hit his head on one of the many sunken tree trunks. They are everywhere on that shore. Wildlife habitats."

Kayne said, "No, ma'am. Please shine that light on the back of the head. The back, please. That is correct. Who dives in and twists one's head to the back? Quite impossible. In his clothes, yet."

He sniffed the nose and opened his mouth for a second sniff.

"You will find no alcohol in the man's blood."

Brother Martin said, "He was abstemious about imbibing spirits."

Kayne said, "Please observe."

He took a pair of tweezers from the ME and pulled at the wound in the skull. He held up about an inch of dark, wet, and bloody debris.

"This is Black Ash, *Fraxinus nigra*. When the sun comes up, you will find the only ash wood in St. Joseph's Lake is Green Ash, *Fraxinus pennsylvanica.* I also need to inform you that the only stand of Black Ash in this forest is there on the closer bank of St. Mary's Lake. Did the deceased hit his head in St. Mary's and drown in St. Joseph's? This unfortunate man was murdered."

He drew back and buttoned his shirt.

"Please note carefully, this man was murdered and dumped here, in the lake before us. The evidence is irrefutable."

He stepped closer to the corpse and turned the hands of the dead religious. There was something of interest about the condition of the right hand.

"Please hold that light closer. Thank you."

Kayne smelled the fingers and rubbed the surface, taking an extremely close look at what appeared to be a stain. He spoke to no one in particular.

"Green. But why?"

The Medical Examiner offered, "Lake algae, pond scum."

Kayne shook his head.

"Hardly."

He gestured to the water behind us.

"There is none."

Alice Dunn looked at the Dean with an expression that I read as *What are we going to tell the press?*

Darren Hughes began to cover the corpse's face with the sheet, but Colin Grey stopped him. The Dean reached into his suit pocket and took out a small, purple priest's stole, placed it around his neck, and began,

"In the name of the Father, and of the Son, and of the Holy Spirit."

The priest made the Sign of the Cross over the body of the late Brother Generoso Cataldi.

The Shadow of Evil

Chapter Ten: Sins of the Flesh

Suite 325, The Morris Inn, The University of Notre Dame, Notre Dame, Indiana
Nick Sechi's Journal

We thrashed in the bed. Our lovemaking was riddled with rough and intense play. Shouts, gasps, and profanities punctuated the heavy rutting of two very fit and sex-hungry men. I seem to remember a strap and some bindings, but I could be mistaken. Anyway, the session did not seem to end. Our blood was up, not to stress the obvious.

Finally, he rolled off me and gripped me to him as our bodies lay side-by-side, sweat-slicked and breathing like endurance runners.

"I cannot get enough of you, my love. I am charged like never before. You are an incredible lover."

"Ten minutes, we go again, Boss. This time at hyper-speed. I am taking no prisoners, dude."

He laughed in my arms and kissed me deep, wet, and sloppy.

"It would seem that you are giving me a run for my money in usurping the man whore title tonight. Wherever did you learn to make love like that?"

"A family secret. Been saving it for the right time. We Bronx lads are one in a million."

We laughed and did some more naked hug-ups.

As Kayne inclined his head back on the wet pillow, breathing hard, I asked, "Whatever happened to Rosa Feldenstine?"

"I read where she remarried and pretty much went on to live a secluded life– Müller, I think, was her new last name."

I asked, "Feldenstine was shot, right?"

"Yes, point-blank in his home. His lover was also shot. Mrs. Feldenstine's prints were on the gun."

I sat up and looked back and down at him, my inside hand wandering over the left side of his body.

"Time to talk about Jack Hrynsyshyn. First, are his initials on the Kayne Sorenson Tree?"

"No, my love. I am afraid I made a complete jackass out of myself in that regard."

"Meaning?"

"Meaning, I made the offer, and Jack, very graciously declined. My failure to induce from the evidence was the subject of a momentary lapse and a few scotches. I was all of twenty years old."

"Very cool that you remained friends."

"I should also add that Brother Kick also made the moves on that hot jock and ended up with a bloody nose. He is not so gracious in failure. We are quite the circus act, we Sorensons. Another Mitch-fixes-it situation. Regardless, I have answered your query."

"The accident?"

"I think the expression is 't-boned.' He would have probably been made the district attorney in a few years, despite the Feldenstine fiasco. It was soon after the birth of little Jackie.

"I was in Europe working on my degree, so I do not know the facts. They never caught the guy. Jack's spine was severed. The family is super Catholic, so the new research with stem cells is not an option, so unfortunate."

"Kayne, they are covering up something. Body language and tells going off like firecrackers when they spoke of it. They have secrets that go deep. Did you get any of that?"

"I agree with you, my love."

He took my hand from his abdominals and placed my fingers in his mouth. He sucked each one and then slowly bit into the heel of my hand, insistent but not too hard. Delightful pressure.

Between hot mouth action, he said, "There is something there, and I can't help but see some connections."

He pushed me down and sat up, leaning over me. His raven-black hair cascaded over his handsome face as he licked, bit, and kissed.

"I neglect to elaborate until I receive more information on this issue. Damn, you are a hot beauty. Are you going to do as you are told?"

He grabbed a fist full of my short hair and pulled my head to the side, his dripping lips and hot breath in my face.

"Answer me, you hot slut."

God, I loved this game, and my body gave hard evidence to that very fact.

I grabbed for him and pulled him down on me, legs entwining, torsos slamming together from groin to neck. Mouths feeding on each other.

In the end, the image of Kayne, naked, glistening, with hard muscles flexed, head thrown back like he was howling at the moon, and climaxing on top of me at the same time would burn into my mind and stay in my memory for a long time.

Chapter Eleven: A Warning

Suite 325, The Morris Inn, The University of Notre Dame, Notre Dame, Indiana
South Bend International Airport, 4477 Progress Drive, South Bend, Indiana
Nick Sechi's Journal

"A mixture of religion and sex– the playground of passion. The scorching heat of a mixture of academics, physical endurance, and spiritual ecstasy– this vacation rocks."

"To whom are you speaking, my love?"

"No one. Anyone. Myself."

I should probably point out that we can also be romantic. Our lusty hunt, bind, and subdue manner of making love is a fantasy-based variety of our intimacy-- healthy, consensual, and supercharged. Switching up the modes of play keeps our coming together exciting and highly gratifying. We love the physicality, the boundary-pushing passion, and the taboo circumstances we often find ourselves in.

"How was your run?'

"Killed. You look like who-done-left-it-and-ran. Big Guy– one hot, sexy mess. You getting out of that bed or what?"

I sat on the bed.

Often, our expressions of intimacy are soft, tender, and almost automatic-- a kiss, a caress, a hand-hold, or a touch. Public displays of affection run from the shy, nearly discernable to the "in your face, haters" acts of defiance.

"You should run or lift at the Rock, Boss. Work out the old man kinks from..."

One of my favorite Kayne things is when he places an index finger against my lips, indicating, "Time for silence, my love. You are about to get some lovin' from your man like you wouldn't believe."

All of this is part of our connection but not the totality. We have, on occasion, played with others. And I must say, <u>played</u>... *very* well... very award-winning, but I'm biased. Sex is sex, and love is a much more comprehensive and timeless experience. Hot trouble... fun and adventure.

What I mean to say is that there is love in so many of the big and little things making up a shared life. Providing guidance for Kris has taken our relationship to a new level recently. Suddenly, there are three of us, but Kayne is my Bossman, and I am his love.

"Plane leaves at noon, my man. Rise and shine."

Admittedly, we have had some setbacks. We are working on communication challenges. Kayne is often unable to articulate the emotions that engulf his ever-active mind. My own issues involve somewhat the same thing. Still, my reluctance stems from the resistance to the soft side of my nature-- I abhor weakness but only in myself.

Anyway, he did train. ("Ahhh... the young athletes of summer. My love... male beauty and testosterone fire...")

I packed.

Kayne checked in with the local constabulary. ("Officer Hughes, if you need to reach us, feel free to use Nick's number.")

We met briefly with the Dean to verify the return of the holy objects from the campus post office. ("We will keep you posted, Father, on the follow-up to the murder of Brother Cataldi. The case leads us away from South Bend at this moment.")

"Go in peace, my sons."

And yes, we both made the Sign of the Cross, following his blessing. ("Not to do so, my love, would have been highly improper.")

***

Kayne is looking over my shoulder as I write this with a curious expression as we sit in the South Bend Airport. We're heading to Chicago and then San Francisco.

"I am sorry to interrupt you, my love, but this is your writing at its best. I respectfully advise you to stick to matters of the heart. The details of our cases, in my opinion, are somewhat boring. I do not understand the interest of your many followers."

"They want to believe in heroes, Boss, and like it or not, we kinda fill the slot."

"Flawed as we may be, I suppose."

He tenderly touched the side of my face near my right jawline and cheekbone. Beard burn.

"I will, in the future, soften my lovemaking. These marks of passion, like the bruises on your delicious white... we most likely scandalized the holy Fathers this morning. Well, suffice it to say I will be more careful."

His ice-blues twinkled as he smirked.

I elbowed him.

"Don't you fuckin' dare."

"Subject change. Time to analyze the data. Go."

I was used to this– a total shift in conversation. More and more, Kayne was processing variant sets of information simultaneously. It seemed his awareness was ricocheting with increasing speed— *time for advanced data analysis, my man.*

"Our follow-up with the police– when you're right, you're right, Bossman. Murder and no suspects as yet. The University turned over the stolen objects and is trying to be honest while keeping a lid on this tragedy."

"Yes, they are a highly moral and responsible organization. Brother Generoso had no family but his Order, and they are men of compassion. Our friend, Tamara, was quite upset, to say the least. Chief Hughes is going after 'the fence,' as you Americans call it, but the trail is sparse. The mailing address of the packages is just as I predicted, a complete blind."

He heaved a sigh and continued. "This religion cesspool really unnerves me, Nick. As an unbeliever, I am often at a complete loss."

"Ahhh, the sinful, lost, and fallen away... your agnosticism is pretty hard to overcome, Kayne. I feel ya, Boss."

He looked at me and confessed, "So many upright and lovely people— totally misguided. Tragic circumstances are.... "

He grabbed me and kissed me for a long moment. I came back from the embrace, very confused.

"Sorry, my love. Did I hurt your...?"

Repeat. This time, a bit longer, Kayne's eyes were everywhere but on me.

"Boss, that time you did. What's up?"

I rubbed my sore lip.

He took my hand and turned it over in his, examining it with tenderness. His hooded gaze was out through his long lashes to a place behind me.

"Pardon me, my love. Your head was in the way."

I started to turn but stopped, catching on.

"How long?"

Still faking interest in my hand, Kayne said, "Not long after, we settled here and started to talk. I will admit I was not sensing anything until then, but we may have been under observation for longer. Dark glasses and a dull, dark jacket. Near Starbucks. Cleared airport security, that is obvious."

I jumped up.

"Coffee? Be back in a minute."

Caffeine for Kayne would be like nitroglycerin at this point. I knew better. Got in line for a green juice thing and a grande non-fat latte. The crowd was kinda big, but I tried to be super casual while looking for our stalker.

The spook came nearer as I picked up our drinks. At the same time, a little boy came out of nowhere and grabbed me around the legs. The trolling woman in the dark glasses spoke so that only I could hear.

"Best to keep one's nose out of dirty business, wouldn't you say? Never can tell what may come from interfering in things that do not concern you or him."

Both hands loaded with our quaffs, I turned a bit awkwardly and said, "Excuse me."

"See ya around, handsome."

The woman made her exit through the airport crowd, fleeing from me after taking the young child's hand.

Chapter Twelve: Touch

Mission Dolores Park, San Francisco, California
Nick Sechi's Journal

Chris Evans was shirtless, sweating, and bellowing at the young jock sprawled on the grass in Mission Dolores Park. His cussing came with a killer smile. The man's matinee idol hairstyle was sweat-plastered on his forehead. Grass stains and dirt smeared his muscled, Captain America torso, shins to ears.

He fake-hollered and pointed at the dazed athlete.

"No! 'Cause you said 'tackle,' boy. I was good with touch. Threw a hurt on ya good, did I? Your own blessed fault, ya cocky lacrosser. Playing with the men, now, 'lil studly. Gotta man up."

He pulled Matt Crawley up from the kid's lying face down on the grass position and clasped him in a hug-up. I thought the kid was gonna collapse again because he found himself in the naked arms of one of the Avengers.

OK, so it wasn't Chris Evans, the actor, but my brother-in-law, Mitch, is a dead ringer. We often joked that he was Captain America's stunt double when we wanted to bust balls."

"No brag, but I am much better looking, truth be told, and rocking a whole lot of natural muscle. Do you know if 'Mister Evans' has his medical degree?"

There would follow a good-natured cuff for anyone who teased the eldest of the Sorenson brothers. He continued his remarks.

"Doesn't anyone ever play touch football anymore? Tackle is my husband's favorite when we get into American sports. But then again, Kick likes anything that involves feats of strength in the dirt with super-fit athletes."

Mitch rolled back into the quarterback position and threw the football to Kris, who was down the field, and the boy leaped to catch it in the air.

When he hit the ground, he came at his uncle and his boyfriend. The ball tucked under one arm and the other in blocking position, Kris ran with a bravado that begged to be challenged, dancing in and out.

Mitch called out to Matt, "Let's bring this showboater down. What do you say?"

They came at him from two sides and wedge-tackled the self-proclaimed champion to the lawn. The result was a three-way wrestle-up with Mitch sitting back on his haunches and catching his breath. Kris pulled Matt to him on the grass and kissed him with testosterone-fueled enthusiasm.

The three dirty athletes look up simultaneously at the two spectators sitting on the bench two feet away-- three open mouths and two returning grins. I tossed Kris the forgotten football.

"Holy shit. Uncle Kayne and Uncle Nick, when the fuck did you get back home?"

Mitch cuffed his cussing nephew. When Kris dove into our arms for a homecoming hug and kiss, his lawn-clipping-spattered cowlick stood straight up.

Kayne said through laughter, "My dear Kristof, you remember that your Uncle Mitch has a dislike of the vulgar language."

'Yeah, ya li'l twink. It's not classy, and it's totally unmanly."

Mitch gave each of us a wet bear hug and smooch as Kris rounded on him with a "Yeah? And who's gonna so make me stop cussin'? Not you, woosie man." He jumped on Mitch's back, and they went down on the grass in a second-round tussle."

I said, "Does everyone in this family fight?"

"It would appear so, my love. We are a sporty breed."

Matt stepped up and extended his hand to Kayne, who gave him a sincere two-handed shake. I pulled him in for a bro-hug. Kris had told me that I was Matt's older man, man crush. I wasn't sure I appreciated the appellation. Still, I liked the kiddo, and well, an opportunity to tease... try and stop me.

"'Sup, dude? Everything good?"

I held him away from me and watched him react like a kid on Christmas morning.

"All good, Mr... I mean Nick. I just graduated with honors and started my graduate internship in the fall at San Francisco General."

"Sensational, been keeping The Kris honest and true?"

Matt smiled and looked at the ground. He came back up, saying, "One tall order, Sir. He will always be a challenge to keep as a dude's one and only... or maybe the other way round."

I agreed, "Yep. The boy is a rover. Kinda runs in the blood."

Mitch came up from the tumble with Kris sorta hanging on his neck and shoulders.

"I am getting too old for this... oof, easy tiger...." He did a hold break but was unsuccessful. Nevertheless, the oldest Sorenson brother continued talking.

"It's all I can do... to keep the Hot Mess under control. Ouch, you little... Seriously, thinking of restraints on that one."

He tossed Kris off and instructed, "Go and make out with that hot boy of yours, nephew. Just do not go too far."

We all laughed. Mitch plopped down on the bench and again tried to catch his breath. Matt sat in the grass, leaning back on his arms, and Kris landed on his back, head on Matt's lap. He fiddled with chewing a blade of grass.

Kayne began, "We got in from Chicago about ninety minutes ago. Trasker said that you three were scaring the tourists at Mission Dolores Park. So we hopped public transport, and here we are."

"How was the dear old *alma mater*?" Mitch wrapped a big arm around me, pulling me in and rubbing my head like I was a Labrador retriever.

"Did you show my favorite brother-in-law the sights and sounds of the finest Catholic University in America? And are they still talking about Kick?"

I placed a hand on his chest and turned to him. "All about the Archangel... everywhere we went... bla, bla, bla. Mitch Sorenson, the mightiest fullback on the soccer pitch... leader of the Four Sorensons... bla, bla bla. You are quite a legend there yourself, buddy."

Kayne sat on the other side of his brother and said, "I seem to remember howling with a few of the alumni. We were havin' a coldie and telling old stories. We remembered a certain beefy jock beauty from 'The Red Center' who showed his spectacular arse and a bit more on the stage at Notre Dame. You know, my brother, I denied any impropriety on your behalf with all brotherly love and sincerity. Sorensons – we defend!"

Even I could not keep a civil expression. We howled at the irony.

Mitch pushed Kayne off the bench on his ass.

Kris sat up and called with excitement, "Naked on stage? You, Uncle Mitch? Come on, give. Details... details for the blog, right, Nick?"

He nodded at me.

Kayne said, " And there are pictures."

Mitch made a fist and clenched his teeth. "Kayne Jason, so help me...."

It was a good-natured threat.

Kayne got up and dusted himself off. He told the story as if he were a pitchman in a snake oil show.

"The theater department was doing a production of 'Miss Saigon.' Mitch was a senior, and the rest of us were sophomores. The student portraying Chris, the male lead, got ill unexpectedly just before the final rehearsals."

Mitch growled, "I used to sing a lot in the shower, you know. Passed the time growing up as we did on Inala in the middle of nowhere. Anyway..."

"Anyway..."

Kayne could not stop laughing.

Mitch roared, "He swiped my briefs. The Hot Mess. Kick. You know he did it. Kayne probably helped him. "

"I admit nothing, but my detective skills lead me to believe there was, in fact, an accomplice in the case of stealing the star's knickers. A highly-skilled intellectual and a dare-devil par excellence– the thievery was masterful."

He laughed again as he continued, stepping behind Mitch and placing his hands on his big brother's shoulders.

"It was a quick scene switch. The young Mitchell Sorenson is changing into his military camos, and, O my Lord, no drawers! What will the ingenue do?"

I called out, "The show must go on."

"Exactly, so on he goes, commando Archangel. The hot jock was jockless."

Mitch took up the narrative.

"The bedroom scene was originally staged with the character, Chris, in uniform, but the director wanted a bit of softcore and all that. I improvised with a towel, but when we finished the song, 'Sun and Moon,' I was supposed to embrace the actress playing Kim."

Kayne finished, "Sun and moon is right, my friends. And there it was, beefcake moon over South Bend. "

"I got a lot of offers to go on dates after that, gals, guys, even some of the lads in seminary. Big surprise, right? The dean of students was as mad as a gum tree fulla galahs."

We were roaring with laughter. Mitch was amusingly pissed.

"Brother Kayne, you are one to talk. I seem to remember a few...."

To stop his sibling from reciprocating with lurid tales of improper judgment, Kayne jumped up on the bench and began to shout to the city and the world.

"Hey... Hey... Chris Evans... right here, ya mugs. Yeah... It's true... autographs... selfies... Chris Evans... Captain America!"

The three of us dissolved in laughter. Mitch chased Kayne up the hill to the far reaches of the park.

The Shadow of Evil

Chapter Thirteen: StrEat Food

SoMa, San Francisco, California
Nick Sechi's Journal

"Yeah, so, we gotta do the trucks."

Kris led the way out of the park. We had all agreed that we were super hungry and dressed solely for urban food. We hiked three blocks up Dolores Street and grabbed the number 22 bus at 16th Street. At the Bryant Avenue stop, we walked north five blocks, and there it was, almost under the 101 – the SoMa StrEat Food Park.

San Francisco seemed to have an obsession with food trucks. This unique, South of Market urban playground offered a variety of victuals from a diverse rotation of vendors, serving a wide range of ethnic cuisines. We spread out and made our choices, bringing back savory selections to a table and chowing down. Kris and Matt dashed off after a bit to hit the carnival games.

Mitch said, "This place is great. Is that a school bus?"

I remarked, "Yep, converted into a party space, The Magic Bus. When the Niners or the Giants are home, this place is mobbed. No res, no get in."

"So, my brother. What brings you to the Golden State?"

I added, "And…."

Mitch sipped his Burmese Beer and said, "Yes, yes. I know what you are going to ask. 'Where is the Hot Mess?'"

He seemed to dodge, saying, "This is one great brew, Nick. Excellent recommendation. Cheers, mate."

We clinked.

Thomas Michael Sorenson was named after his father. He was a junior, but in name only. He preferred the nickname Kick to the point of making a fuss whenever any version of "Thomas" was used in reference to him, with the notable exception of when his father called him to accountability.

The meme went, "It's 'Thomas' when Ace got angry and 'Thomas Michael' when he is bloody pissed off."

And Kick was the author of trouble, by no stretch of the imagination. He was absolutely certifiable with Bipolar Disorder II when not on his meds. As evidenced, Kick's depressive symptoms included sadness and/or hopelessness. What usually persisted were the hypomanic symptoms, elevated levels of enthusiasm, outrageous hilarity, and just everyday bat-shit craziness. Sometimes, he behaved like a room full of kindergarteners jacked up on too much sugar. All expressed with a ton of physicality.

With the guidance of his very stable and loving husband, Mitch, a licensed physiatrist, and with regular doses of mood stabilizers for controlling his serotonin levels, Kick was a riot of loveable fun and athleticism, albeit a very astute business person.

The youngest of the triplets, he was an award-winning athlete. An adventurous swaggerer and ultimate risk-taker, Kick was a natural charmer and the most oversexed of the three, which is saying a whole hell of a lot. And Mitch loved him with an almost legendary love.

Ace did not believe in meds and treated his out-of-control son with a regular strapping in the tack room.

"I most likely fell in love with The Mess when he was an ankle biter." Mitch would say. "Our amah would put him into my arms when she had had enough, and I would rock him to sleep. And so we naturally fell into step as the big brother and his little charge."

The bond grew strong as the years went on, growing up on the family ranch, Inala, in Western Australia, aka The Red Center. Their connection grew through university and post-graduate professional life. Although Kick had a very adventurous and high-energy sex life, he accepted when Mitch proposed two years before Kayne and I married. Together, they built a resort and equestrian empire in the Aerie Valley of Colorado, near Aspen.

Taking another sip of his beer, Mitch rewound to answer the question.

"Phoenix"

"And what, pray tell, is Thomas Jr. up to in 'The Copper State,' scaling the heights of the Grand Canyon or shooting the rapids in an inner tube?"

Kick parlayed his high energy and physical gifts into some very impressive X Games sports championships. He was a parkour master on two continents. Winning the Red Bull AOM three times. Kick's kamikaze vault and Triple A-twist were breathtaking physical works of art.

Now, Mitch did a light headlock on his sardonic brother and gave him a quizzical look.

"Pray tell? Pray tell? Kayne, just what century are you from? Sometimes, you use expressions from the Court of Victoria and Albert. Pomp and circumstance from the Great Australian Fuck All. You know what Da would say. He hates pretentiousness."

Kayne scratched his head, turned to me, and said, "Kayne Jason get offin' your bloody high horse, ya drongo. Stow yer fancy airs afore I wallop ya a good 'un."

His imitation of the *pater familias,* Captain Thomas, "Ace" Sorenson, former Australian Marine and Lord of Inala, the sixth-largest cattle ranch globally, was spot on. Kayne ended his Ace imitation, and Mitch continued.

"So, Kick has been asked to serve on the board of the Interscholastic Equestrian Association. Aerie Stables has been a member of Hunt Seat, Western, and Dressage Disciplines for Zone Eight for a couple of years. Do you know it, Nick?"

"No. Sounds interesting."

"With Kick's leadership, Aerie Stables got into it through our membership with the United States Equestrian Federation. So, the IEA introduces students in private and public middle and secondary schools to equestrian sports by promoting and improving the quality of equestrian competition and instruction. To be specific, safe riding instruction, student competition, and education in equestrian sport at the middle and secondary school levels, mostly ages nine through nineteen."

It was easy to see that Mitch was one proud husband.

"You should see The Mess and the little ones. Especially the inner-city kids. Outstanding. Loves to be a guest instructor for those new to riding. Those little ankle-biters go bonkers for him. And, he so dearly loves horses."

Kayne commented, "Very commendable."

"In our family, Kick does the equestrian and stables business. I work in the resort and related environmental industries. And then there's my practice. It is an excellent partnership."

"And you get to nail his fine arse, and he, yours."

Mitch grinned, leaned back, and stretched-- big arms, shoulders, and chest arching up. Some folks at a nearby table were trolling the hot man, and the posture made them stare gape-mouthed. He slowly brought down one arm to the shoulder of the teasing brother and said, "You are talking about my husband, brother, and I will wallop you for your dirty thoughts. I may be adopted, but I claim my rights as your older brother.

He took a bite of his "The Duke" from the *Me So Hungry Too* food cart. Wiped his mouth and finished his remarks.

"Besides, I'm Da's favorite, and you are jealous."

He poked Kayne in the ribs, which caused my husband to chuckle at the pressure on his ticklish spot. Evidently, this was a gesture and reaction that must have been part of their growing-up high jinks.

Kayne raised his glass and clowned, "Who's for another brewsky? Dat down-home enough for ya, bra?"

Kayne left to get our refills, and Mitch asked, "India? Kris was saying..."

"Yeah, pretty wild, bud. Some major Big Bads doing a lot of shit. The country is so beautiful, with the Himalayas, foothills, and the pristine river valleys. Some dangerous and nasty situations, but also many stunning moments. Met the man himself. It was amazing."

"Kick and I met His Holiness, the Dalai Lama, at a reception when he spoke in New York. He took Kick's head in his hands and gave him a special blessing. Said he was a reincarnation of one of the Tibetan holy ones, I do not remember the details to be honest."

A returning voice said, "Most likely, it was one of the protectors like Hayagriva, who is connected to horses. They are the defenders of the faith and have no mercy against their enemies."

"That's it. Anyway, should have seen Kick after that. I think his innate cockiness increased by two-hundred percent. It would seem that Kris has a lot of that in him, inherited Sorenson brashness. How is he doing?"

"Kris is..."

Kayne interrupted with a hand on mine.

"Excuse me, my love."

He turned to his brother.

"You are a perfect example of avoidance, Doctor Sorenson. The reason for your visit must be alarming indeed. So here is how we will proceed. We will update you on *The Kris*...."

"*The* Kris– you guys raising a legend? The psychiatrist in me is reeling right now."

I said, "Most times, it would seem that way."

Kayne got back to it.

"Yes, The Kris. Following that, you will be on the couch, so to speak. Please continue, Nick."

I paused a bit, saying, "Gosh, where to start? School-- grades are through the roof. The kid is an honors-caliber student. Athletics-- probably looking at a career in professional soccer, truth be told."

Kayne said, "Not if I have anything to say about it, which I am sure I will not."

"Perhaps an international terrorist, like his father?"

"Espionage, Mitch, not terrorism."

The older Sorenson waved away Kayne's corrective remarks.

"Eric been around much?"

I answered, "Since the case in Eastern Europe, he has been back a few times for some brief appearances. We believe he is still working, globe-hopping and all that undercover shit-- disguises and shadows, you know. Kris just idolizes him. That's a hurt, to be sure."

"Feelings of abandonment and self-doubt, most likely. Deep anxiety, wondering why Eric would not want to be with him."

Kayne added, "Yes, to be sure. The lad has steeled his body and mind to prove he can face the dangers which prevent him from being with his father."

Mitch nodded.

I said, "Which has caused Kayne and me to try to keep close to Kris and reassess our frequent separation due to our cases."

"As we have spoken many times before, my love, it is a delicate balance. Kris wants the independence of a college freshman but also needs the loving support of a father, or in this case, fathers."

"The self-objectification is a bit concerning. Can you speak more about that?"

"The Kris is a lad who believes his own press. He is a chronic overachiever and has a bit of a Savior Complex."

"Sorenson."

"And Sechi. Not blood, but attitude-wise, if you know what I mean."

"Yes, not blood either, but often modeling plays a big part in role formation."

We were interrupted by the two college jocks who were done gaming.

"...and The Kris cannot be defeated."

Matt challenged, "I almost had you, ya blowhard."

"And you'd be the one to know about that," Kris threw the jibe as he picked up my glass of beer.

I gently took it back, saying, "So, that would be a no, bud. Unless somehow eighteen equals twenty-one, and they forgot to tell me."

He furrowed his brow and pursed his lips.

"Such a prude, Sechi."

"Such a royal pain in the ass, Sorenson. Bite me."

He faked going for it and nearly knocked me out of my chair. I playfully brought up my dukes.

"Think about it, Your Hind Ass. Gonna hurt."

"OK, OK. Behaving. Sleepover? Cool?" He pointed back and forth from Matt to himself."

Kayne said, "Got studying? Both of you. Tomorrow is school. That comes first. All else has a second priority. Yes?"

Matt said, "Yeah, I got some stuff I have to do for this internship. All good, Doctor S."

I pulled my nephew in close and whispered, "And no yelling. Your room is next to ours, remember."

Kris broke back, wiggled his eyebrows, swatted his buddy on the butt, and they raced out of the park. He spun at the last minute and gave us the "thumbs-up."

Kayne mused, "Guaranteed to yell the house down, nonetheless."

"Cannot be louder than your frisky brother, I wager. All told, it would seem the lad has a healthy emotional life."

"Some fluidity regarding his sexual orientation, but seems to have a yen for the lads."

"Kayne, 'a yen?' He's about as robust in his sexin' as they come… except for his father, who is a bit scary in all of that triple-X bondage stuff. Kris enjoys sexin' up and is not ashamed of who he is."

The Brothers Sorenson smiled. Mitch stood up and signaled that it was time to go.

"Hold on, mate. There is a conversation hanging here like a sleeping bush possum. Give it a go, y'hear."

"Bollocks, you. Back at the Heights. Need to gather my thoughts, and we need a bit of the privacy. Git your arse in gear, muggo."

Sorensons– add alcohol, and the most professional rhetoricians devolve into Outback Bushmen yapping in "Strine."

Chapter Fourteen: In the Heights

221 Baker Street, San Francisco, California
Nich Sechi's Journal

"Welcome home, Gentlemen. I was at the supermarket when you arrived earlier. I trust that your visit to Indiana was a restful one."

"Very fine, Trasker. Thank you for settling Doctor Sorenson in. The East guestroom? Excellent. That one has the best view. I believe he went up to clean up."

"Have you eaten, Doctor Sorenson?"

"Yes, we are fully sated, thank you."

I said, "We are just going to kick back out by the pool with some wine. Say, Trasker, how is Andi working out? Is she a help to you?"

Jessie Trasker was no easy piece of work. She was a traditional domestic and suspicious of anyone and everyone who threatened her domain, most notably my mother, who competed for the crown when she came to visit. Trasker is formidable, devoted to the Sechi-Sorensons, and an expert shooter. Her weapon of choice was a bolt-action .22 long rifle, and she could hit a lit cigarette at 100 yards.

At her trial, Kayne had provided clinical evidence that she was justified in shooting and killing her abusive husband, a clear case of self-defense. Her loyalty to him was unshakeable. She adored our little prince and ensured he behaved and kept to his studies when we were on assignment.

"Well, the getting used to period has ended, and we are both in agreement concerning promptness and how things are to be done around here."

"Your way."

"Needless to say, Doctor."

Trasker was in her robe and nightclothes and was finishing a stack of turkey sandwiches.

"Master Sorenson?"

"Yes, he and young Mister Crawley arrived about an hour ago, and...."

She looked up at the ceiling in the direction of the second-floor bedrooms.

"Supposed to be studying."

Trasker said nothing further. Sometimes, silence can be thunderous.

"Nice of you to fix them a midnight snack."

"I will set out the wine glasses if you and the Doctor would like to change."

"Thank you, Trasker. Regarding that tray, you may want to just leave it on the table outside Kris' door and knock. There will be five for breakfast."

"Very good, Doctor."

Kayne went to the wine steward in the butler's pantry. He had it uniquely designed for the house. It featured a touch screen, which brought up a list of the bottles in our cellar. He tapped an icon and put the robotics into action.

"Hello. This is Castello Banfi 2015 Excelsus– intense nectar from the sun-drenched hills of Tuscany. We have a total of eight in the cellar below."

I goofed with my pretentious wine steward imitation.

"It has a very fruity nose accompanied by more complex notes of jam, spices, tobacco, and coffee. A superb and spectacular varietal that exhibits layers of blackberry, cassis, and black cherry– a wine for the ages...."

"You are reading that over my shoulder, ya mug. Just for that, two bottles."

"... with just a soupçon of man ass. Make mine a Mic Ultra. We don't have chi-chi wines in Da Bronx."

He cuffed the back of my head.

The computer beeped, and the two bottles of Excelsus appeared behind the glass doors at the back of the cabinet. What a country!

***

The summer night was brisk. September and October would bring warmer, sunnier weather. Nonetheless, Mitch was doing laps in the pool when Kayne and I joined him. Foggy and breezy, the atmosphere outside our Pacific Heights home reminded me of the moors of Scotland in <u>The Hound of the Baskervilles</u>. Somewhere, a foghorn sounded in the direction of the Golden Gate, and through the haze, searchlights pierced the darkness. The city's homes and buildings glowed around our hillside residence like half-hidden jewels.

I wore a hoodie and long track pants. Kayne was in a robe and silk pajama bottoms. Trasker has set out the open wine, breathing alongside assorted munchies and the glasses on the tray.

Mitch finished his swim and came up the steps, sheets of night-sparkling water sluicing from his body.

Holy shit? Gotta say it one last time. One breathtaking specimen of a major Australian alpha male. Kick, you lucky dog.

He reached up and shook the water out of his hair. He looked at me and extended both hands.

Kayne whispered, "Toss him the towel, my love."

"Huh?"

"You are holding it in your hands."

"Oh yeah, sorry. I ahh..."

I stuttered but regained, calling out, "Your room is good?"

Kayne had placed a terrycloth robe on the third chair. He began to pour the wine. Mitch put on the robe, turned his back to us, and slipped off the speedo. He tied the belt, sat, and stretched his long legs as he took the wine from his brother. The speedo was hung over the fourth chair.

I had seen him in the altogether before. Always a beauty to see it again, and the dude was almost forty. OK, OK, OK. I will stop-- brain reset.

"Wow, this is grand, you guys. Betting it is Italian." Kayne handed him the bottle.

"Impressive. Strong and savory."

"Excuse me a minute."

I walked to the pool and stripped. I dove in. The water was icy cold, a shock to the system. My head immediately began to clear of my inappropriate thoughts. As I emerged, Kayne hit me in the head with a rolled-up towel.

"Cover that sweet arse, naked boy. There are children around the place."

I wrapped the towel like a sarong and put my hoodie back on. Chair, wine, and I was ready for the convo, brain-focused and thinking pure, altar-boy thoughts.

Kayne's ice-blues flickered in the ambient light as he began. He addressed his brother.

"This is not about Kick. Your hedging and reticence throughout the afternoon indicate that this is new territory. You are at an impasse in dealing effectively with the problem.

"The bracelet on your left arm is new. The leather shows no aging. The design is Wardandi, no, excuse me, Ngaanyatjarra. You are returning from Western Australia. This is about Inala."

Mitch said nothing, sipped his wine, and looked grave.

"As a business person, there is nothing about corporate affairs that would flummox your mind. *Ergo*, Sorenson Industries AU is not in trouble or under any stress that you could not bring to a successful ending. You are the president and CEO of your own company and have much experience in the world of corporate affairs.

Mitch was silent. He let his brother continue and sipped the Excelsus.

"Kick was put out to pasture, literally, and you went alone. You decided that he would make matters untenable and wanted to address this on your own. Your only rational brother, me, was left out of the loop, so this is very curious. The talisman you wear on your wrist is an insignia of healing and strength."

Kayne brought it in for a landing, saying, "Your saving wings are showing, Doctor Sorenson. The Archangel is ready to make a play for good sense and diagnostic intervention.

"Mitch, my brother, what's going on with Ace?"

Chapter Fifteen: Burn

221 Baker Street, San Francisco, California
Nick Sechi's Journal

"Organic blows, man."

"Kris, it's all in the benzene ring configuration, and then it's alkanes, alkenes, and alkynes."

Matt was obviously distracted. His tutorial remarks were spoken to the window pane.

"Huh? My exam tomorrow is on exothermic reactions. I said I was not doing organic next semester because this fulfills my chem requirement and..."

Matt did a crotch adjustment and remarked, "Sounds good."

"Right. You had better tell me what is going on in that dirty mind of yours, bud. If I have to draw my own conclusions, it's not gonna be nice."

Matt turned from the window in Kris's room. On the second floor, the view was across the back lawn and gardens to the patio, the pool, and the parkour course. He was in his boxers.

"Thinking of my practicum in critical care. My supervisor is a ballbuster. Wanna do my best so I can keep the internship and stay here and hang out with you." He reached for the near-naked Kris– a mostly briefs/sometimes jock boy.

Kris snapped a chemistry book closed and jumped up off the bed. Matt met him and tried to move them both away from the window.

"I call BS, dude. Whatcha looking at?"

Kris took the restraining arm and led Matthew back to the view of the men at the swimming pool. Mitch was emerging, wet and shining, and Nick decided to go at a bare-arsed run-in for a dip.

"You are such a horny bugger. I am shocked. Shocked."

He swatted his jock bud's behind.

"Ow. What?"

"They are my uncles, dude. You are trolling, and it is a sin."

"Load of crap, man. Since when are you getting all holy?"

Kris was goofing big time.

"The good fathers who taught us religion at the Lycée Français Victor Hugo in Sofia made it a point to give a lot of attention to our sex education and the sins of the flesh."

"I'll bet."

Matt embraced Kris with one arm and slid the other hand into the back of his briefs. He growled and licked the freshman from ear to collarbone.

Kris continued to tease with a bit of an unsuccessful shove.

"Naw, naw, naw. Not today, Satan. Just because your older man lust has not been depleted-- ain't gettin' none o' this. You sin by your dirty thoughts."

"You Catholics-- tons of guilt and bad sex."

Matt became more insistent. His moments of voyeurism had stoked the fires of carnal desire, and he would not be deterred.

"Ummm, have I told you of my sexy interest in a certain younger man? Yeahhh, bae... makes me so fuckin' hot... this boy's gotta have it. Oh yeah... keep doing that... Ohhh shittt, Kris."

The underwear ended up on the floor in a heap as the young couple moved back towards the bed. Kris reached up and pulled at the back of Matt's hair, causing him to move his head backward. Kris growled into his bud's ear while licking his neck.

"Which of the members of the Sorenson-Sechi stud stables do you want in that bed with you tonight?"

"Only the hottest and most energetic."

He pulled Kris down on top of him.

***

Kayne sat back, all attention on his silent brother, and steepled his fingers.

Mitch crossed his long legs and scratched an ear. Closing one eye, he said to Kayne. "Impressive. As time goes on, you only get better with the inductive reasoning process. But before we go there, Kayne. What happened in December, after the Asian case?"

Kayne pushed back his pesky bang and looked my way. "We went to Australia to help. It was a major disaster on a national scale. In addition, keeping the nephew from coming along proved to be a challenge. He loves danger and adventure."

"Interesting. Kris is quite headstrong, it would seem."

Kayne spoke more about the wildfire disaster.

"Inala was incredibly spared despite the scalding season temperatures believed to contribute to the country-wide conflagrations. The ranch lies a bit nearer the center of the state, away from the sea, as you know. Most of the disaster was up and down the country's southwest coast, from Geraldton, north of Perth, all the way south to Albany.

"The fires caused massive environmental damage. Tens of thousands of hectares of flora were destroyed. When we arrived, Da was in South Australia, meeting with the Emergency Ministers from that state and Western Australia. They were formulating a plan to combine local firefighting resources to protect the population and rescue what wildlife they could. The program would involve a ground force of the military, politicians, firefighters, as well as trained volunteers, farmers, and tourism folks."

Mitch asked, "Stirling?"

I chimed in, "Yeah, awful. Ace asked Kayne and me to join in with the best of his stockmen and help out there. The fire tore through the Stirling Range National Park just after we arrived, around Christmastime. Authorities are claiming it was a lightning strike, but...."

I stopped and looked at Kayne.

He said, "There is more to that part of the story, Mitch, but we are in delicate waters here. We have been officially asked by the government not to reveal, at this time anyway, the results of our investigation into the Stirling Wildfire."

"Yep, 'The Case of the Billabong Inferno' is locked until it is safe to go public. Kayne and I are in agreement that the results would provoke the fall of the government, sure as hell."

Kayne went on.

"Da was a whirlwind. He commandeered most of the wildlife rescue components near Stirling. He put out the word and underwrote getting university students in the animal husbandry and environmental biology fields to Inala. Room and board, and training. Then, the project flew hurt animals to eight rescue stations on the ranch. They figured Inala was safe for humans and animals, away from the fires."

"Kayne piloted a few of the flights using your Da's planes."

Mitch said, "I heard Ace also got the First Nationers to get their people and many of the whites into temporary shelters. Da was always a great advocate of getting the various ethnic groups to work together. Some major network is doing a story on that."

I said, "The conservationists are wild. With the extent of the fires, especially in the national parks, the loss of rare and unique flora and fauna is pretty substantial. One day, we brought in four families of quokkas and a group of wombats. Little guys were so fuckin' cute, man."

Kayne added, "The whole experience took a physical and mental toll on Ace. Darana was on him to be careful, but he is such a bloody risk-taker.

The oldest Sorenson brother said, "Assuredly the source of the infamous family trait."

Kayne said, "We remained through the winter and spring in Australia, returning to San Francisco in April. Summer brought Alumni Days at Notre Dame, and then we returned here. That brings you up to date."

Mitch examined his glass of deep red wine as if he were turning an archeological relic in his strong hands-- carefully, slowly, and with a certain intensity.

He began.

"I got a call from Darana about three weeks ago asking if I could find a reason to visit Inala on my own. Actually, just that day, I accepted an invitation to present a paper on inherited neurological disorders for the International Psychoanalytical Association. One of their presenters had recommended me in an attempt to fill out the conference. I had completed the clinical studies for the monograph last year."

"Please allow me to guess."

Kayne finger-counted off.

"Bipolar Disorder, Schizophrenia, and ..."

He pointed the last finger to himself, saying, "Attention Deficit Hyperactivity Disorder. Actually, mine is not a disorder but rather an enhanced state of consciousness. Correct me if I am wrong, but there is research to support the theory that schizophrenia may also be a genetically caused altered state of mind."

He poured another round of the Italian wine. I could tell that his divergence was an indication that he was a bit nervous about what Mitch had to say. Sorenson family affairs, like my own, were highly emotionally charged-- powerful personalities all around, usually, an express trip to Crazy Town.

Mitch said, "So, Eric really is a fallen angel. I should have brought the complete set of triplets for a ... a... whatchamacallit ...."

I said, "Show and Tell."

"Right. What a bloody sight that would be, eh? Good on ya, Nick. Cheers."

He raised his glass to mine. The accents and the Australian slang came on in full force with both brothers. So true to form-- the night, the drink, and the topic.

Kayne reached out to touch the shoulder of his older sibling, saying, "My loving brother, Inala, Ace. Please continue."

"I packed Kick off to Phoenix and headed to the Lucky Country. Presented my paper at the conference in Darwin and wound down to Alice Springs and the old homestead.

"Da was out on muster and was expected the next day, so Darana and I got down to the business at hand without him around. She and I viewed the operation on horseback."

Mitch looked into the soft San Francisco night and continued.

"Darana had a lot to say about your heroics, both of your courageous exploits and the partnership that Sorenson Industries had with the Aboriginal and Torre Island Straits peoples...."

"The true custodians of the land...."

"Right, Brother."

I nodded.

"Anyway, the ranchers have been taking good care of the livestock, but it was an intense and exhausting six months. Everyone was struggling to get back to normal with the ranch. Da was a fanatic about the wildlife care installations and regularly visited the veterinarian students and the stations. Plane loads of the injured animals along with scientists, veterinarians, members of the National Guard, not to mention equipment and volunteers... his military training was found to be just the type of leadership the project needed."

Mitch sipped and then added, "The paddocks out to the eastern hills were filled with rescues and infrastructure for their care. The army engineers actually expanded Inala's airstrip for the project. What impressed me most when I viewed the work over there was the admirable cooperation between the First Nationers and the other ethnic communities. Not only was Ace part of the council for the rescue of Australia's wildlife but he was also committed to keeping the cattle station operating and ensuring the safety of Inala's livestock.

"So there it was. Darana said that since you both returned to the States, there have been some incidents with Ace."

"I see. Go on, please."

"Bill Harrington, the head roustabout, sent him home just before my arrival. Ace had fallen off his horse and was showing signs of exhaustion. You know him. He was bellowing to be back in the saddle and out in the bush. Darana said there was some bruising, swelling of tissue, and a bit of confusion.

"Mitch, what was the color of his skin when you saw him?"

"Bluish tinge. Yeah, I immediately thought of heart disease. And of course..."

"No doctors. He has no trust in them since the circumstances of our mother's multiple births."

"Between the two of us, Darana and I got him to Alice Springs and his cardiologist. He agreed to the tests after a very animated harangue. First up was his blood pressure, which was very high. They managed to get it under control. The diagnosis is coarctation of the aorta. It is uncommon in adults, but he has it."

Kayne explained, "It is a congenital condition usually afflicting children. The large blood artery that branches off the heart has narrowed for a variety of reasons. Many times, the anomaly is not detected until adulthood.

"Mitch, the treatment for this condition is usually successful. They can replace the narrowed section without opening the chest. You seem to be in near panic mode. Why?"

"Because it's Da, and he is Ace-- total shitstorm mode for just about anything like this. He is in denial, has a lot of anger, and is reacting with his usual bullheadedness. Also, there may be complications, including severe hardening or inflammation of the arteries."

Kayne said, "*Takayasu's arteritis.*"

"Yes, it's what happened next that was even more concerning."

"Please go on."

"When we arrived back home, Da set us down and broke out the plan. He asked Darana to get him a personal lawyer.

"I want a black bloke, Darana. Ya can trust 'em more'n the blasted whites."

"Ace, I am your corporate and personal lawyer. Have been for years."

"Naw good, gal. I'm changing my will, and you need not be a party to all o' this. Set up an appointment as soon as you can.

"Mitch, I made some decisions over the years regarding my assets. For a while, I intended to split everything between my four sons. Not sure I like that picture anymore. No bad blood, lad. It's just that Inala's power and pride are in her size. Breaking her up will lead to fightin' and a decline in her productivity.

"You are all on the Board, anyway, except for Eric. I could do a trust make you co-owners, but... call me old-fashioned, Mitch, that seems like a lot of bureaucracy, and often here, decisions have to be made in a tick– a–bloody–instant.

"My sons have very different lives and their own interests. To run this business with a deep commitment to the land, the people, the wildlife, and the livestock-- there can be no other shit going on.

"Also, I am afraid the federals will break up this Inala, and my Da would come back from the grave and wreak havoc if that should occur."

He tapped the table for emphasis.

"Sides. Even though Inala has made me a fortune many times over. It ain't my land or the Fed's, for that matter. You know that's the God's honest truth, son.

"Anyway, this ranch, this Inala, is a model of how people can work together for mutual benefit and keep the planet thriving, ya see? Naw-- need a firm hand at the tiller, lad, with one focus only. Which of the four of you would relish living here in the Red Center?

"You and Thomas have your hands full with Aerie and its subsidiaries. Kayne and Nick are bloody international superstars. Who knows if Eric is even alive after the shit in Trieste. I have someone in mind, but it will take a bit o' time, provided I have some time left in my life."

"Two more things, son, my grandson, Kris. I want him here. He will be safe here, not in fancy-arse San Francisco. The crap arses what came for

94

'em before will do it again. Lookit it this way. Eric pissed off a lot o' bad blokes while trying to hide his son in the royal house of Bulgaria. Did not bloody work. Am I right? Now Kayne and Nick-- righting wrongs as fast as a goose can shit. The kid has himself in the sites of too many vengeful fuckos. He needs to be with me.

"Kris'll complete college here. I can pull some strings. I am up to my balls, contributing to many institutions of higher learning. They bloody owe me."

I said, "Whoa. I can't say that I like that part of the Ace Sorenson Succession Strategy at all. Kris, Master of Inala-- no, no, no. And the reasons are many and obvious. Does your father ever consider the desires and aspirations of the other folks he ropes into his plans?"

Mitch and Kayne answered me in unison.

"No."

"I agree with you, my love. I think that his father would take him away and keep him from ever seeing the family again. The lad himself would not want this. He is far too ambitious and worldly for that kind of life. Why, he hopes to spend some time this winter with you and Kick in Colorado, hobnobbing with the international ski glitterati. This is quite unacceptable."

Mitch said, "I concur. You both act in *loco parentis,* which matters greatly even though he has come of age. The entire concept would inhibit the lad. He is still very young and trying to find his authenticity.

"Eric. Ha. He and Da have been trading 'fuck yous' for more than thirty years. This is Ace's ultimate revenge. Eric robbed him of a son. For Da, turnabout is fair play, it would seem."

"There's more."

"Medical decisions: I want more information about this heart condition crap 'fore I agree to anything. It's going to be like this...."

Darana said nothing up to this point, but now she interrupted.

"Excuse me, Captain, but this is exactly how it will go. Initially, you will do everything Dr. Horton advises, and I mean everything. The doctors cannot do much until they have your blood pressure under control, and

that will not happen if you continue to run this place as you have always done. You are surrounded by competent employees. Give up the reins until we know what the future holds. It will most likely be temporary. Ace, you will step back."

"Darana is right, Da. You can take a sabbatical for a bit or die on the throne, and that outcome will most likely come quickly."

"Darana, get that file from the office, please. You know the one I am talking about."

She left the room.

"Mitch, I do not want the triplets to know all of this, but I leave that to your discretion, especially my namesake. He will go more nutso than he already is".

"You underestimate Kick, Da. You always have. He is a grown man and handles these types of things well with love, a good deal of common sense, and compassion."

"I'll believe it when I see it. Bloody Hell, man. That boy's name is 'Thomas.' I give him that name. It's my name... goes and gives himself another moniker, shit."

He softened a bit as Darana re-entered.

"A man reaches a point in his life when he has to make right certain things he has done in his life if his soul is to rest easy. Reminds me. Darana, I want to see Pete Djiwali. Tell him it is some holy man stuff."

He looked at his companion and added, "Yes, girl. Don't look at me like that. I want some o' that good 'ole Dreamtime rab jab you blacks are so good at.

"Also, when the time comes, get that bloody priest to come out here. Watsname... Father Davis. Got a whole lot to unload that'll make his head spin. Damn priests, anyway."

"Confession is good for the soul, Captain."

Ace harumphed and reached for the file.

Chapter Sixteen: Rapture

The Church of the Shadow of the Lord, East Bakersfield, California

"Let the grace of the Lord rain down and heal these sinners. Let their corrupt souls be bathed in the mercy of Jesus. Heal and be saved. Amen, and amen!"

The preacher was tall, animated, and loud as he practically danced across the platform of the sanctuary. In his shirtsleeves, he held the bible high in the air as he pranced. His head was thrown back in ecstasy, gorgeous black wavy hair crowning his ruggedly handsome features. He called upon the three persons in the one true God and brought the glorious power down to his people.

"Look down upon us, Lord, and we shall be saved, covered over by your Holy Spirit. Hallelujah! Amen!"

The assembly screamed their ascent, clapping and music accompanying their great slaying in the Spirit of the Christian God. The musicians underscored the frenzy with rocking rhythms that shook the hall. The keyboardist pumped bass notes and rode glissandos up and down the keys like a runaway train.

In the choir, a few members collapsed with the outpouring of divine energy. Deacons and deaconesses hauled them off into the wings, but not until the congregation could see their surrender to the force of divine power. It was holy pandemonium, and the crowd ate it up.

Candidates for baptism swayed on the edge of the stage in dazzling white robes. A few were convulsed in tears. Pastor Amos Kern of the Sumner Assembly of the Lord's Shadow in East Bakersfield, California, approached each of the seven candidates and laid a hand on their heads. He screamed the devil out of each one.

"I charge thee, Satan, in the name of Jesus, to leave this poor sinner! Begone in Jesus' name!"

Time and again, the congregation yelled, "Amen." Each of the new members, in their turn, fell back into the arms of an attendant who placed them gently on the floor. Attendants provided cold compresses and sips of water to those who were "slain in the Lord."

Lighting in the sanctuary was amped up to give the central action a heavenly glow. As the hall began to resemble a holy war zone, Brother Kern brought the service to a close with a shouted prayer, a roar of music, and a climactic ascent. Leaving the fallen, the church staff moved among the folks, collecting tithes and offerings. They particularly zeroed in on newcomers for private conversations on membership and financial commitments.

"Brother Kearn will be contacting you personally to discuss the salvation of your soul. Have you filled out a covenant card?"

"We still have not received your financial statement. Do you need another form?"

"Such a beautiful family. Are they all saved?"

***

Archdeaconess Davilla Hernandez brought the pastor a fresh bottle of water. He ignored it for the time being and removed a bottle of bourbon from his desk. He was much too wound up to sit, so he paced the office and took a couple of hefty slugs.

"Are we ready for the television crews? We have had enough time to prepare. This is the big time, Sister."

The woman went through a list. "Makeup, hair, set dressing—all are checking in. The new logo backdrop is being installed tomorrow. A detailed blueprint of the installation and the new podium is there on your desk."

"How about the audience?"

"Exclusive invitations for the VIP section have been extremely hard to obtain for weeks now. The event will be SRO. Pastor, the marketing campaign led by your wife, Sister Summer, has been most effective. The media push is a great success. Putting Christian evangelization in Bakersfield back on the map."

"I want the Crystal Cathedral shot, Davilla. The New Hour of Power will be us. Since the decline of Robert Schuller's organization, this is our time. The Lord is leading our ministry to greatness. Make way for the Shadow of the Lord, you sinners."

The Reverend spoke with determination as he poured another half glass of the liquor.

"I want to spend some time with the financials today. I am concerned with our present tithing structure for our members, as you know. We need to be more aggressive. The Lord's work does not come cheap. I want a meeting with the finance committee of the Board by no later than Tuesday."

"Sir, have you given more thought to the land issue for the new church?"

"The Sanctuary of Assembly of the Lord's Shadow, a monument to the work of our organization. We need that parcel at the north end of the valley, plenty of space for a church that will accommodate the largest crowds. And more attendance means more support. Church Headquarters is most insistent on this."

"The Vance family is not responding to our overtures for the donation. The pressures you spoke of previously may be needed."

"Let's call our strategies 'encouragements to give.' I believe the family is concerned about the salvation of the granddaughter. We need to meet with them and offer our, for lack of a better word, assistance."

"I will set up the meeting. Announcing our plans for a megachurch is an excellent way to launch our television presence and lead off the World Wide Outreach."

The pastor stood at the window and gazed at the last of the departing vehicles in the parking lot. His thoughts ran to the future.

Ford pickups, Ram trucks, souped-up minivans... the new facility will have Mercedes, Teslas, and Jags. Attendants in suits and ties, fashionable attire. Our day has come.

He lowered the blinds.

"I have spoken with our Worldwide Headquarters in Honolulu, Sister. They will proceed with enrolling the girl in our Transformation of Life Program. Hawai'i does not allow conversation therapy, so leadership in our youth ministry branch has redesigned the teen sexuality components. It's pretty obvious with this conservative administration in the White House, resistance to God's laws is at an end in this country."

The Archdeaconess let the man rant. It seems he was grandstanding a lot these days.

"There is a lot of paperwork we will need to get from the family, the Aldens, correct?"

"Yes. All of those permission forms. Once the girl is under our care, the family will appreciate our efforts to bring her back from sin and perdition. I understand that there is still some work to do as she is resisting all efforts to help her."

The young woman refreshed the pastor's drink, reached for another glass, and poured a three-finger shot for herself.

"We are confident she will come around. Our methods of peer persuasion seem to be quite effective. Peer influencers at her school are making life a bit difficult for that kid."

Amos Kern stepped closer to his number one and took her glass of Jim Beam. He dipped his index finger in his drink and ran the tip of it over her mouth, encircling her lower back with his free hand. She tasted the smokey, oak-caramel brown coating and took the rest of his finger into her mouth, sucking past two knuckles.

Sister Davilla made sure that the door to the office was locked.

Chapter Seventeen: Defensive Block

Bohna Middle School, East Bakersfield, California

Chöle Alden made a face of disapproval. She slid down the tiled wall of the gymnasium to sit and sulk.

"I was so in the key, Coach, lotsa times, and Frannie never wanted to hand off the ball. She is such a gunner ass. Six times, man, I hauled that ball down the court, passed out, then in, just like you taught us. Nothing. What's up with that?"

"We'll work on it, Clo, setting it up, but you need to keep a heads up on the defense. You are open, yes, but it's always the same moves. They are reading you and doubling up to keep you covered. Get that ball out sooner— no showboating, girl. Out quick, back in, then go look for your opening. Sometimes left, sometimes right."

The girls' basketball coach, Rose Dvorak, came up from a squat next to her star player. She pointed at the point guard's bruised right cheek.

"Black eye, kiddo. Get some ice on it pretty soon. Not supposed to be a contact sport, you know."

"Why tell me that? Harry Kruder and her big elbows are the reason. Huge foul."

As if on cue, Harriett, the team's power forward, came over and bent over the seated player.

"You OK, Clo? I'm sorry about that block. If this had been a game, I most likely woulda been benched, right, Coach?"

"Yep."

"It's OK, Harry. Doesn't hurt, and I will look like a superhero-- the Black Widow– kinda cool."

Chlöe stood up and grabbed her backpack. She hit a stance and mimicked a badass Scarlett Johansson, fists raised.

"See you guys."

Harriet ran to the vestibule and out to meet her ride.

"So what's going on, girl?"

"Home is bad right now. They want me to quit basketball. Not for proper Christian ladies, my mother says, and I don't want to. They are super strict about my friends, don't like how I dress, and I get in trouble a lot. Saying I should be more like Daisy Kern and Cindy Albright, but they are a couple of real 'B-words.'"

"Tell me more about the friends stuff."

The player and Coach sat on the bleachers in the near-empty gym. A school maintenance man walked the gym floor, tracing connected north-south lines, pushing a wide grey-green dust mop.

"I like hanging with Cyril and Cooter and Big Danny. Also, Stringer and … um, Sharon. My folks don't like any of them. Say they don't go to Church and are sinners. Coach, they are just kids, like me, ya know?"

'Sharon Getz."

"Yeah, what about her?"

"I see you two goofing around a lot. Anything you want to tell me?"

"Um… naw… nothing."

"Sharon is a good student here at Bohna Middle. Looking to get an honors scholarship to Archbishop Riordan. Her family is good county people. What's the problem?"

"So, their Anglicans, first off. My folks are strict, um. Eva.. whatcha… evangel…."

"Evangelicals?"

"Yes, Shadow of the Lord Church out in East Bakersfield. I hate it, Coach. Is it OK not to like Church?"

"Back to Sharon, Clöe. You know, Middle Schools can have a lot of gossip going on, and it really brings people down."

The eighth-grader could not bring herself to meet her Coach's eyes. She looked off at the man mopping the floor, now about a quarter completed. The girl squirmed a bit as she answered.

"So, we were... up... just trying stuff some time ago. Not a big deal like my mom and dad told the preacher."

Tears welled up, and Chlöe used the sleeve of her hoodie to wipe her nose. She kept her head down.

"I'm not allowed to hang out with her anymore."

Big wet sniff.

"Wanna tell me, Clo?"

"Like... kissin' stuff. Nothing but that. We thought we... we were alone, and then that ass-wipe, Rhonda Ferguson and her big mouth caught us back by the fieldhouse, and she told Daisy and some of their friends."

"Experimenting?"

"Yes, just trying some things we heard about. Then my folks freaked and told the Reverend, and I got grounded, and no cell phone-- and I was in big trouble."

"First time?"

Chlöe Alden paused. She had visible trouble answering this one. The star player finally responded to her basketball coach.

"No. Summer Jesus Camp. Only other time. That's when my folks told my aunt and uncle, who were visiting from Santa Barbara."

Silent tears dropped onto her sweatshirt.

"It's OK, sweetie. You are just trying to find out who you are."

The coach asked, Do you still have that information I gave you on the Rainbow?"

Before the girl could answer, they were interrupted by a very formidable woman who came into the gymnasium and made her way to them.

"Check out that flier, Chlöe. Lotsa kids in your shoes. It's a supervised chat site. Not dangerous at all… Hello, Mrs. Alden."

"Chlöe Grace, I have been sitting in that car since four-thirty. What is taking you… What happened?"

Mrs. Alden turned her daughter's jaw and saw the bluish scrape on her left cheekbone near the eye.

"Just a block, Mrs. Alden. Afraid we got to talking and didn't get ice on it. Sorry. Nothing serious."

"You look like you have been fighting. Your father will be furious to find you in such a state. Get your things, and let's go. I have dinner on the stove."

Chlöe looked forlorn as she stood up to follow her mother out.

"Oh, Miss Dvorak. You might not want to count on Chlöe for the team. We have decided it is not in her best interests."

"But, Mama, I am good. I'm the point guard."

"She is excellent. We sure have missed you and your husband at our games."

"We will discuss this at home, Chlöe. Let's go."

The woman turned to have the last word with the educator.

"Miss Dvorak…"

"It's Ms. or Mrs. to be somewhat traditional."

Mrs. Alden's tone dripped with sarcasm. Assuming her forbearance face, she folded her hands at waist level, just below her ample bosom.

"How very nice, and what does your husband do?"

"My *wife* is a partner for Kramer, Whiteside, Harriman, and Dvorak, Attorneys at Law. She specializes in civil rights litigation."

Nancy Alden was unable to hide her expression.

Rose Dvorak waved a hand.

"Mrs. Alden, you have a nice evening."

Chapter Eighteen: Just One Look, That's All It Took

East Bakersfield, California

"Daughter, are you listening to me?"

Dinner was a disaster.

"For one thing, your hair is way too short. You are going to grow it out. And while we're at it, I'm not happy with your clothes. We bought you those beautiful things for school and even some very chaste makeup. We are getting rid of your jeans and a T-shirt look. Most of the girls at that school look like girls."

"Mom, I like the way I look."

"You listen to me, Chöle. I'm signing you up for the church youth retreat. You need the Lord in your life right now."

"We don't have the money right now to send her away. They are cutting positions at the corporation. We need to consider what may happen to my job, Nancy."

"Rolf, I am going to speak to my father. He can help us. I want Chlöe out of that school. No basketball, no people of sinful lifestyles, and none of those disreputable friends of hers, giving her bad ideas. She should be learning to be a good Christian lady."

"Mom, my friends are good guys. Why are you always putting them down? Please let me stay on the team."

"Chlöe, you are learning some things that are not acceptable in this family. I will not have my daughter exposed to sinful ideas. Sexual behavior against the Word of God is not permissible. I continue to forbid you from using the internet. What's on there is the work of Satan."

Rolf Alden remained silent. Family dynamics were split along traditional lines. He brought home the paycheck, Nancy took care of the home, raised the children, and ensured everyone got religion.

However, his tolerance for his wife's obsession with rightist, religious morality had just about reached its limit. Nancy had been talking to the pastor of their church, the Reverend Kern, about sending the girl on a month-long religious retreat, out of state, to Ministry Headquarters--tons of hellfire and brimstone.

"I need to be connected to do my homework. You slapped all that parental control filter stuff on my Google account. I can't get into anything. And you won't let me have social media. It's not fair."

Nancy Alden passed the vegetables and said, "It is how the devil leads children into sin. Not good, Chlöe. It is our responsibility to see that you grow up to become a fine Christian woman, marry a good Christian man like your Father, and have children who are brought up in the ways of the Church."

"I think I like girls."

Nancy Alden struck her daughter across the face and turned red with anger. She shook with righteous indignation.

"No!"

All action in the room stopped. Chlöe did not cry. The hurt ran deeper than tears. Her mother seemed to have trouble breathing. She raised her hand to repeat the punishing act.

"No. You are not doing this to us."

Rolf stopped her.

"Nancy. Enough. Chlöe, go to your room."

"No, Dad. Why am I always being punished? Sent out of the room? It's like you two don't even like me. What did I do that's so bad? I kissed Sharon. It felt nice. Why is that a sin?"

Now, on the verge of control, Nancy called out, "It is against the Bible. You cannot choose to be that-- one of *them*. Lesbians and gays are destroying family life. You will not do that to us."

She rounded again on her daughter. Everyone was standing now. Rolf reached for his wife's raised arm to prevent further violence, but Nancy shook him off.

The petite fourteen-year-old caught her mother in a deadly stare. Nancy froze mid-swing. The girl pointed at the florid woman.

"Mom, do not ever hit me again."

***

It was impossible to sleep. Chlöe's parents had yelled and hollered long after dinner had ended. Nancy wanted the church people to come over and talk to the child, but Rolf resisted.

"Let the kid sleep, Nancy. She has school tomorrow."

"That school, I want her out of that school. She is not going back there."

"Nancy, let's take this slowly."

"You're the reason, Rolf. This is your fault. You wanted the son I never could give you, and she was your little tomboy-- swimming, baseball, basketball. Daddy's girl-- you spoiled her. Getting her to wear a dress or play at girl things was impossible. And now, it's up to me to save her. Do you want her to burn in Hell?"

"You don't make kids that way, Nan. Kids just are the way they are."

"No. Don't give me that. We raised Chlöe right, sent her to church, and read the Bible to her until she could read it herself."

Chlöe got out of bed.

She pulled up the backpack's flat bottom panel. Chlöe reached in and took out the cellphone, a gift from a teacher. She put in the web address from the brochure Coach Rose had given her. The splash page for the Rainbow Youth Project led her into the chat rooms.

She hated the "No Cell Phones In School" rule. Chlöe was an expert at getting around the restriction. One of the computers in the school library was positioned so that there was a bit more privacy for users, away from the prying eyes of Mrs. Morton, the librarian, and a member of her family's church. Chlöe often used that one as her portal to the world. Tonight, struggling with sleep, she logged on and looked for messages from kids she had reached out to earlier in the day.

A green light marked those online now.

Avenger Boy: Sup, girl? How's the basketball season going? Heard you have a big game coming up. I hope your team wins.

Black Widow: Pretty bad. My folks want me off the team.

Avenger Boy: Sucks major. Why are your folks so pissed?

Black Widow: They think I am a lesbian because I play sports. Church crazy.

Avenger Boy: Ouch. Sorry.

Black Widow: I think they are gonna send me away to get fixed or something. I don't think they want me anymore.

Chapter Nineteen: Fat Boy

The Church of the Shadow of the Lord, East Bakersfield, California

"Thank you for seeing us, Pastor. We are very worried about our daughter."

"The salvation of our children is very much at risk in this world of perdition, greed, and sinfulness. What is the child's name, Sister?"

"Chlöe. Chlöe Grace Alden. She's fourteen."

"The name of a beautiful child of God. We will add her to our worldwide prayer chain. Church members across the globe will hold your child up to the Lord and beg his mercy on her soul. Tell me, does Satan have her in his power?"

Rolf shifted in his seat. He was having a lot of trouble with the whole casting the child as a minion of the devil thing. He was raised in the church from childhood and received the Baptism of the Spirit, but found as he got older, much of this just didn't make sense— no, that wasn't it. His heart seems to have gone out of this. He prayed silently that the Lord remove his doubts and distrust. In addition, there was something about this guy.

Nancy answered, trying to hide her shame for her daughter's behavior.

"Yes, Reverend Kern. She told us she had unholy desires for other girls."

"Just some kids' stuff, Pastor. Things all kids go through."

"Then she *is* in Satan's power. No, Brother Rolf, our Christian children have to be prepared in their faith to meet the Devil head-on. Tell me, has she received Jesus Christ as her Savior?"

Nancy answered, "No, Reverend. We are planning to have her baptized in the Holy Ghost on her fifteenth birthday, which is in two months."

"I see. I pray we are not too late, but we must have hope in the grace of the Lord.

"The Church of the Shadow of the Lord has been assisting in the salvation of families for years, my friends. We provide counseling and spiritual support.

"I want, of course, to meet with the girl to make a ruling on the condition of her soul. Depending on how far she has strayed... hum. I will be recommending our Teen Retreat Experience before Satan can get a full grip on your child's soul. This year's theme is 'Finding the Lord in Paradise.' Our youth camp, the Daybreak Retreat Center in Hawai'i, is hosting.

"Church professionals and Christian behavioral specialists meet with the youngsters in a controlled environment, free of the outside influences of the Devil. We address their gender disorders from a biblical perspective. Sometimes, in difficult cases, retreatants are required to sign up for an extended stay."

"May we visit her?"

"Not until the program is in its final days, we call them the Days of Sanctification. We must insist on no distractions."

"I am not sure about this, to be honest."

"Understandable, Brother Rolf. I believe that your parents are no longer with us. Am I correct?"

"That's right."

"And a brother."

"We are not on speaking terms, Pastor, a falling out many years ago."

He turned to Nancy and asked, "But your Father, Charles Vance, is the girl's living grandfather, yes?"

"Correct, Reverend Kern. Our daughter is his favorite grandchild."

"And you have one sister?"

"Risë Vance Hrynsyshyn, she and her husband live in Santa Barbara with their son, John Jr."

"For me to do a complete assessment of Chlöe Grace's condition, I will need to meet with all involved family members. We contribute in so many ways to the spiritual health of our children, parents, grandparents, and siblings. Don't you agree, Sister Alden? I will ask Sister Davilla to work with you to set up our meeting."

"I need to think a bit more about this. I am not sure how our daughter will respond to...."

"Brother, allow me to be very clear. It is not up to the child. As her parents, you hold the responsibility for salvation in your hands like water. If you have doubts, if you hesitate, it would be like opening your fingers, and the water falls out. The girl will be lost to the Lord."

The preacher stood to signal that the meeting was over. He took the hands of the Aldens and bowed his head in prayer.

"Come upon us, Most High God, with the favor of your grace. Allow us to stand in the shadow of your love. Drive from our hearts all...."

Nancy Alden heard a voice in her head as she was filled with the emotion of divine supplication.

"Fear not."

***

Joey Santoramo just didn't like the way this kid looked. Fuckin' little DIT– Dyke In Training. He turned to his buds, Arnie and Crisco, for a quick conference.

The Crisco Kid shook his head, "She's just a kid, Jay. C'mon."

"Shut the fuck, fat boy, lesbos deserve all they get, fuckin' freaks. Leave if you got no guts."

In the end, it was The Kid who saved Chlöe's life. He pulled Joey off from stomping the crumpled, dirt-covered girl who was bleeding from the head.

Chapter Twenty: Hate

East Bakersfield, California

"I skipped practice and walked Sharon home. We had a good talk. I knew Mom would be at the school around four, so I made sure that I had time to get back.

"They were three guys from Center Valley High. I never saw them before. They asked me if I was a boy or a girl and made fun of me, the way I dressed, and my short hair and stuff. They called me names and told me that I needed to go away because I was making our town a dirty place and I was a filthy gay. Then they started punching me. I fell down, and they stomped me.

"I tried to fight back, but they were bigger, and I couldn't run away."

"What did you and Sharon talk about?"

"Really, Nancy?"

Rolf continued, "Chlöe, is there anything else you can tell the police officer about the boys who attacked you?"

"One had a super bad complexion, the dark-haired kid. The other one had a cast on his... left, yeah, left arm. The big kid, the heavy guy-- he actually stopped them. I forget, though."

The police officer asked, "Any names?"

Chlöe wiped her nose and eyes.

"Not that I remember. Those guys sure cussed a lot. Wait. The main guy, he called the big kid, Fatso, and he had a ripped earlobe like someone pulled out a piercing in a fight or something."

Chlöe Alden was picked up by the police after the attack and hospitalized for three days. She had awakened from the coma about four hours ago.

"Someone must have seen something, Officer. I want those guys found before they hurt another kid."

"We have been questioning around the High School, Mr. Alden. No one is talking, but I think we need to give it time. Kids talk eventually."

"She's awake. Now, all we have to do is get her smiling."

Risë Hrynsyshyn pushed her husband into the ICU unit and said, "Your Uncle Jack persuaded the staff to allow us to come in. How are you feeling, Chlöe? You look better awake."

"I guess OK, Auntie. Just some hurts on my side."

Jack said, "We understand that the head damage was the main problem. The other issues seem to be healing up or starting to anyway."

Nancy said, "My word, Jack, you sure have a way with the medical people, getting all this family information."

Jack looked at his sister-in-law.

This woman has been through hell and back. Much of it has to do with her own doing. Let it go.

He did a wheel rock and winked at Chlöe.

"It's this chair thing— super instant sympathy. People cough up. Comes with getting the reserved parking spaces."

Rolf shook his brother-in-law's hand and introduced Officer Shanahan. He kissed Risë on the cheek as Nancy looked on with her usual scrutiny.

"Thanks for coming. How was the trip? And how's the Spud?"

"Two and a half hours. I married a lead foot."

"Jackie's fine. With Jack's momma. He sent his cousin, his favorite Teddy."

Risë pulled a big, worn bear from her purse and gave it to Chlöe. The girl snuggled the stuffed toy.

The police officer decided to pursue her questioning another time and chose to leave. She turned to the Aldens and said, "We will keep you posted on the case. Maybe a hate crime ruling on this one. We will want to know more about that. Our detectives are talking to folks at both the middle and the high school."

Nancy became slightly animated, saying, "No, no, no, Kids start all kinds of rumors all the time. Chlöe shouldn't have been anywhere near those bigger kids."

Rolf was stunned. The other family members and the police officer looked at the girl's mother with disbelief as the ICU nurse came in, checked her vitals, and spoke to the patient.

"How are you doing, honey? I like your bear."

"Thank you. I am sleepy."

The very expeditious medic turned to the adults.

"Gotta go, family. This baby is good enough for a private room, and one has just opened up. She needs her rest. Gonna take good care of her. Don't worry."

***

"We are fortunate that Chlöe's head injuries are not all that serious. Her coma was most likely brought on by trauma. Brain scans do not show issues of grave concern. The wrist will heal nicely as long as we keep the cast in place for the needed time. One rib has been fractured, as well as the nose."

The doctor added, "Most of this confirms what we spoke of soon after she was admitted. I would like to keep her here for a few more days, just to make sure."

Nancy said, "When can she return to school?"

"Let's give that another week of rest at home. Then, she can ease back into her school life. She tells me that she is anxious to get back to playing basketball. When the wrist is completely healed, we can get her back on the court."

"My husband and I have decided that Chlöe is not going to play basketball anymore. There are more lady-like activities she will be pursuing– more involvement in our church."

"Are you sure? Returning to her normal activities…."

"Yes, Doctor, we are quite sure. Thank you."

"I hope I am not intruding."

"Reverend Kern, thank you for coming. This is Chlöe's Doctor and my sister, Risë, and her husband, Jack Hrynsyshyn."

The family exchanged a greeting with the man of faith.

"It is very nice to make your acquaintance. Tell me. Are you saved?"

Jack chuckled, saying, "Not a chance, pastor. We are both lawyers."

Risë added with a humorous edge, "Correct. Libertine and lost."

"Left out the liquor, Sweetie."

"Yes, temperance is not among our virtues, Father. Plus, we're Catholic. Always liked that denomination. Not as rigid and filled with condemnation. More sin than sanctity."

Kern's smile froze. He was distressed by the frivolity of these two. He turned to the Aldens.

"We, at the Church, were so distressed when we found out your daughter was attacked. We continue to pray for both her physical and her spiritual recovery. I wonder if this is a good time to speak with the girl."

"Certainly, Reverend. She is getting better every day. I will show you to her room."

"That won't be necessary, Sister Alden. Children often like to speak to a spiritual counselor without a parent present. They feel they can unburden their soul with confidentiality. I know you understand."

No one said anything.

"Thank you, I will find my way."

The Preacher left the visitor's room, as did the Doctor, who couldn't hide his smile.

Risë turned on her Sister.

"Nancy, you amaze me. You threw out the basketball coach like she had the plague. Not even accepting the flowers from the team. Yet you allow this pompous jerk, who, by the way, both Jack and I have met before, access to Chlöe."

"That woman is a lesbian, Risë. Ever hear of recruiting?"

"Ever hear of bullshit? Believe me, I'd have a lot of issues leaving Jackie alone with a man of the cloth and no trouble with asking any of our gay and lesbian friends to babysit. What the hell is the matter with you? You really are the limit."

"Just what I like to see. It seems like old home week. You two have been arguing since you were both in diapers. And who's that guy that needed me to leave so that he could hear my granddaughter's confession? What does a fourteen-year-old have to confess anyway?"

Charles Vance was a robust man of sixty-eight years, a widower of seven years. He not only filled the doorway but commanded the room and anywhere he went. Vance made his fortune in the early days of Silicon Valley, bought a lot of California, and sat back. The tycoon refused to retire from running his agribusiness empire. That being said, he looked and acted like a very unassuming businessman, easygoing but serious about what needed attention.

"Daddy, we were disagreeing, that's all. Reverend Kern is not hearing Chlöe's confession. We do not believe in that."

"He asked to speak to me while I am in Bakersfield. A contribution, no doubt. So, let's see what he has to say. What's his interest in Chlöe?"

Charles looked at his son-in-law, who was noticeably withdrawn, seated, forearms on his knees, staring blankly.

"Rolf, boy. You look like your cat just died. The girl is going to be fine."

"Sorry, Dad. Work stuff."

Nancy said, "Reverend Kern has been offering spiritual guidance to Chlöe. She has been having some issues lately."

"What sort of issues?"

Nancy hedged, "Oh, the usual teenage...."

"She told Rolf and Nancy that she feels attracted to girls," Risë said.

Nancy was furious.

"What? Don't look at me like that. He is her grandfather. If her sexual identity troubles led to this attack, he has a right to know. Family of secrets. Not good, Nancy. Not good."

"This is a spiritual matter with my daughter, which may threaten her salvation, and I will thank you to…."

"She's fourteen. What the hell kind of spiritual peril could she possibly be in, Nancy?"

"Do you understand the power of Satan that has my daughter in its grip? Do you have any idea about these degenerates? They get hold of these kids and seduce their minds. They turn them from God. With all we've taught her, she wants to be a… a… God forgive me. I cannot even say it."

"You are even crazier than I thought you were. Are you insane enough to believe the poison with which that Church infected your mind?"

"Enough!"

As Charles spoke with authority, Rolf's head seemed to sink lower during the exchange between his wife and his sister-in-law.

"Nancy, get in that room and be a part of whatever is being said between Chlöe to Reverend Kern. Now. And close the door."

Nancy Vance Alden followed her orders. Charles Vance lit a cigarette.

"Dad, there's no smoking …."

"Risë, you can tell everyone else on God's green earth what to do except me. Hand me that plastic cup."

"Jack?"

"No thanks, Dad."

He looked at his other son-in-law, who shook his head, also refusing a smoke.

"So, Chloe thinks she is a lesbian."

He raised a fist, shook it, and said, "No granddaughter of mine…."

He started the last sentence with a mighty fury but stopped. He looked at his family.

"Figured that's what you were gonna hear, huh? Well, I have news for you."

The three looked at the old tycoon as if he had two heads.

"Jesus. At fourteen, I thought I was Superman. Growing up at that age is a bitch. You all listen to me. My granddaughter can be whoever and whatever it is in her nature to be, so long as she is loving and giving... like her grandmother."

Jack said, "Shit, Charles, you are such a ballbuster."

"Famous for it. Now tell me what support services the school has to offer. Kids dealing with grown-up stuff like sexual orientation have to have a hand in her positive development. We pay enough fucking taxes."

Risë said, "Dad, there are counselors, support groups, and straight allies. I have been checking around."

"Is that true, Rolf?"

"Dad, yes. I guess so. I really am not sure."

Charles stood up and approached his granddaughter's father.

"Now, you listen to me, Son. You better get your head in the game, and I mean right away, or that woman in there is going to let some Bible-waving jerkoff mess with the self-esteem of your only child. And that will be more damaging than anything you'll ever dream of. Am I making myself clear?"

Rolf looked up at his father-in-law and said, "I lost my job today. The company's going under-- salary, benefits-- all gone. Nancy doesn't know, but this is gonna send her completely off the rails."

Vance put his hand on the shoulder of the younger man. "Like she needs anything more to push her over. You need this like a damn hole in the head right now. I am sorry, Son."

He continued, "Rolf, you have to put that German pride of yours in the back seat and make what is going on with Chlöe your first priority. I have been telling you to come and work for me for years, but you do not want to be your father-in-law's lackey.

"I am telling you again. Rolf. No one gets a free ride at AgroVance. I'm not talking about nepotism, Son. Enough of that bullshit these days, even on the highest levels. My companies are expanding so fast that I have positions I cannot fill quickly enough, especially with these new farming methods. I will work your ass off. No special favors club."

Rolf nodded and did not say anything at first. He patted Charles's hand and said, "Thank you."

The elderly gentleman turned to his other children.

"Gotta get over to the coast soon. How's my Jackie boy?

Jack answered, "Lil' Spud is fine, Dad. Getting bigger every day."

Charles Vance smiled and said, "Good... good...." His voice seemed to trail off, and the smile faded. His three family members waited for him to come back into the conversation.

Staring off into the distance, the man then said, "I am very concerned about that girl."

"Chlöe?"

"No. Nancy."

***

The man of God saw the woman's husband coming toward them down the hall. He finalized their conversation by saying, "We can help your daughter turn back to the Lord, but only if you have great faith. When the time is right. Bring her to me. The Lord will take care of the rest."

Nancy Alden nodded.

Chapter Twenty-One: Andi

221 Baker Street, San Francisco, California
Nick Sechi's Journal

Trasker had an excellent breakfast prepared. Andi Rodriguez, our part-time clerical assistant, had eventually taken on some responsibilities as a domestic when the occasion arose. This meant she helped Mrs. Trasker. It was all about acknowledging that the older housekeeper and cook was the queen bee.

Andi was a street kid with a lot on the ball. Kayne and I seemed to collect the Miserable Ones every so often, and Andi's story was a tough one. She came to our attention when investigating the death of a prostitute in the Tenderloin, specifically near the intersection of Eddy and Mason. This was still an impoverished area despite gentrification. Like Andi, the dead woman was transgender. The women were fellow sex workers, flatmates, and friends.

Andrés Rodriguez had been thrown out of his home in San Jose at sixteen. The latest trouble at school was the last straw for his family, who were struggling to understand the boy's gender conflicts. So, he hit the streets of the City by the Bay and soon found friends and plenty of makeover advice. There was also money to be had turning tricks in the high-crime neighborhood, where violent street wrongdoing such as robbery and aggravated assault was commonplace. Andrés became Andi and learned The Life with very little trepidation, saving what little she could for gender reassignment surgery.

She was pretty shaken up by the death of her "big sister" and close to making some very harmful choices.

"First, you will come and work for me. Nick and I need a competent administrative assistant, and an eleventh-grade education will not do, my good woman. You will get your GED. There are fast tracks, the purpose of which will be to get you enrolled in a state college and in a degree program of your choice. When you assure me that these components are in the making, we will work on better lodgings."

"In San Francisco, Mister? You been paying attention, Sherlock? A low-income, professional woman of the evening like myself can't afford anything but shit for housing and other whores for roommates. This town is for millionaires only. Gringoes. Lemme tell you something, detective man. This doll is left with Jack and Shit, except Jack just left town. This ain't happening."

"Ms. Rodriguez, you must never refer to me as Sherlock. Next, your life expectancy on the streets is another two years at the most, with death from the same terrible circumstances as that of your friend's murder. Think hard, young woman. Never look askance at second chances."

The petite woman had already begun to look older than her years, some of which was by design. She adjusted her blouse and undergarments with a pat to her lustrous mahogany hair and smirked.

"Second chances? I'd give anything for just one chance. One chance to make somebody happy. One chance to show I am as good as the next person. And one chance to earn somebody's trust and make them believe that true love still exists."

She paused, trying very hard to keep emotion from her voice.

"So, before you go giving out second chances, blue-eyes, just remember that some people would do anything for just *one* chance."

That was six months ago. This morning, Andi, who had survived the battle for the household throne and had remained in Tasker's good graces, passed a plate to Kayne. My Bossman was seated with Mitch and me at our big kitchen table.

"I hope your eggs are as you like them, Doctor Sorenson."

"They look great, Andi. Thank you."

I quipped, "Hey, Andi, what's a Dingo's breakfast?"

She looked at me with a sly smile and said with a comic accent straight from the bush, "A yawn, a leak, and a good look around."

Mitch and Kayne exchanged a look. The older Sorenson said, "Hold on, you two, with the ribbing about 'Straya.' One of the things we do very well in the Lucky Country is brekkie."

Kayne added, "Mornings at Inala with the 'big fry-up.' Nothing beats a plate of beautifully cooked farm-fresh eggs, smoked bacon, grilled tomato, and mushrooms. Sausages, hash browns, or beans would be optional extras."

Trasker refreshed our coffee.

"Extraordinary, Mrs. Trasker. Was it difficult to learn to make coffee as we have in Australia?

"It was a laugh a minute, to be honest, Doctor Sorenson. But I got the hang of it."

I went into the butler's pantry to grab my ashwagandha supplement. Andi carried in dirty plates.

Our new assistant nodded to Mitch in the other room.

"Is he sure he's married?"

An unusual professional slip.

"Ohhh, quite sure."

I went back to the table. We were interrupted by two college jock boys practically falling down the back kitchen stairs. Kris and Matt spun through the kitchen like some morning football play, dodging, scooping up food and drink, and settling into two empty chairs.

Kris kissed each of his uncles good morning. As he bent over me, I touseled his hair as Mitch did a fist bump with Matt. Trasker and Andi busied themselves away from the bustle with cooking and clean-up.

Kris pulled out his phone.

"Oh, shit. I almost forgot. Have a look, Uncle Kayne."

Kayne scrolled Kris' mobile.

"Our friend, young Master Jamison Lathrop Welton, attending the Silverman Academy up in Marin County... fascinating."

I teased, saying to Mitch, "Big time crush on The Kris— loves him some jock handsome."

Matt smiled, and Mitch did an eye-roll.

Just what his inflated ego needs.

"Nephew, leave the kiddies alone."

He gestured with his fork. "Got you quite a man for yourself right there."

I thought Matt would float up to the ceiling.

I explained who Jamie Welton was and his role in our last case.

"Look at this, my love. Our lad is quite the private investigator."

Sup, Kris? Hope all is going well, big man. Any more soccer games this season? HMU when you have another match. I'll come and watch your game. Be a blast staying over (hint, hint).

Loving school, big time. No fights, lotsa sports, and the teachers are really cool. Learning a lot. Maybe I'll get to go to the University of San Francisco like you.

I looked at Kris and said, "This boy has it bad. No mention of Mr. Matthew... humm. Interesting."

Matt chewed his eggs and rashers and said, "That dude would throw me under a bus."

So, I agreed to be an advocate for a young gay group, the Rainbow Youth Project. I chat with guys and gals who are struggling with sexual identity issues. They trained us on how to help. We are supposed to let them know that they are not alone in this world. I got this one friend I am worried about.

Her family is super religious, and she came out to them. They took her to their church to get her fixed. Anyway, I lost contact. I think she may have run away. The only thing I know is that she goes to a middle school in Bakersfield and plays basketball. I hope she is going to be OK.

I looked at Kayne and said, "You don't suppose this missing girl is...."

Kayne stared out the window for a bit, cognition in full gear. When he came back, he said, "Mitch, what time is your flight back to Aspen? It looks like Nick and I will be flying down to Santa Barbara. We seem to have a case developing that could prove very interesting."

***

It was a time when my fear of flying seemed to be in remission. I had flown with Kayne all over Europe and Asia, usually numbed and sleeping, thanks to Xanax. Lately, I have been working on my meditation and getting this and some other fears under control. Tight places still brought out some deep terrors.

The four-hour trip offered us some important time to review what seemed to be coming together as a very sinister case. We walked Mitch to his gate, and Kayne assured him.

"Nick and I will get down to see Da soon, brother. I believe we can help him come to a reasonable frame of mind regarding that with which he is dealing."

I added, "We will work on his insistence on having Kris become the next Master of Inala. Trying to convince the Captain he is wrong about something will be super tough."

"Believe me, I know. Please keep me in the loop. I will join you if you believe it is best. Right now, however, I need to get back to Kick. Some minor issues, plus I miss The Mess like all get out. Come for the winter fest, lads. We will show you a good time."

I said, "That sounds great, Mitch. Give our love to Scott and Gints."

Our two buds back at Aerie were of great assistance on a few of our cases, providing muscle and cyber information. They met at the resort and fell in love. They have been together for over a year.

"Will do. By the way, I forgot to tell you guys. I found out that the board approved the hiring of Scott Iverson as the head of Aerie Corporation's Technology, so he will be in charge of the resort, the ranch, and the lodge. And Kick is behind making Gints a member of our security staff. I think that is also a good move."

Kayne smiled and said, "Capital. They both will do very well—competent and very professional blokes. I hope we can continue to use them for our research gurus."

We hugged up and went to our gate just in time for boarding.

The Shadow of Evil

Chapter Twenty-Two: Risë and Jack

East Bakersfield, California
Nick Sechi's Journal

'It was Nancy. Best we can tell, she went to the church with Chlöe three days ago and came back alone. Refuses to talk to anyone about it. Says that she signed the girl up for retreat camp.

"Rolf is beside himself. Talking to his lawyer after going to the church and demanding his daughter. Kern refused to see him, and his assistant gave him a copy of a signed permission form."

Kayne asked. "What do the authorities say?"

Jack answered this time.

"They are not addressing the situation. Claim the family allowed Chlöe to enter the program and agreed to the conditions of confidentiality and non-interference."

Charles Vance charged onto the veranda.

"You two are lawyers. I want you to represent Rolf and me against your sister, who has gone completely off the rails. Get a restraining order on that pastor and his church people. I want her back. We need to do something with Nancy, but for the life of me, I do not know what."

Jack said, "Dad, this is Kayne Sorenson and Nick Sechi, private investigators. I went to school with Kayne. They have done amazing work advising law enforcement around the globe."

Vance shook our hands.

"Heard of you two, the gay detectives. I read about your work with that huge scandal in Colorado. Turned out all right. Justice served."

Kayne did his best enigmatic smile and said, "Yes, and you are the straight head of California's largest agri-business corporations. Your fame precedes you also."

Vance got the point.

The man added, "This is a mess, Doctor Sorenson. Abduction... extortion... Do you know what that minister had the nerve to talk to me about? A donation of land up in the valley... Belongs behind bars."

He continued, "I don't understand these things, I will admit, gentlemen, but I feel my granddaughter is in danger."

He settled into a chair as Jack rolled over with a cocktail.

There was a shout as another invader commandeered the patio.

The boy raced around the adults and exclaimed, "Papa! Papa!"

Charles swatted the boy gently on the behind as he scooted by. The man took his drink to the side as a call came through.

I scooped up Jackie and sat him on my lap. He showed me his Avengers action figures. We played a rescue scene in miniature, Iron Man soaring overhead and the Black Widow knocking the aliens to the table with her tiny martial arts moves.

"What's that one, kiddo?"

"She's Captain Marvel. She is very good and can fly."

I whooshed the blue and gold figure over the coffee cups with appropriate sound effects as the boy giggled.

"Hey, Mom and Dad, watch what Nick taught me."

The little boy raced to a nearby bench just off the patio on some soft grass and climbed on top of it.

"Jackie, be careful, Spud. No hurts, OK?"

"OK, Dad. Watch. Watch."

I stood up to help the mighty mite if he needed it. The little tyke jumped off the bench and landed on one knee, head down, looking at the ground. He then looked up with a dramatically stern face.

I faced the audience, arms wide, and said, "Superhero landing."

"Superhero landing, superhero landing. Wanna see it again?"

We watched Jackie's descent to Earth, ready to fight crime, three more times.

Jack said, "You two need one of those. Ever consider it?"

Kayne mused, "Got one, actually. Our nephew is in college back home. A bit older but the same parental skill sets."

We all smiled.

Kayne checked his watch and said, "I do apologize, but we need to leave. Thank you for your hospitality. I will talk to you soon."

The family joined me in, looking a bit bewildered.

"Come along, my love. Tomorrow's Sunday, and we do not want to be late for church."

Chapter Twenty-Three: Slain

The Church of the Shadow of the Lord, East Bakersfield, California
Nick Sechi's Journal

The banner above the church welcomed the faithful and, in our case, the skeptics. It announced:

"Resting in the Lord's Shadow – The Spring Healing Crusade."

The graphic was an ethereal pair of healing hands, above which was a divine light and below, what appeared to be a darkened veil.

Another caption read, "World-Wide Outreach."

I did an aside to Kayne.

"Got any ailments you want to be cured this morning? I could most likely fake something."

He wasn't paying attention to me. Two women were engaged in a blistering conversation in the shade of a large pecan tree, a bit off to the side. Kayne positioned himself to eavesdrop, facing me but concentrating on them.

"Quite interesting, Nick. It would appear there is trouble in paradise."

Both women had very big hair. One was a tall blonde in gold and diamond accessories. The other was a petite brunette. The glamazon was fashionably dressed in a designer's spring line original and impeccably tailored. The other was in a choir robe. Her dark chocolate brown coif was expertly styled to frame her face and cascade down her back to her shoulders. A gold chain encircled her neck and held a large cross between her breasts.

The women parted in what appeared to be a retreat to neutral corners. Kayne swept in as the deaconess attempted to avoid the assembling crowd and hide her light up of a smoke.

"I beg your pardon, Sister. I would like to speak to the Reverend Kern before the service on a most urgent matter."

The woman looked us over carefully. Her response was programmed, it seemed.

"Impossible."

The clergywoman shot a glance at her departing rival.

"He is... at prayer."

She flicked ash. Again, she scrutinized us.

"I know who you are and what you are. Furthermore, I know why you are here."

Her gaze narrowed as she added, "You are Doctor Sorenson... and you would be Sechi." She pointed with two fingers and the lit cigarette.

"I'll save us all a lot of time. The girl is gone. He won't talk about it... police and family have already been here. Their lawyers, our lawyers-- bla, bla, bla... The mother signed a confidentiality agreement: religious freedom and parental rights, all in the mishmash. You aren't gonna get anything out of him. I expect the Grandfather will get the media on this any minute now.

"That's why, except for services, Kern is MIA. By the way, you both actually look better in person. Those Webshots don't do you justice."

She flicked, puffed, and pointed again.

"Anyway, Kern doesn't see sinners like the two of you anyway."

I said, "Interesting that a man of God cuts himself off from anyone. I thought you guys were in the soul-saving business."

"Ha! That's rich."

Kayne became insistent.

"Sister Davilla. Where is Chlöe Alden?"

The minister looked away for a long time. It seemed this was "make or break time." She dropped her cigarette and sighed. When Davilla Hernandez next spoke, it was more like she was talking to herself.

"What the heck? I am pretty much fucked, no pun intended, when the Honorable Mrs. Kern—she's the blonde bitch I was talking to, sets the situation to rights. Maybe it's time to get lost– not going to jail for that jerk."

She hiked a thumb in the direction of the worship center.

Kayne clarified his request, saying, "I am not interested in the Kerns right now, or you for that matter. Where is the girl?"

"The candidates for the youth retreat are sent to Hawai'i, Church of the Shadow of the Lord Headquarters on the Kona Coast. The Alden kid is scheduled for a month-long special program, and you can pretty much figure out why."

Kayne shot his forelock and was about to say something but stopped. Behind us, the service was beginning, loud music greeting the last of the entering faithful.

The deaconess took off her pectoral cross and chain. Ms. Hernandez said, "But Professor, Chlöe Alden is not at the retreat center. Even the family doesn't know this part, and I don't know how long he intends to keep it secret. We got word a few hours ago that she ran off."

The Judas, Davilla Hernandez, reached out her hand for mine. She placed the chain and cross in it.

"Do me a favor, kid. Put this in the collection basket. The Reverend will know exactly what it means."

The Shadow of Evil

Chapter Twenty-Four: *E pur si muove*

Los Angeles to Honolulu
Nick Sechi's Journal

I usually include in our cases how much I hate flying. Leaving the planet filled me with fear– the Triple-A kind, acrophobic, aviophobia, and agoraphobia. Pharmaceuticals, meditation, a cocktail or three, and alternate means of travel, when practical, have lessened my terrors of soaring in the skies above. Also, Kayne was an excellent flying mate and pilot as well. Usually, we reviewed cases or caught up on the history of our destination during the trip.

"I am afraid I can only report to the congregation of the holy brothers that our investigation of Brother Generoso's murder has led to an endless series of dead ends. I cannot find any connection to the theft of church artifacts of the kind we encountered at the University of Notre Dame."

"We've met some genuine nutsos in our investigations, Boss. Some Big Bads-- an oligarch or corporate head who imagines himself as a religious figure and will go to any lengths...."

"Murder?"

"Seems so... to surround himself with the trappings of the God connection. But Boss, a bell and an umbrella? Gimmie a break. A papal crown or that death cloth of Jesus...."

"The Shroud of Turin."

"Yep... would have made more sense."

Kayne steepled his fingers and stared into space.

"May I bring you anything, gentlemen?"

The first-class attendant leaned over our seats. Kayne was lost in thought. Slowly, his eyelids with the impossibly long, black lashes closed. I answered for both of us.

"Thank you. Two of the same."

First Class, LAX to Honolulu courtesy of AgroVance Inc.-- so far, the accommodations were excellent. My mind went back to our discussion of the healing crusade in Bakersfield. We had been rounding up in the Hawaiian Airlines Lounge, awaiting our plane.

Kayne pointed out, "Regarding science, medicine, and intercessory prayer, the scientific data on faith healing are inconclusive. Religion has been concerned with healing for thousands of years. There has been quite a bit of research on the matter in the modern age. But the variables are extremely complicated."

"What are we talking about here?"

"Studies have been filled with a variety of assumptions. The results are often a disaster for both science and theology-- suspect results. What I find most interesting in these studies are the Hawthorne Effect and the Rosenthal Effect. Think about it."

He continued.

"The patient is studied in a comforting and caring environment, and prayer lessens the symptoms. This is the Hawthorn effect, which states that individuals modify an aspect of their behavior in response to their awareness of being observed. This can undermine the integrity of research, particularly the relationships between variables. The patient is relaxed, unconsciously wanting to please-- *Voila!* A lessening of the medical symptoms."

He continued.

"Observer expectations also muddle scientific results. This is the Rosenthal effect. So, the tendency of the rater to expect symptom attenuation across time may result in the attachment of lower significance to reported symptoms."

"I don't get it, Boss. If prayer works, couldn't it result from some unknown mental energy? Why presume God is involved?"

"Excellent point. So, we come to a series of fascinating theological questions. Is the nature of God such that God can be manipulated with behavior that science can predict? Is God's loving care for individuals based on the quantity and quality of prayer, the sincerity of the praying community, or the patient? Are petitions from sinners like us not answered? What if the targeted person is of another faith or even a non-believer? Furthermore, why would God be willing to submit to experiments that attempt to validate God's existence and constrain divine responses?"

"Sounds like a mess." I thought for a moment and then rejoined.

"Kayne, the crutches, Lourdes."

He shook his head.

"As I stated, the theory of miraculous intervention is conjecture at best. Something obviously happened with these crippled folks, divine origin, hoax, psychosomatic responses in accord with the two effects I mentioned – we just don't know."

This was Kayne at his utmost best, challenging ignorance and faulty science. He brushed back his bangs and continued.

"I think it is essential in all of this to remember Galileo. He said, 'The aim of science is not to open a door to infinite wisdom but to set a limit to infinite error.'

"Plainly said, religion is based on conditions that cannot be proven. We call that faith. Science must be verified with proof. Therefore, randomized controlled studies cannot be applied to the study of the efficacy of prayer in healing. In fact, no form of scientific inquiry presently available can suitably address the subject. To assume otherwise is totally absurd."

I jumped in.

"So what you are saying is, God may indeed exist, and religious petition may heal, but God shows no logical and proven preference for humankind. This obscure divinity is highly unlikely to cooperate in scientific studies that seek to test his existence."

"Precisely so."

"So can the Reverend Amos Kern really...?"

Back on the plane, my reverie was interrupted by the attendant who brought our drinks. A low baritone at my left shoulder crooned.

"You are thinking of our Galileo conversation."

"Holy shit, Boss! No way you could have..."

"Here is what I observed when you thought I was meditating. You had your resting, heavy-thinking face on. Three times as you stared off between typing, you touched your neck cross. I believe you told me it was your Father's. From there..."

"I call BS, Boss. You are starting to believe your own press, dude, but..."

Kayne reached for his Hibiki Rocks and smiled devilishly.

"You were so engrossed in writing your blog entry, my love. I peeked over your shoulder at your laptop. There, I have 'narced' myself, as you would call it."

Chapter Twenty-Five: A Phone Call from The J. Edgar Hoover

Los Angeles to Honolulu
The Case Files of Kayne J. Sorenson, Ph.D.

"Got it, Boss? Looks like it's for you."

"Kayne, I sure hope you bad boys are behaving. I may have to put my agents on you if you are not. I would fear greatly for them, however."

I moved nearer to Nick and put his mobile on "speaker."

"Special Agent Chaffee, such an unexpected pleasure to hear your voice. Nick sends his love."

"I am so much more at ease, knowing that he has you under control and vice versa. Our work together has taught me that his crazy matches your crazy. And so, you cancel each other out-- meaning your behaviors are less wild-assed."

"I believe you have not been paying attention to the blog, Mary. Whereas my husband does have a tendency to drift into hyperbole, our hair-raising adventures continue unabated."

Mary laughed at the other end.

"A fine example for the young and innocent Bulgarian Prince."

"Young Kristof has his arse in a tub of butter, my girl. And he is far from innocent. Plan on paying us a visit and see for yourself."

I grimaced, shook my head, and glanced at his mobile screen.

"Sorry, Kayne, dead spot. I hate the Hoover Building. You would think the FBI's D.C. Headquarters would have the best WiFi. Heading to the Miami Office in three days, anyway. As usual, there are some extraterritorial issues there that we need to take on. "

"Seriously, love to see you when you can get to the Bay Area. Presently bound for Hawai'i on a case."

"Yes, my sources keep me informed. The nature of your work is becoming more of a Bureau interest."

"Translation, we have a file on you, and Big Sister is watching. How can we assist you, Mary?"

"Kayne, you are well aware that concerning local law enforcement, we try hard to respect boundaries. It's a partnership. Recently, some cases facing our Honolulu office may have the potential to threaten national security."

"Please continue."

"My sources tell me that you have been asked by the family of Chlöe Alden to assist in finding her."

I pulled at my forelock and shot Nick a glance.

"You are, as usual, very well informed. But the FBI does not deal with runaways. This is not a kidnapping."

"Kayne, there could be a larger context to this drama."

"So now we have become a prophylactic for national security, is that it?"

"You know what I mean. Do not bring sex into this, please. And speaking of-- hi Nicky, you total sex bomb."

My hot man called out, "Agent Chaffee-- mind your manners, gurl. Hello, and give us more on this, please, crazy woman."

"Sorry. OK. So, I need you to get with Hawai'i PD. We believe there is a potential shitstorm brewing related to the death of a guy who jumped into a volcano on the Big Island recently. The deceased is Damien Kuhio Aloho, a researcher for EnVitro Tec, Inc. His family is from Puakō on the Big Island."

I asked, "Sounds like local law enforcement is where this one belongs. Why are you interested? "

"Well, I am really not sure. Call it intuition. The thing is, there is this religious group that keeps popping up, and we don't know why. The

142

pastor guy has the highest political connections. Evangelicals are where it's at in the new, conservative America.

"I get the feeling that we're looking at a spider's web of intrigue, to be honest. Too many connections."

Nick took some notes on my laptop. I did research on the EnVitro Tec and its church ties based on keywords.

Mary went on.

"We are observing this church organization with interest. Some smuggling accusations, possible cases of human trafficking, fraud--it's a long list. They keep coming up clean. This brings me to the Alden girl. These Jesus folks had Chlöe Alden in one of their programs. Four days ago, she disappeared.

"So, we are looking into it, unofficially, and bingo. Sure enough, these church yazoos have an interest in biotech. My, my, my... sure enough, we're looking at EnVitroTec, a company whose purpose is highly secretive and seems to be tied to the church. The ministry denies this, however."

Nick and I exchanged a look. Mary added, "See what you can find out, please."

Nick asked, "Got a name?"

"The Church of the Shadow of the Lord."

The Shadow of Evil

Chapter Twenty-Six: The Royal Hawai'ian

Honolulu, O'ahu, Hawai'i
Nick Sechi's Journal

"Welcome to Paradise, my love."

Somewhat fortified, I braved a look out the window. The sky and the Pacific were a soft blend of every shade of blue and green, with turquoise and cobalt fighting for dominance. White clouds, like my grandmother's sheer curtains on the windows of her apartment in the Bronx, seemed to part. The vibrant emerald, brown, and white chain of islands appeared, rising from the sea like jewels. The closer we descended, the more this heavenly island chain was revealed: mountains, beaches, cities, jungles, and farmlands. Most of the archipelago's lush vegetation was on the northeast side of the eight major islands, in the path of the trade winds.

Our final destination was the state's most populous island, O'ahu. As we settled into ground transportation and spirited away from Daniel K. Inouye International, Kayne began his narrative.

"Once an independent nation, until 1898, Hawai'i has a pretty controversial history of American Imperialism. In the 19th century, many migrations of workers resulted in a culture that is strongly influenced by North Americans and East Asians, in addition to the indigenous Hawai'ian culture."

"Looking forward to clearing up this case and enjoying some of the sites and leisure activities, Boss. Vance has us operating out of the Royal Hawaiian, Waikiki."

The next thing you knew, we were zipping down Kalakaua Avenue to the famous resort crowned by an iconic pink hotel. Our room had an excellent view of the beach as far east as Diamond Head. As we settled in, we were informed that a member of local law enforcement was waiting to speak with us. We were directed to a private area of one of the hotel's spacious lanais on the beachside.

Detective Makoa Lopaka (his name means warrior of shining fame) was a striking example of a male *Kanaka Maoli*, the indigenous Hawai'ian

People. He flashed a brilliant smile below dark but sparkling eyes. *Yeah... but... hiding something? I wondered.* Still, some evidence of a no-bullshit personality from the get-go.

"Yes, my ancestors go back to the *Ali'i Nui*-- the royal elite who ruled this nation for centuries, even before the islands were united by His Majesty Kalani Pai'ea Wohi o Kaleikini Keali'ikui Kamehameha o 'Iolani i Kaiwikapu kau'i Ka Liholiho Kūnuiākea."

Kayne said, "Kamehameha I?"

"Yes. I just like using his full Hawai'ian name. Learned it in school when I was a kid."

"Mako" was impressive at about 6'3" and 225 lbs. His handshake was firm and friendly. He was dressed in a tight HPD polo shirt and tan dress slacks, brown loafers, and air hose (no sox). Tribal tattoos illustrated his right arm, starting at the wrist and disappearing under the upper arm band of his shirt. A sea turtle design hid out on the underside of his left bicep. His Polynesian features and dark coloring were total Hollywood.

"I was a Navy man over in Pearl City. Gave me a leg up in law enforcement. HPD loves a native man on the force. Helps with public image."

He stood up as a woman entered the space. I made her out to be in her early forties, Asian, and very professional. She carried a tablet and was in the process of ending a call and dropping her iPad into a stylish shoulder bag.

"This is my partner, Rachel Takeda. We have been asked to assist in your investigation of the missing girl."

Officer Takeda drew back one side of her shoulder-length, straight black hair and extended her right hand for a shake.

"*Aloha*, gentlemen. It seems we have a mutual friend. I went to college with Special Agent Mary Chaffee. That's before she went to Quantico."

She motioned for us to be seated and pulled up a chair.

Kayne said, "That woman's first class. Her blood's worth bottlin', that one."

"I gotta say, I feel like I know you guys. I follow the blog. Great stuff-- kicking criminal butt. Going outside the norms... fascinating, Officer Sechi. Too bad-assed to be bound by legalities... my, my, my."

I said nothing. I simply smiled. Cops knew cops.

Officers Lopaka and Takeda produced HPD badges. Kayne steepled his fingers and half-closed his eyes as Mako began.

"This is what we know. Four days ago, the Shadow of the Lord Youth Retreat Program outside of Kahakuloa on Maui reported that Chlöe Alden, Caucasian, age fourteen, did not show up for morning chapel services. Records show that she was in the camp at bed check the night previous."

I asked, "Her friends, camp counselors, program administrators-- are they giving you anything to go on? What did she take with her? Speculate on her method of escape, please, Officer."

Mako paused to look me over, then said. "Your police force roots are showing, Mr. Sechi. Pretty cool. Anyway, no one is talking. It's like the girl vanished into thin air."

"Hey, can we do the first name thing? I understand life here in the Aloha State is pretty casual."

Rachel chuckled, reaching out to stop my hand.

"Mako, Nick, Rachel, and Kayne-- do not do the surfer dude, 'hang loose' hand thing, Nick-- a touristy dead giveaway."

Kayne and I laughed.

Rachel said, "The Department has pictures of Ms. Alden at all the airports and ferry slips. It looks like she either left the ranch on foot or hitched a ride. There were some deliveries that night, but our investigations haven't turned up anything."

The hunky Hawai'ian added, "This is an archipelago of about 130 islands spread out over about 1,500 miles. It is easy to get lost if you want to."

I commented, "Someone must have seen her or been aware of her plans."

Studly cop guy said, "How likely, if you are fourteen, is it that you have a plan, Nick? You feel threatened, you see an opening, and you go."

Rachel said, "I would say she is not likely to be trusting anyone about now."

"How soon can we get to the compound where the girl was last seen?"

Mako checked his watch, "We have a seaplane standing by at Pearl – forty minutes ground to ground."

Fuckin' great.

Chapter Twenty-Seven: Kahakuloa

Pearl Harbour, Oahu. Hawai'i
Kahakuloa, Maui, Hawai'i
The Case Files of Kayne J. Sorenson, Ph.D.

I will admit that my opinion of my husband's blog has changed during the time we have been together. This is not to disparage his writing skills or the accuracy of his reports. I am just amazed at the fandom that our cases have created. While widespread recognition sometimes helps us in our investigations, I find it somewhat restricting to be on the verge of celebrity. Also, I will not tolerate any intrusion into our family's privacy. My notes often fill in the gaps in his reporting when he is indisposed or acting independently.

Officers Takeda and Lopaka accompanied us to Joint Base Pearl Harbor-Hickham, where we prepared to board the Cessna 206 Seaplane for the flight to Maui. The aircraft bobbed in the harbor just off the pier, an HPD Investigation Division logo on its tail.

"Please allow us a moment."

Nick and I walked to the other end of the pier. Around us, the military installations, air and sea craft, and heavy equipment were a hive of both armed services and civilian activity. From here, the United States commanded the Pacific.

We looked out over the harbor and the sea beyond. Gigantic skies presided over gently rolling ocean waters. Off to our right, the Pearl Harbour National Memorial was alive with tourists and schoolchildren. I stood behind Nick and gently placed my hands on his hips. I modulated my voice so only he could hear.

"Look at that black and gray curtain of rain under that thunderhead off in the distance, my love. It descends into the dark blue waters like a veil, a storm amid sunshine. Nature awaits and calmly releases her gifts. Listen and breathe in the energy and strength."

He slowly closed his eyes, putting his mind in a safe spot. Our practiced meditation brought calmness and regular breathing to the lad. We stayed that way for several minutes.

I admit that, whereas my persona would imply that I am far too cerebral and detached, my husband continually brings out my sensual and more spiritual side. Standing close, the sensations of touch, feel, and smell of Nick were among the most delicious experiences I have encountered. I kissed the side of his neck, lingering a bit over his trapezius muscles. I felt an energy connection, almost electric in nature.

Behind us, Mako and Rachel went through a systems check with the pier personnel. The four-passenger Cessna was ready. Nick checked his SmartWatch for pulse rate and got his Bronx-cocky back. He swaggered up to the seaplane, checked our guides, and said, "We gonna do this or what?"

***

I had been to the islands of Hawai'i before, long before I began teaching in Florida. In Ft. Lauderdale, I met and fell in love with Officer Nicola Michael Sechi (known to his mother as 'Nick Baby') of the Wilton Manors Police Department. He is the absolute love of my life.

The previous incident of which I speak involved a missing cache of jewels. With the help of a very able local friend, I was successful at uncovering a band of thieves who had ransacked the royal regalia in the basement of the Iolani Palace, home of the kings and queens of Hawai'i.

The robbers were holed up on Maui, in the rainforests on the fabled Road to Hana. My companion and I were able to restore the "Eye of Lona," a large natural pearl, in myth linked to the goddess of the moon. It had been initially set in the Queen's scepter. We returned it with the other regalia to a very grateful Minister of Culture. Days and nights followed in the "Valley Island" with my island companion. An account of the details of that interlude is not pertinent to the present case.

As we approached the verdant green paradise by air, Officer Lopaka pointed to the Island's rugged north shore.

"There is Kahakuloa Village, and to the east, that rise is Kahakuloa Head. Kahekili II, the warrior king of the island, was said to leap 200 feet down to the water from this hill in the mornings before eating breakfast from a spot we now call 'Kahekili's Leap.'

I had done some research and found that the tiny Kahakuloa settlement is on the sea end of a valley carved by erosion of the western shield volcano, Pu'u Kukui. The land is a natural watershed with fertile volcanic soil, creating a lush agricultural center. We could see cattle roaming the hills. Pineapple plantations stretched up the sloping valleys, and where the lowlands were wet, taro farms carpeted the valleys. The little village could not have supported more than 100 people.

As we flew over the town center, Rachel pointed to a wooden structure on the highway. A steeple crowned a red-tiled roof supported by green walls.

"That is the Kahakuloa Hawai'ian Congregational Church— Church of Christ— very Pentecostal. If it's not in the Bible, these folks are not gonna do it. Restored after a fire that pretty much leveled the historic structure. And speaking of religious evangelicals, there, have a look."

We flew over to the northern shore and circled a large ranch off the main highway. Poetically, the sun grew lower in the western sky and cast a bit of shade on the Community of the Shadow of the Lord. Officer Lopaka came in from the compound's waterside and taxied to a pier hosting a few boats. We entered from the dock to the paddocks through a wooden lynch gate surmounted by a cross.

Soft afternoon shadows reached down from the verdant hills like the gray fingers of a mysterious dark hand.

Chapter Twenty-Eight: The Missional Mindset

Kahakuloa, Maui, Hawai'i
Nick Sechi's Journal

Our appearance at the Daybreak Retreat Center seemed to be a stressful encounter from the start. The ranch seemed to be rather large, consisting of a sizeable chapel, a school building, and assorted outbuildings. Extensive grounds provided occupants with sports fields and what appeared to be a farm. It seemed that not many visitors came to this remote place, and so hospitality was mixed with suspicion.

We settled at a picnic table in the shade of a banyan tree as a security guard wandered off in search of the appropriate staff to address our visit. Kayne nodded to the young retreatants dressed in black skirts or pants and white shirts. For the most part, the kids ignored us as they moved through the compound. I whispered, "They look like automatons, Boss, brainwashed and totally passive."

Mako said, "This was once a Catholic boarding school for boys. It was bought and renovated by the Evangelicals. They turned it into a retreat center for youth. These kids come from all over, wherever the church has a presence. Folks from five continents are represented."

"Officer Lapoka, have you found the girl?"

The speaker was a petite woman, conservatively dressed. A name badge identified her as "Director Margaret Ocampo." Smaller script identified her country of origin, the Philippines. Most likely, this detail was an attempt to inform visitors and students of staff diversity and the worldwide embrace of the Church.

"Not yet, Doctor Ocampo. Law Enforcement wants to continue to review details of the case with the folks at the Center to see if we can gain additional information."

Mako and Rachel introduced us as private consultants working with the Hawai'ian Police Department and the Vance Family. The woman was slightly unnerved as she asked to see our identification.

"I am afraid, gentlemen, since you were brought here without an appointment, we are unable to spend any time with you. A tour of the facilities is out of the question. Our program requires focused concentration, prayer, and reflection to discern what God has in mind for them. We carefully control the environment of our guests so that they may be open to the invitation of the divine in their lives. These experiences are highly emotional and powerful. Program counselors monitor our students carefully. The children are already very distracted by the recent defection of the Austin girl. Such occurrences mitigate our work with them."

And speaking of distraction, Kayne, as usual, was preoccupied. He seemed to be watching a soccer scrimmage a short distance away.

I asked, "How about the camp staff. We would like to speak to folks who were working when Chlöe Austin was last seen on the grounds."

"I am afraid, Mr. Sechi, that is not possible. This has been done with the police and the administration. We are understaffed and cannot have our workers neglecting their responsibilities."

Kayne stood up and walked toward the soccer group.

"Doctor Sorenson, I am afraid... where are you going, Sir? You are not allowed..."

Kayne did a pirouette as he walked. Not stopping, he called out, "I need to use the loo. I regret that this is unavoidable, and I beg your indulgence. Thank you."

Rachel attempted to gain the woman's attention, asking, "What is the procedure for the students leaving the campus and going into town?"

"Only in groups no larger than three and not without supervision, and only after they have been assimilated into the program. Chlöe was not yet comfortable here, so she was confined to the Center."

"Did she have any friends?"

"No, the girl was quite antisocial."

The response was too fast to not be a lie. I asked, "What precisely goes on here?"

"At this Center, the Lord refashions teens with a purpose and gives them a mission. We provide the tools to carry out a peer ministry that reaches all Christian denominations. We are about facilitating maximum impact for the kingdom. The Lord Jesus Christ wants to use our young people to influence their world, and it all starts with being intentional about sharing the good news."

"What happens to a student who is having questions of sexual identity?"

The Director unconsciously traced a design on the top of the wooden picnic table, pausing to look over her shoulder for the whereabouts of my husband. I noticed a security person hurrying from the sidelines to the men's room.

"Our young people will endure many struggles and triumphs as they follow the call to accept Christ. We encourage them to know the scripture and trust in the Lord's designs for them. We teach Christian morality with frankness and loving care. Repentance and transformation are always possible with the Lord."

"If they resist?"

"I assure you, we have very little of that, Mr. Sechi. The students themselves create an atmosphere of support for the struggling ones. We gather disciples with a deep passion for Christ, who, in turn, support the creation of other disciples. Our students are mobilized to share their faith."

"Go ye therefore, and teach all nations, baptizing them in the name of the Father, and of the Son, and of the Holy Ghost, teaching them to observe all things whatsoever I have commanded you. And, lo, I am with you always, even unto the end of the world. Amen."

Kayne had rejoined us. He finished his sermonette.

"Matthew 28, 18 to 20."

"Yes, Doctor Sorenson. I am afraid I need to assemble my team and... unless there is...."

Kayne said, "You could not be more anxious to escape our presence, Madam. Room seven, Grace Hall. Open it for us, please."

The Director blanched.

"Not without a warrant, Sir."

"Ms. Campo..."

"It's <u>Doctor</u> Campo."

"I see... well, we can discuss academic credentials another time, as well as that scandalous affair— where was it, Liberty University?" He popped a look at my phone.

"Did I mention my researchers work very quickly?"

He positively glared at the woman.

"So quite to the point, a child is missing, and the traces of her disappearance drip like a stain on the Shadow of the Lord ministries, dark and deadly."

Kayne was using his father's "voice of God" baritone, an inherited skill, it seems.

"Just who, exactly, do you think you are dealing with, Madam? I remind you that we are seeking the granddaughter of Charles Vance, a man with vast resources and influential friends-- among them, members of the Federal Bureau of Investigation. My husband, Mr. Sechi, is a cyber reporter with an excess of two hundred thousand followers across the globe. Take us to our requested destination or stand aside."

***

"There's always some unfortunate youngster hiding from sports activities at school. Fear of bullies. The boy's name is Billy Springfield, and he gave me this."

Mako, Kayne, and I were in Number Seven, Grace Hall. Rachel was questioning the requisite security guard in the building. The room, set up as a dorm for four students, revealed very little despite Kayne's thorough search methods.

It was apparent that Mako, our Hawai'ian police officer, was pretty uncomfortable. I wondered if he regretted hooking up with two hotshots from the mainland. He approached Kayne and said, "May I see that?"

Kayne handed the cop a scrap of paper.

"Maracaibo Bubble Gum but the inside..."

Kayne explained, "It is a doodle in ink of six squares piled in a pyramid. A highlighter colored the drawing a pale yellow. Only the wrapper, no gum. Courtesy of the boy, Billy Springfield."

"Did he say anything to you, Boss?"

"Not much,"

A girl of about fourteen stumbled into the room. She called out to the guard, who was still talking to Rachel.

"Gotta take care of something very private, Sir. Will only be a minute."

She went to a drawer in one of the bureaus and snagged a feminine product. She was about to shove it into the pants of her soccer shorts when she stopped. Not closing the drawer, she cocked her head, motioning for us to step closer.

"This is not a good place. They are very strict with us. Those who need reprogramming are separated out, and we get some extra religion classes junk. The boys have a super rough time. Billy told me he was... Anyway, Chlöe hated it and gave 'em a lotta shit. She got out. 'S all I know."

We were interrupted by the guard.

"Let's go, Mei Lin. No talking to the visitors."

She faked-dropped the maxi pad, which Kayne retrieved and handed back to her. Using the delay in her exit, Mei Lin said one more thing as she exited, "Try the... no, get some shave ice."

The sentry returned and escorted the girl to the hallway.

"Shaved Ice?"

Mako was about to say something when Kayne opened his hand. Another gum wrapper uncurled, a secret handoff from Mei Lin. He handed it to the cop. On the inside was a drawing of a stick figure with three legs. The middle leg was longer than the other two. The man looked at it for a bit but responded to my query.

"No such thing as shaved ice, Nick."

"Huh?"

"It's Pidgin— Hawai'ian Japanese vernacular. 'Shave ice.' To cool off, immigrants in Hawai'i used their tools to shave flakes off large blocks of ice and then coat them with fruit juice. Never say 'shaved ice.' You will immediately be recognized as a *haole*— a foreigner. Big matter of distrust with some of my people...

"And, boys, the best shave ice is right down the road at Mama Ululani's. Let's get out of this place."

Chapter Twenty-Nine: Come Out, Come Out Wherever You Are

Kahakuloa, Maui, Hawai'i
Nick Sechi's Journal

Mama Uluani's was a roadside hut on a turn in the highway passing through Kahakuloa. The stand was a short walk from where our seaplane was docked. It was green all over, from thatched roof to wooden walls, tables, chairs, and counters. A chalkboard out front advertised, "Mama's Fruit Stand, Banana Bread, and Shave Ice." On the roof, attached to a small gable sporting an upside-down American flag, a handpainted sign named the establishment for the owner.

A utility pole next to a bedraggled sandalwood tree brought electricity to the stand. The clapboard walls were latticework. Fruits in palm-woven baskets, kitschy island gifts, a variety of sweets, plastic containers of macadamia nuts, and be-ribboned, plastic bagged tins of freshly baked banana bread and other cakes were piled on the counter and stowed in hanging racks. At the rear wall, a big tin basin held a large block of ice sweating in the warm air next to a chest refrigerator holding squirt bottles of juices and flavors. A stack of piled, pointed paper cups guarded the block of ice.

In the shade, we settled against an outside counter, slurping our cool treats and mopping drips with paper napkins. Mako drew two gum wrapper symbols and six others on the napkins.

Rachel leaned over his shoulder and nodded. "I think there are more, but these are the main ones."

Kayne caught on immediately and remarked, "Oppressed people have ways of communicating with one another when assisting in escape tactics. In the South, in the 19th century, the conductors on the Underground Railroad would hang quilts outside with communication symbols to guide passengers to freedom in Canada."

Mako pointed to the stickman's long middle leg and said, "This is not what you think it is. It is a pole holding up...."

I jumped in.

"A scarecrow."

"Yes. And this? Remember, the blocks are yellow."

"The Yellow Brick Road."

Mako touseled my hair and said with a heavy Polynesian accent, "You smarty pants, *haole* boy, eh? Two for two. You make your mama and papa *haaheo loa* – very proud."

Kayne stood near us without any of Mama Uluani's treats. He leaned against the sidewall of the hut. His expression was one of amusement. However, Kayne seemed a bit reticent to chime in. He watched the exchange between cop and former cop, waiting for the other shoe to fall.

The Royal Hawai'ian went with me through the rest, indicating them one by one.

"Oil can... heart ... fuckin' easy man. Um ... a wand... a flower... oh, I got it... a shoe."

"Yeah, the last two are always red. So it's a..."

"A poppy and one of the Ruby Slippers."

Rachel said, "Friends of Dorothy. Queer kids coding each other using the iconic story."

"What is that one?"

Kayne examined the triangle with a squiggle coming out of its bottom center.

"Obviously, this is a symbol for a flying monkey. Signifying danger."

Mako said, "Proceed with caution-- they are looking for you."

He continued, "The Yellow Brick Road tells the youngster that they have found a way out, a way to freedom. Scarecrow-- someone is coming for you. The heart– be brave – hang tough. The red poppy means a runaway can sleep here and usually get a meal. The oil can identifies a conductor– a friend.

"However, this one is the most ominous, the Flying Monkey. It means danger is close by here. Glinda's wand tells of a happy ending, and the Ruby Slipper is also meant as encouragement. It points the way home. This is a secret language, but LGBTQ+ kids get it."

Rachel shifted as she continued the explanation. "In Hawai'i, as in most places in this ruthless world, gay, lesbian, and trans kids are in danger of being swallowed up by human traffickers. They are sold as sex workers by drug cartels who make them addicts, prostitutes, and mules. They end up either dead or severely health-compromised among the houseless population of the big cities."

Kayne was no stranger to rescuing the street kids. Back in Fort Lauderdale, he employed a small army of ragged spies and informers from among the juveniles no one seemed to want. He had stringent rules of conduct, ensuring their safety and continuing education.

I said, "Chlöe met student conductors at the camp who got her out and to the next conductor, but who?"

Kayne stepped away from the wall. Behind him was a small drawing of a silver oil can.

"Kindly introduce us to the proprietress of this establishment."

***

"You fuckin' bastard, how come you bring the white boys to my place, huh? Hello, baby Rachel, give Mama a kiss."

The stout native woman was in a colorful *mu'umu'u,* hair braided tightly to wrap around her head, and with one hibiscus flower behind her right ear. A fresh lei of plumeria flowers paired with one made of kukui nuts— both surrounding her neck and lying on her ample bosom. The formidable *mana wahine* looked us over with annoyance. Mako introduced us in Hawai'ian.

She waved us away and spoke with flashing eyes.

"Yeah, who gives a shit 'bout you? Eh? You see dat flag up dere? I sovereignty movement gal. You fuckers robbed our land and are ruining it. *Aloha,* my fat ass. You standin' on stolen ground."

Mama Ululani looked at the remains of our snacks and said in a totally different style, "Oh, you bought stuff. You tip Mama's jar?"

Kayne took a twenty in two fingers, reached over, and donated.

Mama pulled out a bottle and some shot cups. She smiled a toothless grin and said, "Here, drink dis, you bastards. Mama's special bourbon brew."

We tossed back a shot and were refilled. Our host toasted to *"Kukoa,"* freedom. The taste was a homemade bourbon with some unique Upcountry Maui ingredients, particularly fresh pineapple.

"You have the blue eyes of the sea god, and fuck you, you are a hot fire creature... my Mako and Miss Baby Rachel-- dese manly boys, huh? What 'cho want with Mama?"

Kayne placed the picture of the runaway before the woman. Her eyes grew wide, but she slipped back quickly into her Bloody Mary persona.

"I tole *māka'i* fuckers, I don't know shit." She punched Mako's big upper arm. "Police already been an' you know dat. Wha' 'cho doin' back here, den?"

Kayne pointed to the silver code image on the side of the hut. He took Mako's pen and drew the wand symbol on the palm of his left hand.

Ululani stared as tears welled up.

"Dey slap dat baby around, you know. Fuckers. She in bad shape-- ver bad when she come to Mama. Tree day ago. I fix'er up, give her food and supplies, and get her a ride Souf, Lahina, most likely. Safe driver guy-- friend doesn't harm kids. From dere? Who knows? Next, oil can... send her to another island hideout or da mainland. Dat child not sure where she goin'."

I wanted to ask why the woman did not get Chlöe into Children's Services. Still, I remember many times discussing with Kayne the obstacles and failings of the system. So many runaways commit suicide rather than accept help.

Mako had stepped away and leaned against the sandalwood tree. I could not read his expression, but I would say it was grave.

I asked, "The name of the driver, Mama?"

The Hawai'ian woman did another shot. She gave me a mean look.

"Go fuck yourself, fireboy."

She picked up her bottle and headed back to wherever she came from. Her exit line was directed at the brooding Mako.

"Hula kāne kāne hula"

He explained, "Mama Uluani is māhū. In Native Hawai'ian culture, a māhū is recognized as a third gender identity. Mama is filled with both male and female spirits, but she is not confined to a traditional gender binary. Māhū have historically played important roles as healers, teachers, and keepers of knowledge within Hawaiian communities.

I asked, "Mako, what did Mama say as she left?"

"Hula kāne kāne hula. She was referring to the two of you."

Kayne said softly, "Dancing men dance."

The Shadow of Evil

Chapter Thirty: The Emerald City

Kahakuloa Head, Maui, Hawai'i
Nick Sechi's Journal

"The meme is so apt. It's like there and not there. Only if you look for it."

"I'm not sure I understand, Rachel. What do you mean?"

We took the trail up and to the east, away from the village of Kahakuloa, into the hills known as Kahakuloa Head. Settling beneath some shady coconut palms, we could see the seaplane docked below, the retreat center, and the town. Behind was the West Maui Forest Reserve, green and waving above the heart-shaped leaves of the taro fields, like steps cascading down the slopes. We found a place to sit on boulders and fallen logs. Mama's Shave ice stand looked minuscule from our perch above the sapphire-blue Pacific.

"Think about it, Nick. In the movie, Dorothy is a runaway, looking for a place of safety-- somewhere over the rainbow. No one in Kansas understands who she really is."

"Along the way, this girl who is different from everyone else finds allies to help her out. They're broken, like her, but together, they get it done. What everyone else considers deviance is found to be a gift and was there all the time."

"Think you're stretching this way beyond the issue as far as talking about the gay kids."

"No, it's true. These kids have most of the entire world telling them they are no good, sinners, and, in some cases, worthy of abuse and even violent death. A guy I used to date was a lawyer. His firm did outreach to LGBTQ+ youth. Even in this island paradise, services in Hawai'i need some major improvement.

Kayne jumped in, "On the mainland, four-point-two million youth experience homelessness each year. Lesbian, gay, bisexual, transgender, queer, and questioning youth count as much as forty percent or one-point-seven million gay juveniles. Staggeringly disproportionate since gay youth are believed to be about seven percent of those aged thirteen to twenty-one. So, in reality, an LGBTQ+ youngster is one hundred and twenty times more likely to experience homelessness."

Mako was MIA. The Police officer was physically present, but his mind was wandering. The magic and mystery of the island seemed to have hypnotized him or shrouded his consciousness with veils of memories he longed to forget.

Kayne was aware that our bud had spaced out, but he continued. "I happen to know these stats because our nephew, Kris, and some of his university mates volunteer at The Ark of Refuge in San Francisco. This group assists homeless LGBTQ+ young adults with food, shelter, health, counseling, education, and related services.

Rachel said, "My ex used to work with True Colors. Despite these sobering statistics, there are currently no federal programs specifically designed to meet the needs of gay and transgender homeless youth. This means that, in many cases, these young people are left without the resources and assistance provided to other homeless populations. Among other things, True Colors is working to level the playing field for these kids and fill in the service gaps not provided by the state or federal governments."

I asked, "What's Hawai'i doing to serve these kids?"

Rachel said, "The State law does not explicitly criminalize running away. Some laws allow youth to receive services and even health insurance independently, without the courts getting involved. However, no legislation exists to provide essential intervention and emergency services for homeless kids.

"Hawai'i needs to include a strategy to address LGBTQ+ youth in its plan to end homelessness. The State also should create an Office of Homeless Youth Services, which designs, implements, and evaluates all such programs."

Kayne said, "True Colors sponsors research in care for LGBTQ+ youth in all fifty states. Comparing three benchmarks, law and policy, systems, and environment, the Aloha State received a grade of 47 out of 100, my friends."

I offered, "The state has banned conversion therapy for minors based on sexual orientation and gender identity or expression. However, more and more, we are seeing these laws challenged under the guise of freedom of religion."

Mako finally spoke, "Such Bullshit." He seemed to be talking to the sea and not to us.

Rachel said, "I serve on an *ad hoc* committee in the State to address the need for the staff of runaway and homeless youth systems to be trained on issues specific to LGBTQ+ youth.

"Like what?

"Nick, our goals are to create safe and inclusive environments in runaway and homeless youth programs by providing protections for sexual orientation, gender identity, and education in healthy sexual development."

She seemed to be struggling with a bit of hopelessness as she continued.

"It's so regrettable. These runaways hit the ground with so much against them. Do you know that the research shows that the primary reason for homelessness among LGBTQ+ minors is that they were forced out by their parents? Throwaways. That and running away because of their SOGIE."

I shook my head.

"Sorry, Rachel– lost."

"Sexual Orientation and Gender Identity Expression—articulated by an equality/anti-discrimination bill proposed by the Congress of the Philippines. I guess LGBTQ+ kids everywhere are looking to get over the rainbow to the safety of the Emerald City. Somewhere, ya know?"

In my head, I seemed to hear the high-pitched voices in the film. They were singing to the four runaways. I listened to the choir's background track telling the girl and her four friends that they were out of the woods, out of the dark, and out of the night. Safe haven just required them to...

Step into the sun, into the light, march up to the big green gates and bid them open.

Open. Open.

Chapter Thirty-One: The Dancing Fire

The Port of Lahaina, Maui, Hawai'i
Nick Sechi's Journal

"Mahalo nui loa.[2]"

The performers greeted us with traditional expressions of *aloha,* beautiful leis, and double-cheek kisses. Mako was bro-hugging some of the male performers and kissing some of the women in their exotic costumes. It was Polynesian Fitness Central, and I was in frisky jock boy heaven – gorgeous beauties.

With even more flowers in her straight black hair, Rachel spoke to the concierge, insisting that we receive special seating near the open-air, ocean-front stage. She pointed to one of the owner's tables and got assuring nods in return. Kayne and I were about to follow her to the low, sit-on-the-ground space when the fight broke out.

I say "fight," but it was more like jocking around.

One of the dancers was saying, "You are a fuckin prince, *'īna'i*. Fine Hawai'ian studlies don't dress like *haole[3]* Polo models. Gimme that shirt. Rock that *mea ali'i* bod, Brah."

Mako gave in and joined us, wearing a crown of ti leaves and a matching lei that dropped like a stole to his thighs. He dropped cross-legged on the mat next to Rachel. Kayne had his "resting jealousy face" on, so I must have been acting like a jerk, ogling the hard bodies.

The *lū'au* crowd was about eighty and was seated off to stage left. There were multiple performance spaces with stage lights and a band placed throughout the garden setting.

Behind the guests, a large tent served as an outdoor canopied kitchen. Cooks prepared island dishes of chicken and long rice, Hawai'ian sweet bread, salmon, sweet potato, and squid-- all made in the style of the

---

[2] Thank you very much
[3] Foreign. A term used to indicate non-Native Hawai'ians

ancient culinary arts. A smoking pit fueled by hardwood, the *imu*, served as the oven for the main dish, *kālua puaʻa*– Hawaiʻian roast pig. Chefs were busy uncovering the bounty, removing the hot stones inside and out, and peeling off the pounded banana tree stalks and ti leaves. The fragrances were intoxicating as they wafted across the banquet space.

As the setting sun painted the sky and the waters of the Pacific, the outdoor lights lowered, not wishing to compete with the breathtaking twilight display. Against a darkening sky and calm beach surf, a Polynesian warrior stepped into a spotlight and raised a conch shell to his lips. His call filled land, sea, and air. It was echoed by the *oli*, the chants filled with spiritual energy that brought wisdom, well-being, and the preservation of the people's history in a unique culture that had no written language.

"E ola kakou. E ike kakou. E ola na kini e. E ike ka lokahi e. Aloha e. Aloha e. Aloha e."[4]

The soft narrator's voice began the story as dancers joined the warrior on the stage, calling people from the sea with swaying bodies and exquisite hand and arm movements.

"Three hundred years before the common era, Polynesian settlers from the Marquesas Islands, guided by the gods across miles of ocean, landed their outriggers on these islands."

Torchlit outriggers sliced through the lagoon waters, and dancers, singers, and drummers alighted, scrambling onto the performance spaces. The enthusiasm was infectious, promising an unforgettable experience.

The ensemble told the story of Hawaiʻi in song and dance. The story unfolded as chapters, the Kapua Era of the high chiefs, the arrival of the Europeans, the Spanish, the Russians, and the English claimant to the kingdom. The arrival of Captain James Cook brought a new dance with a distinctly different dress. The Christian overlords of this period would outlaw the *hula* as sinful.

During the action that described the history of the House of Kamehameha, the drums became war-like, and the dances more forceful and lightning-fast– the *urʻa pau*. The narrator and the performers told the

[4]Let's live. Let's see. Let's live. Let's live. Let's see unity. Love. Love. Love.

tale of the unification of the islands and the establishment of the Kingdom. Finally, the stage was set for the dissolution of the nation.

I turned to Mako but was surprised to see a troupe member sitting in his place, grinning like a mischievous child. He pointed to the stage and said, "Da Bright Warrior Man dere was a member of dis company not too long pass. Tonight, he take my place. Now you will see sometin', eh?"

HPD's tattooed Hawai'ian prince stamped into the lowering stage lights with two fire knives, lighting up the darkness and the muscled planes of his glistening body. He threw his head back and sang, "*E mālama nā luna ki'eki'e i ke akua o ke kaua a kaua a me ke ali'i nui.*"[5]

Kayne said, "The warrior calls upon his fellow chiefs to fight beside the great King in the name of the god of war."

The Hawai'ian smiled and said, "*Pololei 'oe,*[6] Doctor. I am Dani Kale' Okapa, by da way... good buddies with Officer Makoa Lopaka. *Mahalo,*[7] my boys."

Rachel waved to the guy and pointed back to Mako, "He's good."

The pants had been replaced by a floral pattern *malo*-- a loincloth cut high on the dancer's flanks, allowing freedom of movement and an excellent view of his muscled butt. Wrists and ankles were bound with bands of dark green ti leaves. His necklace was of animal teeth with a wild boar's tusk at its center. Black stripes of warrior makeup stretched across his face from ear to ear.

Mako jumped, leaped, and whirled with god-like power and grace as the singers took up the chant, and the drums underscored a high-risk performance by a skilled professional. The flaming machetes cut mesmerizing circles of light as the warrior twirled them up, down, and side to side, jumping over and into the flames with blazing expertise. Toss and catch maneuvers brought gasps from the crowd. The act's finale was a host of men and women, flaming sticks in their headdresses and hands twirling heat and light behind the exuberant star.

---

[5] "The high officials will take care of the god of war and the war and the great king."

[6] You are right.

[7] Thank you

The fire warrior went down into a split, burning knives held high, with the drums rolling up to a last staccato shot as all action stopped. The audience was on its feet as the stage lights came up. The *wahine* and *kane* dancers reached out to teach the guests how to snap and sway their hips and tell the stories with graceful hands, making smooth and seductive movements of the once-forbidden dance.

Chapter Thirty-Two: A Tropical Night

The Port of Lahaina, Maui, Hawai'i
Nick Sechi's Journal

"Damn, spectacular, bud."

The star of the show came over to Rachel, Kayne, and me and placed a crown of flowers on our heads. Mako signaled the waiter for another round of drinks. He plopped down next to Kayne and accepted compliments all around. Rachel got up to dance with Dani.

Our drinks arrived, and we clinked cheers. Mako looked at Kayne and flashed a left arm of solid muscle.

"Do what you are famous for, consulting detective. Have at it."

Now, this is getting even more interesting.

Kayne needed no further encouragement. He came very close to touching the sweating athlete as he said, "This sea turtle, symbolizing the voyager, is made of Maori and Samoan-inspired motifs. The inner triple twist design itself is a Maori symbol representing the meeting of two different cultures, the union of two peoples. Stylized shark teeth symbolize strength and adaptability.

"Frangipanis, the flowers inside this design on your right arm, are typical in tropical areas, particularly on the Pacific islands, and they mean shelter and protection. The markings on your body illustrate a journey from Earth to the sky. Please turn to your left. Thank you."

The policeman's broad back came into view, and Kayne gestured to Mako's dorsal surface as if the big cop's hard muscles were his teaching notes projected at the front of his classroom.

"This hammerhead shark snaking from your right deltoid to your waist is a very complex design. It is made of many symbols representing the virtue of strength. The spearhead motif on the inside of the beast's body tells of difficulties overcome, also shown in the moray eel design in the shark's tail. Octopus tentacles and shark teeth inside the head symbolize adaptability and intelligence, tenacity, and determination to reach success. That theme is repeated here-- the sun is made of shark teeth in the head.

"Please stand, Officer. Again, thank you."

Mako did. Kayne tastefully moved the loincloth to the right and continued his lesson.

"This is the path of Kamehameha along the outside of your left leg, ankle to pelvis, representing a journey full of challenges, finally leading to glory. The hands of a tiki on the design are symbols of protection, and the two chasing birds symbolize help to the loved ones."

Mako stood above his seated guests like a Hawai'ian tribal chief guarding his outrigger, big arms folded and thick legs apart.

"You have outdone yourself, Sir. Impressive."

"Your body art is from your youth, indicating that you were raised in the ancient traditions, a child who struggled with many personal issues, an orphan raised by the community. The forces of strength and courage are somewhat overstated, mate... hence my inductions."

He pointed to the stage. "... a community where you learned to be a champion dancer, athlete, and protector of the people. You are an accomplished rugby player-- your dance moves give that away, gestures modified from sports to the arts. There are other personal struggles evidenced in your behavior, but I will stop there."

The teacher and the student exchanged a knowing look.

"Boss, how do you know all this?"

"During that previous trip to these Islands, in my younger days, I met a diving instructor, a Hawai'ian. He was well-versed in many traditions of these islands. The lessons of his body art were quite educational."

I smiled knowingly. "Got it."

Dani slid in beside his friend with a very familiar hand-on-shoulder gesture. Rachel checked in with, "What'd I miss?"

She quaffed about half of her cocktail and eyed the plate of *haupia*, the traditional *lū'au* dessert. She fought temptation.

"Doctor Kayne was demonstrating his methods. I was acting as the specimen."

Kayne said, "This really is too easy, my friends. Officer Tanaka, or should I say Reverend Tanaka?"

Rachel smiled, "You Googled me."

Kayne shook his head and indicated the woman's hands as she reached for the dessert.

"No, Officer. You wear a cross ring on the third finger of your left hand. You are a believer working in a very secular world. The cover of your iPad is embossed with *'Pro Deo et Patria.'* That's the motto of the United States Army Chaplain Corps-- for God and Country. Like your fellow officer, you were greeted by many past associates when we were at the Pearl Harbor Base. Your knowledge of Christianity has made itself known more than once in the short time we four have been together."

Rachel raised her glass. "One plus one equals two, Doctor Kayne. I left the service. Pastoral guidance of souls turned out not to be my strong suit. I am a much better cop. Sort of the same dynamic-- pastor, police officer-- keeping the folks safe, get them to follow orders."

The woman smiled and continued. As Rachel took over the lesson, Dani and Mako were all ears and eyes. She pointed to Kayne with a fork.

"You were his teacher, and you fell in crazy hot love. Nick was a cop in South Florida and, from what I gather, a real institutional pain in the ass. Been there, guys."

Her dark eyes swung over to me.

"Your personal struggles involve a fear of heights and of flying. Both you and Kayne are total warriors when it comes to hand-to-hand combat."

Mako nodded and saluted with his drink.

"Doctor Sorenson is a crime-solving genius, which also pisses off the authorities. Your profession translated to the classroom-- psycho-criminology or everything you wanted to know to trap serial murderers, kidnappers, drug lords, oligarchs, and corrupt politicians. Your cases have taken you all over the world. Your family members run the gamut from colorful to insane, likewise, your friends and colleagues. And I gotta say this, although it is highly unprofessional...."

Rachel took another swig of her drink and grinned, holding her audience in the balance.

Dani said, "Tell it, Rache. Don't give us da suspense."

"The two of you sex up like you invented it."

The other two Hawai'ians high-fived and said something in their native tongue. They did the thumbs up and clapped Kayne on the back.

The look on my husband's face was one of seemingly general amusement. Still, I had a feeling I was in for a "Come to Jesus" in the immediate future about my blogging.

Somewhat emboldened by the Mai Tai, Rachel went on.

"Oh, yeah, you both are verse. No telling who's a bottom or a top."

This time, Kayne did a spit take. Dani touched my face and snickered.

"Yeah, bud. You blush like a virgin at an orgy."

Laughter and more salacious comments-- Kayne shot me a glance that confirmed my inklings that a verbal spanking was on its way.

He remarked, "My husband loves to titillate his readers even if it means breaching the boundaries of propriety."

"Bullshit, Boss. Truthin' is my game. It's only sex, and Rachel is right. We are very accomplished in that avocation, and so are a close group of our friends. Great fun and high drama."

Kayne brought the laughter and relaxed camaraderie to a sudden shutdown. He turned to the handsome dancer and said, "Dani, please tell us where the girl is."

Chapter Thirty-Three: Dani's Secret

The Port of Lahaina and Honakowai, Maui, Hawai'i
Nick Sechi's Journal

Dani Kale' Okapa stood up with a grave look on his face. Mako was confused, as was Rachel.

The lithe dancer looked around the *lū'au* assembly, now in the semi-darkness of a tropical nightclub. Tiki torches provided soft dance floor lighting. The darkness had a thousand eyes and ears, and the dancer was alert to the point of fear.

Dani bent over from behind his seated friend and placed his hands on Mako's broad shoulders. He spoke softly.

"Not here. *Honakowai.*"

He turned and left, heading for the performers' dressing rooms.

Three of us turned to Kayne.

"What the fuck, Boss?"

Kayne took a gulp of his Hibiki and placed the glass next to my mobile. He pointed to the phone.

"Research my love-- Scott and Gints in Aerie. Came in during the performance. Dani Kale' Okapa-- about a year ago, he was brought up on charges of human trafficking. The evidence was found to be inconclusive. The plaintiffs were the parents of a runaway with close affiliations to the religious right.

"He is suspected of being a conductor for the Yellow Brick Road— a pipeline for getting runaway gay kids to safety. Did none of you see the stylized oil can tattoo on the inside of his right forearm?"

Mako came up from a head-in-his-hands position and said, "I am embarrassed. Dani is a very close friend. We met… well, that is not important. He has had a tough life. Strict family upbringing… big time

Jesus people. At the ripe old age of fourteen, he was a pushout when his folks found out he liked men.

"Lots of trouble with the law growing up. The details are not necessary. Mama Uluani took him in and got him sober— off drugs and off selling his ass. Enrolled in school, got a job, driving for the growers on the island. As you saw, the kid has a kick ass body. Sports and dancing were a cinch for him."

He looked at us and added, "I had no idea, but it seems he is involved in this."

Mako's distress was sincere and genuine.

Kayne placed a hand on the police officer's right arm.

"My young friend, it would seem that Laka is indeed blind."

I said, "Who?"

Rachel explained, "Laka is the Hawai'ian goddess of love."

***

Honakowai was a resort on a bluff overlooking the sea, not too far from Lahaina on the western shore. It was not actually a resort, more like a commune for native Hawai'ians and their friends. Tucked into the hills near the sea, there were common buildings for eating, bathing, and other group activities, nestled in a lush, garden-like environment. A series of sleeping platforms for private living spread out through the park. They were open-air, covered by thatched roofs, and afforded privacy by walls of long white, opaque curtains. Each platform had an enclosed bathroom and a fire pit area for outdoor cooking and living. No one was far from the sea breezes and salty smells of the ocean.

Tikis, colorful surfboards, Hawai'ian art pieces, and island trappings were everywhere. A group of outriggers owned by the resort were piled near the curved path to the beach. Fishing nets hung between poles, drying for the next day's catch. Other guests and owners could be seen gathered around welcoming fires. Laughter and friendly shouts often broke the serene and sandalwood-scented silence.

Dani had set up two guest venues for the group adjacent to his own. The enchanting boy had started up a fire pit in the center of their accommodation area. He was dressed in a blue and green *pāreu*, in a colorful Tahitian motif. A loop of small shells encircled his neck and dropped to his pecs. His right wrist sported a matching bracelet. Mako held up a hand as we entered the compound and approached the dancer.

They spoke softly in their native tongue. Mako turned and explained.

"This is Mama Uluani's share of the commune, and we are her guests. You can tell her politics-- the many symbols of nationalistic protest against the United States government. She is a legend in the solidarity movement of Hawai'i. She holds a meeting here and plans civil action. We must respect tradition in this place, my brothers."

He looked slyly at Kayne and me in our white boy tourist kit.

"Oh, you mean our clothes, right, Big Guy?"

"Yes, Nick. Mama and her family are strict traditionalists-- they do not allow *haole* clothes in the settlement. I have placed customary apparel in your *lumi lumi* on the bed. The *pāreu*, as Dani wears, or, if you are feeling adventurous, a *maro*, the warrior's loincloth, as you saw at the *lū'au*."

"Got it."

We headed up to our sleeping platform to get native.

The bed was big and swathed in white sheets and pillows. There were towels near the washroom door. Bedside tables with lamps bookended the bed. A scowling Tiki mask adorned the only solid wall outside the small sink and toilet area. An outdoor shower with a wooden privacy screen was provided for the shy types.

Kayne said, "Our roommate is Ku, the Hawai'ian god of war. Perhaps I will wear the mask when I ravage your nubile body tonight."

"Oh, hell yeah, bring it, Boss. Been a while, and the hot island fever's got me."

He removed his shoes and socks while sitting on the bed.

"We must continue our investigation first, my love. Young Opaka must explain his involvement. He walks a dangerous line in this."

As we continued undressing. Kayne picked through the four articles of clothing on the bed: two sarongs and two loincloths.

Kayne lifted a brown and green *pāreu* to the soft light. It was colorful but pretty flimsy. "This will show off that sexy jock arse of yours just fine, my love."

"Fuck no, Boss. You heard the police officer. I am feeling super daring."

Naked, I wrapped a dark green loincloth around my manly charms before exiting our *lumi lumi*.

"Let's go, Boss. We need to find out what Dani has to say."

Kayne grabbed the other sarong, blue and sea green, and quickly did a "rat tail," snapping the end against my bare ass. He dodged my roundhouse and dashed after me, tying the cloth around his waist.

"I won the bet," Mako smirked. "Knew the choice would go this way. But Kayne, c'mere bud."

Mako looked into Kayne's eyes and said. "I'm gonna touch you, bud. Cool?"

Without waiting for an answer, the big Hawai'ian, rocking his own loincloth on some world-class haunches, pulled off Kayne's covering.

"It's not a beach towel, Brah. Supposed to be worn like this."

He took the rectangular cloth and folded it diagonally into a triangle.

Both Mako and Dani were so checking out the spectacular Kayne Sorenson body.

Dani pulled Kayne's hair into a savage warrior bun with long tresses on each side. Mako wrapped the *pāreu* around Kayne's waist and then gathered the two ends and tied a slip knot on his hip.

They stepped back and admired the transformed *haole*-to-*kānaka maoli*[8] standing before them. Dani tied cowrie shells in Kayne's coif and around his left bicep.

---

[8] Foreigner to Native Hawai'ian

"Two knots at the hip if you wish to prevent an accident. One if you are feeling... adventuresome, eh? We will leave it at that."

"You come to Dani, Red Sechi. I gonna fix you up like a hot *koa*—fierce as hell.

Using stage makeup, Dani painted half of my face with aesthetic tribal designs. A temporary tattoo covered my right shoulder, down to my upper arm, with a series of intricate Polynesian signs, spear patterns, lines, and symbols. He moved aside my loincloth to create some transient body art from my left lower back to my right buttock and halfway down my thigh.

"Now, *ha'a* stance for me. Bow-legged and dose big gunz up. That's right. Open eyes wide and stick out tongue. You gonna kick some *hoki kanaka ino*".[9]

I stomped my right foot and crouched with legs wide-- my best warrior dance pose for the boys, front double biceps of steel, fierce face and all.

"Lord Jesus, yes! You look mighty, mighty, Ni'ko. Do not worry. Wears off two three days dat tattoo shit, yeah."

Kayne ran a hand over my back and whispered. "*A'o nō i ke koa, a'o nō i ka holo.* Learn bravery, learn to run."

Rachel came into the circle just in time to get a glimpse of some nearly naked Kayne and Nick. She looked like an island princess in a yellow and red sarong. Our friend commented on the tie-up.

She fingered the cloth knot on her chest.

"One if you like to tease." She winked at me and added, "You guys sure keep fit, lemme tell ya. Counting eight on each of those washboards. Shoulda brought some laundry."

I did a torso plank but still blushed. The firelight and shadow disguised my reddening.

---

[9] Bad guy ass

Settling next to Dani, Rachel set a tray near the fire pit with beer and one glass of whiskey on the rocks. Rachel placed a hibiscus flower behind each of our left ears and distributed the drinks.

"This is Big Swell IPA from our Maui Brewing Company. It's actually an excellent craft beer. And this, Kayne, is Old Hana Road Whiskey on the rocks from the Ko'olau Distillery on Oahu. It will rival your Hibiki, I'll bet.

"All of this creates an exceptional island mood, my friends, but we still have a lost girl to find." Kayne turned to Dani and continued. "After Chöle escaped from the youth camp, you made contact. Tell us how and where you took her."

The young Hawai'ian stared into the fire. He poked at the burning wood with a stick as he explained. As he spoke, his accent seemed to get more pidgin, and he used additional Hawai'ian words as if the setting drew out a more native persona in this man. Old memories crammed into the boy's awareness as he attempted to explain.

He addressed Kayne very aggressively, "You listen to me, *haole* man. I drive that girl. No ting' more. You hear what I say?"

Kayne nodded, "*Hilina'i wau iā 'oe, e ku'u hoaaloha.*[10] I make no accusation. Dani, where is she?"

The boy took a deep breath. In the firelight, his large brown eyes sparkled with fought-back tears.

"*Olu'olu nā mea a pau, ke kāne.*[11] Cool– very cool. Ever t'ing is cool, men.

"First off, dares Mama. It was Mama Uluani. She call me to say we had a runaway seekin' safe haven. I had to move fas' because dat church place– dose fuckers suspect Mama as da *wahine*[12] the kids turn to when dey are trying to get away. Time to time, dey give her shit."

He looked at Mako and Rachel.

---

[10] I trust you, my friend.
[11] All is well, man.
[12] woman

"No police, you know? Runaway gay kids dey do not want to be sent back to dere parents. Only makes more trouble. Don't look at me like dat, Brah. You know what I'm talkin' 'bout. 'Member dat suicide last year?"

Mako stood and walked away from his friend. The accusation was obvious. Rachel said solemnly, "Not fair, Dani. That boy was fifteen. So very tragic. The police were only doing their job."

"Dat Chöle girl made it clear that if she were returned to her family, she would take off again, the first chance she got."

Kayne asked, "Where is she now, Dani?"

"She is safe, Doc."

He made eye contact, flames reflected in his brown eyes, and lights danced along the planes of his face. The firelight made his expression all the more determined.

"You gotta understan'. I know what dese kids are going through, *ke kāne*. Fuckin' torment and no one, no one to help you, to understan' dat stuff. No kid deserves dat shit."

He stirred the fire and gazed intently at the burning embers as if they held some secret revealed only to those with the courage to be brave in the face of danger.

Dani continued. "Yeah, yeah, believe me, bra. I know what trouble I got me now. Been down dis road before with the *māka'i* boys. No jail time for dis boy. Take my canoe out dere and get los permanent before I give it up."

He gestured in the direction of the sea.

Mako paced off to the side. His conflict with his friend, who had acted very irresponsibly, was palpable.

"Let's go, Brah. The important thing is the girl."

"I said she safe, *hoa momona*. Why don't you let it be? Huh? Trust dis man. What you all gonna do? Huh? Make dis situation betta for dis *kaikamahine*? How you gonna make dat happen? You fuckin' tell me ri now."

183

I said carefully, "The girl belongs with her family, D-man. It is the law. She is a minor."

Kayne was conspicuously quiet. We had disagreed, with some disastrous results, in a similar situation when we were working on our first case. Right now, it seemed he had checked out-- listening to the conversation but focused somewhere far off.

"I picked her up from Mama two nights ago, right here at dis compound. I get her to da Big Island. I got a cousin wid a fishing boat. He take her. Dat cousin, Jonah Kalanianaole, and his wife, Marie, all very *pau*, you know? You swear you never gonna get dose folks in any kina trouble, see?

"But here's da t'ing, *ke kāne*, dat lil' girl, she got some dope on dose God people. Ver bad shit, ya hear? Dey up to no damn good. Chöle gal, she got da evidence, man, ta hang 'em all."

Kayne said, "How fast can we get to the Big Island?"

Mako replied, "First thing come sun up. There is a storm in the way right now. Best not to make the trip tonight."

After a beat, Dani said, "Forgot to tell. I give her dat number. Ya know, Runaway Switchboard number 1-800 sumptin' sumptin.' Always keep dat in my truck for dose kids.

"But hey, gotta go slow with dis, *e na hoaaloha*.[13] She will run if we spook dat kid. Tellin' you. You listen to your Dani."

He stood up and spoke an aside to Mako in Hawai'ian. The police officer, struggling to suppress his frustration, seemed to argue that the young dancer had stretched the boundaries of their relationship in this situation. Dani tried to reassure his buddy with a hand on his shoulder. In the firelight, the two men were a study in frustration and passion.

***

Mako walked us back to our *lumi lumi*.

"So, here's the thing. First, Rachel's gonna stay on Maui and keep that youth camp under observation. She is working on an official visit with

---

[13] dear friends

Children's Services and her legal contacts. The disappearance of the Alden girl has precipitated a more extensive investigation. My boss is getting calls from the FBI."

"Good decision, mate. The church folks are up to something with those young people, and, based on the cold reception we received, Nick and I are not among those they trust right now."

Kayne continued, "I am anxious to accomplish three critical things. Secure the girl and get to the bottom of her secret. Also, the man who jumped into Kilauea, Damien Kuhio Aloho – we need to know the details of the connection to the Church of the Shadow of the Lord. His family in Puakō will undoubtedly have important information for us. I fear we are close to great evil with this case, my friends."

Mako turned away. Again, I felt stirrings related to the god-like physique of the native cop. The nearly naked muscled hunk, our host, in his looks and movements, seemed to suggest some carnal play that would release quite a bit of tension related to the case.

The drink is talking, yeah. You're married, Nick Boy. Have some fuckin' class.

Mako spoke softly, almost as if he were revealing something close to his heart.

"I believe Dani has more to tell us on this, but he is holding back. I will work on that."

The ghostly white, floor-length sheers hanging on the four sides of our *lumi lumi* were tossed sensuously by the fragrant night breezes. Soft candlelight illuminated the interior of the covered platform space with its bed and other guest furnishings. Again, I had the sense that Mako was about to suggest a night of sexin' up.

I was wrong.

"I will leave you guys to the mysteries of the Hawai'ian night and meet up in the morning. Our place is just there. I cannot promise that we will not disturb you, but we will try."

He moved the hangings and stepped down, making his way to his own quarters.

"Wishful thinking, my love?"

"Huh? What, Boss?"

He took me in his arms and said, "As I have often indicated before, you are very transparent when it comes to pursuits of the flesh. You like 'em muscled up and on the savage side. And I would have thought, all of this...."

He lifted his arms away from me and hit a porn star pose, big guns up and behind his head. The single knot of his *pāreu* coming apart, the sarong dropped to the floor. Make that partway– you see, it got caught on his...um... his enthusiasm, his rather attentive enthusiasm.

I reached forward and finished his strip and added my own skimpy manhood covering to the crumpled fabric on the floor. We did things to each other fueled by the raw and brutal energy in the hot, exotic night, first standing. One kneeling, switching, and then tumbling over each other on the cool, white sheets.

Far into the first round, we were pausing to change the rhythm of our lovemaking. The searing nocturnal heat and sweat were pierced by Mako's cry, "'*O 'oe e kūlohelohe nei, ke ho'ōla nei au iā 'oe e like me ka hō'ino.*"

Kayne pulled my head to his mouth and gasped in my ear, "Rather obscene if I understand correctly. Truthfully, it gets lost in translation, hot boy... oof, yeah– turn that way... But you should know what we just heard is *exactly*... what I am going to do to you... mmm, give me that hot..."

I was his captive in a lust-filled, savage ritual as old as these islands.

Chapter Thirty-Four: Flying Monkeys

Honakowai, Maui, Hawai'i
Nick Sechi's Journal

I jostled the naked man, sleeping face down next to me, with one arm across my chest. His long hair spread across his face and the pillow like a sweaty black headdress.

"Kayne, Kayne, you awake, Boss? Something's going on. Listen."

The sounds coming from the "room" next to ours were not noises of lust and passion. It was more like a struggle was occurring. Kayne sat up in bed.

"It is just as I feared, my love. Trouble is afoot."

He tossed me my cargo shorts and slipped into his own. We drew back the curtains and dashed over to see what was happening. Just beyond the compound, two heavies had Dani between them and were hurrying away towards the sea. The kid's feet were barely touching the ground as he struggled to resist the capture. Mako was nowhere to be seen.

We raced to the cliffs above the rugged coastline and the raging surf. The trail was challenging in our bare feet, but we managed to keep the abductors and their captive in sight. Now, they pushed the boy ahead at gunpoint. His arms were bound behind his back. They reached the edge of a flat lava shelf above the rushing sea and knocked Dani to his knees.

Dawn was about an hour away. The boundary between the land and the sea was a smudge of mist, fog, and ocean spray heaving up and onto the jagged, black lava. The rocky shoreline was indented with lava pools filled with dark water. The men were arguing and waving a gun at the boy, who kept shaking his head, resisting their attempts to coerce information.

Kayne pointed to the left, and we spread out. A wave came up from below and swept across the rock inches from the three men. It seemed as if the sea were grabbing at the contentious humans. Dodging behind lava boulder outcrops, I attempted to get close to the thugs. I heard Dani scream that he knew nothing about the girl or any missing files from the mission camp.

I pressed my back against a rise of hardened lava and concentrated.

OK, dude, This is where you bust around the corner, dodge a bullet and kick the shit outta those fuckwads.

Hopefully, Kayne, around on the other side, would join in the assault. The dodging the gunfire thing was the hard part.

It sorta went that way, but really not.

I busted out like a banshee and screamed like a chimp on fire. I hit the ground on a shoulder roll. This drew the attention of the would-be kidnappers. Perfectly timed to my antics, Kayne vaulted a rocky rise and landed a kick to the head of the gunman. I saw the Luger skid across the wet rock and land in a tide pool.

Check one.

The other thug pulled a dagger from his belt and made for the kid. Dani was now coming up from a crouch on the rock. As the killer drew back to toss the knife, the flat lava surface beneath his feet exploded, a jet of water blasting 50 feet into the air.

Check two.

The recoil had two catastrophic results. The force of the gusher in the blowhole pulled the assassin into its maw with a horrible sucking sound. At the same time, Dani was lifted off his feet and tossed into the churning, rocky sea.

I ran, scooped up the dagger, and sprinted full force into the turmoil of air, rock, and stormy water. It seemed as if I were watching all of this outside my body. I saw myself put the blade in my mouth as I reached the edge. At a running leap, I lifted my body into an arrow-like, straight-forward running dive, hoping to gain the maelstrom of sweeping, swirling water beyond the rocks where the boy had gone down.

The undertow was like the grip of a giant hand seeking to crush me into the depths of the watery abyss. There were a ton of bubbles and foam but little light. I was pulled down despite the resistance of my strong arms and legs to battle the current and find the boy. Useless, futile, and totally nutso, I went down and tumbled ass-over-head-over-ass-again. No air, lungs bursting. Panic.

Fuck! I lost him...

And then I touched him. His bound arms...

I pulled Dani to my chest and tried to kick out and up to the surface. Fuckin' useless.

And then... and then...

I just let go, not of Dani but of trying to resist the powerful surge of the sea. We continued to descend. I cut the bindings that held his arms behind his back and clutched him like a life preserver.

Drowning... down and down...

The last thing I saw before the blackness was the light in the ceiling of water above our heads– dawn.

The Shadow of Evil

Chapter Thirty-Five: Kanaloa Rising

Honakowai, Maui, Hawai'i
Nick Sechi's Journal

The naked beast man is immense, like fifty times life-size— upper body of a powerlifter, lower body, the sinuous coils of an enormous squid. He has powerfully handsome Polynesian features with long hair of green, blue, black, and white, swirling around his head and powerful shoulders. Large eyes dance above his facial scruff, which accents his grin of flashing white teeth. His massive torso sparkled with curtains of water lights.

The monster's kākau wrapped his face, shoulders, and arms with Hawai'ian tattoo patterns made of repetitive geometric forms and patterns that signify protection, strength, and family. Stylized images of sea creatures move across his upper body, under, over, and around the tribal designs.

But his eyes— totally hypnotic— coral red and sometimes aqua with glints of gold. He breathed water.

Around him, living marine creatures cavorted in the churning water— a sea turtle, blue-grey dolphins, and schools of fish, flashing iridescent scales and fins like angel wings. The mysterious giant seemed to command all around him. The animals, like attendants, were rolling on their backs and spinning through the million shades of blue and white. Strings of bubbles like ascending pearls surrounded him and embraced Dani and me.

Whoever this colossus is, he is amused by the puny human boys drowning before him. His expression is a bit like a father who allowed his sons to reach the brink of disaster after numerous warnings.

I heard him in my head: "There is nothing more powerful than me in the entire universe, ko'u mau keikikāne.[14] Why do you struggle? Come and

---

[14] my boys

give yourself to me. E mālama au iā ʻoe.[15] *I will hold you in my strong arms."*

As we fell, the leviathan reached from beneath us and, on a flat palm, raised us from the watery depths up into the light.

His laughter sounded over the roar of the surf.

***

Fuck me, man. I thought I was gonna cough my lungs up. Water, air, and whatever the shit surged out of my mouth and nose as I gasped, cramped, and spasmed on the hard lava shelf. Kayne was kneeling over me and coaxing me to breathe. He had given me mouth-to-mouth after hauling Dani and me out of the sea. His strong hands lifted and turned me to make sure that I continued to come to consciousness.

Mako stood over us and looked none the worse, although the big cop had a visible bump near his right side hairline from a pistol-whipping. He had one arm around his exhausted bud. Dani had some cuts and bruises from being tossed against the rocks, but it looked like nothing was broken or bleeding badly. He was breathing like a marathoner leaning into the shoulder of the big Hawaiʻian.

He would later say, "Nah, Brah. *Kanaloa*, sea god. He love to make love to his Boy Dani, but Big Daddy, he play rough, you know?" He winked at Mako and added with a smirk, "Rough is insane hot, *ke kāne*. You know what I'm sayin'?"

I arched my back and hurled one last time. Kayne pulled me up and onto his lap.

"You are an amazing hero, my love. You saved the lad and came up alive. I am so proud and thankful."

He hugged my wet upper body against his. The emotion in his grasp and in his voice was genuine. I suspected he was pretty nutso at one point when I wasn't breathing.

"The guy..."

---

[15] I will look after you.

"Rachel is driving with him over to Lahaina Police Headquarters. She got a couple of squad cars here to investigate the death of the other one."

Mako said, "Hired guns, both of them. Hopefully, we can find out the reason for the attack through interrogation of the surviving attacker."

Kayne thought for a moment and said, "They wanted information. Chlöe Alden stumbled on some pretty incriminating goings-on involving the Church. Dani has confirmed that she did not share her secret with him. His brutal abduction underscores the importance of stopping the church's sinister plot. I am convinced that the key to this is the death of Damien Kuhio Aloho. If the girl is safe for the time being, the priority is to find out what the source of guilt was that caused the man to immolate himself in the volcano."

Dani crouched down next to me. He reached out and brought my head to his.

"Dis da *honi*, Ni'ko Brah. We gonna touch our spirits. Dani sayin' t'anks for saving his life."

He touched his forehead to mine, nose to nose, and exchanged breath with me.

Remarkable.

Chapter Thirty-Six: The Company

Police Headquarters, Lahaina, Maui

Rachel Takeda Remembers

OK, Nick, this is for your case files. Feel free to use it on your blog. I hope it fills in the gaps.

I went back aboard the patrol car with the abductor. What a dick, man. Dude by the name of Joseph Haaloa Chung... criminal record as long as his arm. Up on a murder charge last year but got off on a technicality. Youth in the juvenile hall. He was a guest of the Washington State Correctional System. Been in Hawai'i for a little less than a year. About three months ago, we marked him for working for the mob, the Company. His connection is a family thing. His father worked for crime boss Wilford "Nappy" Pulawa.

Yeah, yeah, I can hear Kayne saying that law enforcement put The Company out of business thirty years ago. Not so, guys. Hawai'i's version of the syndicate has deep family traditions. The mob started in the Sixties-- the Chinese Triads. Then came the Japanese Yakuza, Korean Kkangpae, and Samoan criminal families. Nappy Pulawa seized control and pulled it all together to form a Pacific-wide crime syndicate.

State prosecutors in the '80s and '90s waged a winning war, sometimes putting whole families behind bars. The Mob went underground, but, more and more, we suspect the next generation is getting its evil act together.

So, our man, "Crazy Joey" Chung, is cooling his heels here until we get him over to Honolulu. The State Attorney General is doing somersaults.

On another note, while you three are on the Big Island, I am getting some of my folks together and going back to that retreat center. Director Ocampo is in for the surprise of her life.

Chapter Thirty-Seven: Puakō

Kawaihae Harbor, The Big Island, Hawai'i
Nick Sechi's Journal

I was OK on the short flight to the Big Island. I spent the time learning about *moe aikāne*[16] relationships from the internet.

"Hey Boss, did you know that in Polynesian culture, gay relationships, both male and female, were widely practiced and accepted by precolonial Hawai'ian society."

"Correct me if I'm wrong, my love, but the elite class favored their same-sex lovers with no stigma attached, another example of a heterosexual community also accepting homosexual and bisexual relationships. Among men, same-sex relationships usually begin when the partners are teens and continue throughout their lives, even though they also maintain heterosexual partners.

Mako chimed in from the pilot's seat.

"Kamehameha had male lovers. Tales are told that all chiefs had them. Gods and goddesses also had *aikāne*. The *ali'i*[17] women, also. None of it was hidden. Same-sex coupling was considered natural."

I added, "I found a story about Captain Cook that is very interesting. It seems he had this hot guy as a member of his Royal Navy crew. So, it seems that one of the frisky chiefs took a fancy to the young sailor. Cook was asked to leave the stud muffin behind."

Mako nodded.

"It was considered in those days to be a great honor."

Kayne redirected our conversation as Mako brought the plane over the port and skied the aircraft across the water.

---

[16] LGBTQ+ people
[17] royal

"It is essential that we meet with the family of Daniel Aloho. I believe, my friend, that you indicated that they are located in Puakō, here on the Big Island."

"Yes, Kayne. Puakō is down the coast to our south. Waikoloa Estates and the Headquarters of the Church of the Shadow of the Lord is east of there into the higher elevations."

The police officer deftly guided the seaplane into a berth in Kawaihae Harbor. He turned to me and said, "Let's go, scholar boy. You totally missed flying over Mauna Kea, the highest mountain on the globe."

I rubbed my eyes and looked to the eastern horizon to see Hawai'i's only snow-capped mountain.

I swaggered, "Naw, Bro. We were in the Himalayas for our last case. Now there's some big-assed mountains. These cinder cones are...."

Kayne was smiling as if he knew something was coming.

"Oh, nooo. No, no, no, little hotshot...."

Mako made a game-show-wrong-answer-buzzer sound.

"But thank you for playing, Kaikaina."[18]

He shut off the engine, and the plane glided into the slip. Native dock guys in cargo shorts began to secure the craft with tossed ropes.

Mako grinned as we climbed out onto the deck.

"So, mine is definitely bigger– much bigger than yours, little man."

The dock guys overheard and smirked. Dudes, gay or straight, are constantly sizing each other up.

Officer Hunky did a crotch grab but pointed to the mountain.

"You see, most of the volcano is underwater, and when measured from its marine base, Mauna Kea is 33,500 ft, the tallest mountain in the world. Talkin' massive realness here in Hawai'i. The word I'm using is 'massive,' son."

---

[18] Little Brother

"Whoa, brag much, studly?"

We threw air punches.

Kayne… huge eye-roll and smirk-- an indication that I was acting the fool all too typically. I will say the rescue of Dani on Maui boosted me up respect-wise with the big cop. He started referring to me in affectionate terms, albeit teasing, like "Little Brother and Little Cop Boy." The modifier "little" is getting in there way too much for my liking.

"Great place to dive, there."

He pointed across the harbor.

"Kawaihae Reef. In some ecological danger right now, but the state is working to restore it. Again, big-- biggest in Hawai'i."

"I got a Great Barrier, I'll show ya sometime, Muscle Head."

More jabs, dodges, and grabs as we walked the quay to the waiting police transport.

The Royal Hawai'ian jeered, "Big, Jack. The Big Island, big, big, big."

"If I could interrupt your rather sophomoric slap and tickle party, gentlemen, we have work to do. Puakō, remember?"

"Sir, yes, Sir. Aye aye, Sir."

***

The truck with the green, broken triangle logo was parked near the side of the house. The passenger's side window had a black plastic trash bag duct-taped to cover the space where the glass had been removed. Kayne opened the unlocked door and extensively examined the vehicle's cab. Using nitrile gloves, he picked through the debris on the seats and floor mats, stashing some samples in small plastic bags.

"No telling how many have been in this conveyance-- a stampede of bungling evidence destroyers. The graphite powder still remains from the police crime scene investigators. However, it has become smeared on the steering wheel, as would be expected.

Mako watched and said, "I reviewed the police report. Not much in it to go on. They are tracking down the prints. Two sets. Figuring not a passenger but a robber after he parked."

"Take a look at this, Officer. Someone ate what would appear to be a cut lunch on the passenger side. The individual does not like bread crusts. Teeth marks– see here, would indicate the size of the person's mouth is that of a child or young person."

"Cut lunch?"

I translated, "Sandwich."

Kayne went on, "The plastic on the dashboard is cracked and has snagged a bit of material. Most likely torn off in a hasty move to grab something-- the food, no doubt. Missed because it dropped beneath the fissure in the break. Observe, please."

As Mako took the plastic-enclosed scrap and passed it to me. A woman in a colorful apron interrupted us.

"She's at work. Shame about her brother. Poor Mia'ila."

"Where can we find her?"

"Big cop guy... thought you guys would know all about this. Puakō Petroglyph Park, just down the coast."

Kayne thanked the neighbor woman and turned his attention back to the evidence. He asked, "Nick, what color were the uniform shirts of the students at the Church's Retreat Center?"

"Ahh... gray, Boss."

Kayne tapped the torn cloth.

"Cadet gray, to be precise."

Chapter Thirty-Eight: Kii Pohaku

Holoholokai Beach, The Big Island, Hawai'i
Nick Sechi's Journal

We joined the hiking tour.

The 30s-something woman was in the blue and green uniform of the staff of the Puakō Petroglyph Archaeological Preserve. She led a group of a dozen or so tourists through a relatively unmarked trail. The guide pointed out the carvings in the lava rock between the brush and the Hawai'ian Mesquite Trees.

"The park is 2,223 acres and has more than 3,000 ancient petroglyphs. We call these lava rock carvings *kii pohaku*. Many date back as far as 1200 AD. We do not know the true meanings of the designs. Still, we think that these carvings tell of the births, deaths, and other significant events in the lives of the people who lived on the island of Hawai'i long ago."

Mia'ila Aloho continued her tour, winding among the lava outcrops. Carvings in the stone showed stick-figured humans, canoes with sails, and turtles, among other forms.

"The concentric circles indicate family. The human or anthropomorphic figures are of different types. Here are pregnant women with swollen bellies squatting in a birthing style. See the difference in these human carvings. The triangular body-shape characters are the more vital community members-- aggressive and war-like.

"We don't know why people lived here. The land is quite inhospitable; it is not immediately next to the ocean, and the *kiawe* forest is very thorny and dense. The soil is unsuitable for agriculture, and rain on the Kohala Coast is scarce.

"Further, toward the sea, we find the glyphs depict the ocean creatures, fishers, and the sailboats, indicating that there was an ancient harbor – a port for arrivals and trade."

The sun began its descent into the Pacific to our west. I asked Mia'ila if there was any folklore connected to the site.

She nodded.

"The Night Marchers – apparitions have been seen in the forest and out to the tidal pools on the beach. They are spirit-like beings who carry torches and beat drums as they wander down from Mauna Kea to the seashore. The native people have great respect for these ghost walkers. It is forbidden to look at them directly. To do so invites evil.

The hike ended at the tidal pools near the shore. We all sat cross-legged on the rock, watching the ever-changing canvas of sunset on the Pacific.

Mia'ila stared at the three of us.

"I thought you were the police again. I wonder if you have something more for me on Damien's death."

The woman's expression was somber as she looked out over the calm waters and gently rolling waves to the black sand beach as if an answer to her brother's death lay somewhere in the breeze blowing from the sea to the land.

Kayne introduced the three of us and expressed our collective sympathy.

The woman said, "Suicide is so strange, you know. The ones who suffer are the family. You never stop asking, 'Why?' Why didn't I see it coming? Was this a clue? Did this or that have a significant meaning? When exactly did he get lost along the way?"

She shook her head, choked back tears, and continued. "So let me cut to the chase. No substance abuse, no depression, none of that. Damien was a science geek with a graduate degree in biology, specializing in genetics. He was quiet and focused, with no time for much social interaction. He worked. That's about it."

Kayne asked, "His work colleagues?"

"Damien had a history of excellent performance reviews. Lately, he confided that he was dissatisfied with what was going on at En VitroTec. He never complained, but the project he was working on disturbed him. He kept nothing on his home computer but video games and geek crap, graphic novels, and that sort of thing."

"Did he keep a journal?"

Yes, he always had a flash drive in his pocket. I saw it a few times when he pulled out some change at the ABC store. I asked him about it. He said they were supposed to keep all technology at work, but this was private stuff and homework. He managed to sneak it out and in."

"Was he religious?"

"There for a while, he was. Caught up in some fundamentalist stuff and got really zealous and shit, but that died down in these last years. He was a member of the Church of the Shadow of the Lord. They gave him this."

Damien Aloho's sister reached into the collar of her shirt and pulled out a gold chain and cross.

"He stopped wearing this about a year ago, right around the time he stopped going to church. They found it in his truck."

I asked, "Ms. Aloho…"

"Please call me Mia."

"Mia, do you know of anyone who would know why Damien would have ended his life?'

The woman thought for a bit, punctuating the silence between the four of us by tossing pebbles into the tidal pools.

"The night before Damien died, I saw them. I was working late and used to take long walks. That night, I wandered out to the beach. As I turned back to the visitors' center, I saw them coming down through the trees, walking like some primitive army – drums, spears, and blowing conch shells, an ancient Hawai'ian army by torchlight."

Her eyes grew dreamy, and there was a sing-song-like quality to her voice as she continued.

"The old ones… they were fearsome-looking with masks and trailing torn clothes. Their bodies seemed to be transparent, and I remembered they marched, but they never touched the ground. There was a whooshing around them, like mourning, wailing, death-like and eerie."

She stared into the coming darkness.

"I watched them. Did I bring evil into my brother's life? Is all of this my..."

I remember feeling a coldness come over me as she broke off. The other hikers followed the park signs back to the parking lot as night came on. The cries of forest creatures mixed with the gentle sighing of the surf. An owl hooted somewhere inland.

As we were about to leave her, Mia turned to Kayne and said, "I know someone, yes. She can tell us what we want to know."

Chapter Thirty-Nine: A White Dog

The Lava Fields of Kilauela, The Big Island, Hawai'i
The Case Files of Kayne J. Sorenson, Ph.D.

The blind woman was chanting.

Mai ka Lua a'u i hele mai nei, mai Kīlauea,

Ke kui 'ia maila e nā wāhine o ka Lua ē

'O Puna lehua 'ula i ka papa

I 'ula i ka papa ka lehua o Puna

From the crater, I've come from Kīlauea,

The women of the caldera have strung leis

The foundation of Puna is crimson, covered in lehua blossoms.

Sacred is the fountain covered with the lehua blossoms of Puna.

Mako whispered, "She is the High Chieftess 'Aila'au. The people believe she is an ancestor of the first Tahitian *ali'i* on the island. Mama 'Aila calls the goddess. She is a keeper of the spirit of Pele."

The ancient Hawai'ian was dressed in a red and white *mu'umu'u*. Her long grey and white hair was crowned with a circle of *ti* leaves, symbolizing her high rank and divine power. Also signifying Aila'au's *ali'i* status was her lei of sleek black kukui nuts. She was small, wrinkled, and easily over eighty but moved with ease and some grace on the arm of her niece. Her eyes were covered with opaque, milky cataracts. No walking stick guided the blind one. It would be a desecration to pierce the lava body of Pele.

We parked the Jeep to the east and walked the hardened lava flow to the caverns to the south. The horizon was lit by a fiery ribbon of the living lava stream slowly coursing down from Kilauea to the sea as we hiked. Steam, fire, and boiling water spewed where the two forces of nature collided. The youngest island of the Hawai'ian archipelago was still being born.

Mako pointed to the broiling sea and explained, "Pele, the goddess of fire, and her sister, Na-maka-o-Kaha'l, the Hawai'ian sea goddess, are eternal enemies. You see the titanic conflict as the lava, the blood of Pele, is consumed by the boiling sea waters, the body of her sister."

To the south, beyond the spectacle of earth and ocean, thunderclouds spewed tridents and forks of lightning, adding to the night sky pyrotechnics and rumblings of this desolate stretch of the Big Island. It was easy to imagine supernatural forces gathering around us that would defy explanation and foretell a terror yet to come.

Nick backed off the prospect of descending into hell, eying the dark maw of the cave opening. He held back, preferring to remain outside and allow the séance to go on without him.

"Tight spaces are... yeah, yeah... no fuckin' way, Boss. I'll wait right here. Don't let anything happen to him, Big Brother."

He took off his hoodie and flopped down on it, using the jacket to cover the hard ground. Mako, the young woman Mia'ila Aloho, Mama Aila'au, the ancient Keeper, and I entered the extinct lava tube.

I remember the ground was warm, and the cavern we approached was dark and glowed a soft red in its deepest recesses. There was something powerful and death-dealing back there in the red darkness. It seemed to throb, just out of sight.

Damien's sister, Mia'ila, scattered frangipani flowers as we entered the cave. As we drew closer, the rear of the underground expanse glowed with an eerie red light. Circular and bloody, with peremptory flashes and animalistic roars, it seemed as if the passage leading deeper into the earth was indeed the very gates of the Inferno.

"Give me the *ki'i* and sit down on the Earth-Eating Woman."

We settled on the black, hardened, scarred body of the fire goddess. Mai'ila handed the Keeper her brother's bracelet of a dolphin. The cavern was immediately filled with another song of the sightless oracle.

Lapakū ka wahine aʻo Pele i Hawaiʻi

ʻOaka e ka lani noke nō

ʻEliʻeli kau mai

ʻOaka e ka lani noke nō

ʻEliʻeli kau mai

ʻUhī a ʻuhā mai ana ʻo Pele

I ka lua aʻo Halemaʻumaʻu

Pele is active in Hawaiʻi.

Continuously flashing in the heavens.

May profound reverence alight

Continuously flashing in the heavens.

May profound reverence alight indeed.

Rumbling, puffing, Pele comes

To the crater at Halemaʻumaʻu.

There was wind. Soft at first, but then stirring the hair and garments of the four occupants in the sacred circle with the deep opening into the earth at our backs. Faint rumbling-- not from the gathering storm outside but deep within our passageway-- made its way up and around us.

Mama Ailaʻau seemed to disappear. Eyes closed, her visage became blurred and ghost-like. Her voice was almost a cackle as she spoke.

"The goddess comes to us. Be brave."

She began to rock on her haunches and to keen in the ancient language. Miaʻila translated in a solemn voice.

"We pay homage to the builder of these islands. We venerate your body and those you allow to dwell here. We ask permission to address the goddess. I am your *akua noho*. Enter into me and bestow your sacred power, your *mana*."

Aila'au's hair and garments seemed to be lifted around her as if she were sitting on a grate of hot rising air. She threw back her head and convulsed in a full-body clench and a silent scream. The ancient woman seemed to be made of flame and smoke. When she brought her head back, she opened her eyes. In the place of a white film, her pupils had become fiery red. Her voice was deep and soft, seductive, and foreboding. It had the tenor of a much younger woman. Again, Mia'ila translated.

"I hear the sound of the great god, Kane-hekili, breaking through heaven, bringing the thunder and announcing my presence. He fights with the owl, Kukauakahi, who has not finished his hunt this night."

The Keeper, now completely possessed, it seemed, pressed her hands together with the bracelet, the *ki'l*, between them. She hummed deep tones as she searched the faces of each of us.

She spoke in English.

"I have him. He is mine. Why do you want him? The man came to me, desiring to be one with Pele. Much sorrow has been burned away from his heart, no more crimes. He is free. Why do you search?"

Mia'ila spoke.

"Great goddess, we are burdened by the death of my brother. Grief overcomes the *menehune ohana*, the family. Why has he left his family as one so young? What secrets did he bring to your fiery bosom? Pele of the sacred land, how can we atone for his sins?"

The eerie medium began to quake, and the glowing mouth of the cave beyond began to throb. A trail of steam seemed to coil up from the depths to ensnare us, the three seated supplicants.

"Gentle sister, your dutiful respect is noteworthy. You must look into the earth. Evil shadows – shadows of death reach deep into the heart of Pele. There, you will find the reason for his madness. Be careful. This evil threatens the children of Earth. Many will die."

The air in the tunnel turned hotter. The wind grew and seemed to groan. Outside, the thunder rolled. The rock floor of the cavern seemed to shudder. A hiss combined with a muffled tumult came forward from the recesses of the hot lava tube.

The goddess spoke one last time.

"The consuming fire of vengeance burdens your heart. Your family is, however, under my protection. Daughter, I will punish your enemies. Behold, you have among you my *aumakua*, a guardian spirit. He will bring my *mana* to you. Look for *Pueo*, the owl, the one who belongs to earth and heaven. The justice you seek will be his to bestow in my name. Do not waver in your belief, or his protection and divine guidance will become your destruction."

There was a loud whoosh as the goddess departed from the *Ali'i*, and the old woman slumped forward, caught by the Mako's strong arm. Seconds ago, the cavern in which we sat threatened to be a live conduit for the vomiting forth of the largest volcano in Hawai'i. Now, it was again a dark and hollow recess deep in the earth— no steam, heat, or eruption. We climbed the passageway to the outside, and Mako took the arm of the very fatigued Mama Aila'au.

***

Nick was sleeping. He twitched and exhibited the REMs of a deep-dreaming state.

I gently roused him, and he came to a somewhat confused consciousness.

"Hey, Boss. Sorry. I guess I crashed. Did you see her?"

"I am unable to say, my love. It would appear that Mama Aila'au, in the lava tube, manifested the goddess Pele."

Nick said, "No, not in there. I was talking about the young woman with the white dog... she was calling me. I tried to follow her, but I could not move. She disappeared."

The Keeper reached out, and Nick took her arms gently. She touched his face.

"You saw her, my son. Pele was here, calling to you. You have described two of her manifestations: the young woman and the dog. The goddess comes to those she favors in dreams."

Nick looked from the old woman to me and back again. He whispered, "This is either pretty nutso or spooking the shit out of me, Bossman."

I carefully guided Mia's ancient grandmother back into the care of our Hawai'ian friends. We began our journey back to the jeep, hiking across the hardened lava flow. The thunder and forked lightning seemed to lead us out of the volcanic field back to safer territory.

Nick and I fell back and shared a private conversation.

"What happened, Boss?"

"I am not sure, my love. I will confess that I am a Doubting Thomas when it comes to the mystic and the supernatural. From the point of Science, I believe the geothermic sights and sound we witnessed in our so-called séance were simply the manifestations of a standard volcanic vent."

"How about the trance and the divine directions given through Mama Aila'au?"

"I feel it is essential to cite the anthropologist I.M. Lewis, who noted that women are more likely to be involved in spirit possession cults than men are. This research also postulated that such factions compensate for their exclusion from other spheres within their cultures. I would say that this is not true among Native Hawai'ians. Women enjoy a much higher status there than in other societies.

"There is another school of research that shows because of deficiencies in thiamine, tryptophan-niacin, calcium, and vitamin D, along with a combination of poverty and food taboos, bring about involuntary symptoms stemming from these conditions. They affect women's nervous systems and often appear as spirit possession.

"Clinical psychiatry defines trance and possession disorders as states involving a temporary loss of the sense of personal identity and full awareness of the surroundings. It is considered a dissociative disorder like psychosis, hysteria, mania, Tourette's syndrome, epilepsy, or even schizophrenia."

We reached the parking lot and walked into the light of the street lamps spaced between the rows of cars and trucks.

I lowered my voice to convey my conclusion.

"I would also say that your dreams were a subconscious coincidence. So, in summation, Nick, I do not believe any of us were visited by the volcanic goddess Pele.

Nick stopped me and reached up. The others halted and turned around to face us. Mai'ila gasped with her hand over her mouth. Mako let out with a profanity.

"Bossman, what are you doing with your hair?"

My husband reached into the locks on the back of my head and removed three dark-brown feathers.

I held them to the dim light.

"Most curious, my love. *Asio flammeus sandwichensis*, the short-eared Hawai'ian owl."

Chapter Forty: World-Wide Outreach

The Headquarters of the Church of the Shadow of the Lord, Waikoloa Estates, The Big Island, Hawai'i

"It's the White House, Sir. I have the president on the line."

The man in the white suit reached for the handset.

"Seth, how are you doin', cousin? Still, keeping those Democrats at bay?

"Good. Good. Yes, thank you. My little church community and our supporters are all healthy and praising God. We are indeed blessed.

"And your family, Sir? I see Junior made the press again. So much personal criticism. How does your family manage to steer the course? Well, I guess that helps... yes. It's good that your administration has at least one news network taking your side when the mudslinging starts. Now, what can I do for you, Mr. President?"

The Reverend Nathan Lahaye listened to the request from the Commander-in-Chief and made some notes on his computer.

"I am happy to help out, Seth, but you are aware that politics are not really my strong suit and...

"I see... yes. Getting significant pastors on board would be very important for your re-election, I agree... enhance your position with believers... yes, unofficial, I see. Use my influence with the other evangelical pastors... yes, that makes sense. My church does have a good deal of clout when it comes to forming the consciences of patriotic Americans, and there are some favors I can definitely...

"Yes, the rally in Dallas comes on the heels of our Texas Crusade for Christ. I am the keynote speaker, and the whole family will be there. My biggest concern is that right now, we're gearing up for the Virtual Worldwide Outreach."

Lahaye stopped talking and listened. His responses to the President's lengthy description of the critical need for the minister's support in this campaign strategy were single words, agreeing with his cousin.

Finally, he said, "I need to get with my people on this and craft some messages. I am always open to talking points from the White House, I mean, your re-election campaign headquarters. I will get with them.

"Correct. Just what I was thinking, a few dog whistles… ahhh, let me correct myself here… a few key phrases and ideas, and we can steer the faith communities in the right direction. I will touch base in two days, Mr. President. I understand… Arvella sends her best."

He pressed another button on the phone.

"Elizabeth, schedule a team meeting for eleven. Yes, the Executive Council of the Church Elders, and let Reverend Matthison know I will need to see him privately at noon. Find out what he wants to eat. Tell the pastor it's a working lunch. Cancel everything else."

***

The older man stirred his scotch neat and pointed to the Pastor of the Church of the Shadow of the Lord. He was in his late '60s and dressed in business casual.

"You asked me to come out of retirement, son, and be a what… a special advisor and your spiritual director. I founded this Church with your father, which gives me some say-so. I know you want to know what's going on with the Heart of Darkness Project so I can bring you up to date."

"I appreciate your coming in, Simeon. I met with the council this morning to strategize our response to the President's request."

"Fools. When we ran this ministry, Malachi and I never listened to anyone but the good Lord. So, tell me what they came up with."

The CEO took a deep breath and said, "The Church, as the point of religious organization for the re-election of Seth Layahe, has been given the opportunity to rise in stature among the evangelical right in this country. It will raise our ministry to the top of the conservative religious movement. This meeting, coinciding with particulars for the Worldwide Outreach… Well, let me just say that the momentum for spreading our message is amazing, Simeon. This magnifies our mission plans a hundredfold."

"Got it. Your Council recommends the church go all-in on this. Coordinating your message with the White House so that the re-election and the Crusade go hand in hand. That includes... what are you calling it? The virtual assemblies. You know, I think that strategy needs to be killed. Stupid idea. People need to get off their butts and come to church."

"Simeon, the style of evangelism you and my father led with a heavy emphasis on biblical, expository preaching is no longer useful or valid. People are spiritually apathetic. The folks want a 'feel good' message, more secular, which flies in the face of the direct, intentional work of a crusade evangelist."

The old pastor frowned and said, "I surrendered my life to Christ totally and entirely when I was seven years old. I was onstage with a Bible in my hand when I could barely walk. I have spent a lifetime doing God's work. Bringing lost souls into the embrace of the Shadow of the Lord, inviting the lost, and then nurturing new believers as they follow Christ. This is a plan that worked in my great-grandfather's day."

The younger pastor objected. "It is no longer possible to think we can win the world by getting people to come into the church. Many just won't. The action is outside the church walls, removing the idols that supplant the presence of the Lord in people's lives. This crusade will call to action the very thing the church needs in this century– the incineration of false religion. I truly believe the impact of this Worldwide Outreach will have lasting results and will be felt for years to come. The world will explode with the holy fire of evangelism."

Simeon Matthison held up one hand and pointed to his young colleague.

"You and your council just better make sure that this message has a direct appeal for consecrating the assets of believers. Land, cash, securities-- it all has to come to us to do the Lord's work, including getting that sinner, your cousin, re-elected president."

"It's all coming together, Simeon. But a full-frontal assault on secularism and the tolerance for idolatry and sin must carry the day. We have media specialists and data marketers working night and day on this."

"Showboating, Son. But it's your Church now. I will not be the lone voice of dissent any longer. Have at it. Church work is 90% show business anyway."

He took a draught of his liquor and looked out the window at the plantation-like setting of the headquarters of The Shadow of the Lord Ministries Incorporated.

"Heart of Darkness. What's the latest?"

"Your scientists at the Center are close to a breakthrough with the serum. You can tell your armament contacts that what our teams are developing will have the potency of a nuclear weapon, as was predicted. I am told it has a slow buildup, but the results will be vast and devastating."

"And the vaccine?"

"Something about having to develop the strain first. But the lab will control the formula once developed."

"No leaks whatsoever, or this project will be a disaster if it falls into the wrong hands."

Matthison rubbed his hands together and looked intently at the pastor of the global church.

"Nathan, you asked me to serve as your personal overseer on this when you took us down this path. I told you then that I know nothing about any of this. Furthermore, as much as I would like to witness the destruction of non-believers in Christ's name, this project is incredibly dangerous."

The vehemence of Lahaye's response was disturbing.

"The Lord has told us that we are to take up weapons in his name and bring all nations under his Shadow. He will protect his Saints so that we may not dash our foot against a stone in this holy war."

"Listen to me. The virulence of the serum is not the issue here, although considerable caution needs to be maintained. I am speaking of the human factor."

"What do you mean?"

"It seems we have lost something, something important."

The Shadow of Evil

Chapter Forty-One: Thirty Pieces of Silver

EnVitro Tec, Inc., Waikoloa Reserve, The Big Island, Hawai'i

"Find me that girl. I don't care what it takes or how you do it. Find her and bring her here."

"Going to be hard to get that done, Reverend. The police are searching. You know her grandfather is Charles Vance, the industrialist. Big money behind getting that kid back."

"Now, you listen to me. That little dyke, Chöle Alden, has stolen some vital information from EnVitro Tec. She was in Aholo's truck, and I have information from his colleagues that that guy kept copious notes on the project, a diary, or a journal. That kid has it. I am sure of it, and the entire project, Heart of Darkness, is compromised. Do I make myself clear?"

"Yeah, Reverend. Got it."

The man with the scar on his face paused before going further.

"What?"

"We moved on that dancer guy, the one who picked up the girl on Maui. Sorta got our asses kicked. The fag has protection. We lost Jimmy in the fight, and Joey is in the slammer.'

The old pastor grumbled, "One major screw-up after another, Sid. This is not acceptable. Give me the details."

"A couple of private investigators from the mainland. And they are working with that big cop from HPD, also a fag. Damn degenerates are every-fuckin-where."

"Must be pretty tough if they took you guys out. What exactly happened to Jimmy?"

"Lost at sea. They found his body down the coast. Not much chance they will trace him back to the operation. We got that covered, Reverend Matthison."

***

"I don't want to tell you who I am. I got your number when you were around asking questions. Yeah, I saw the girl. She came looking for food. Recognized the logo on the shirt. Stupid kid.

"Anyway, she hangs out right near here, panhandling the tourists, but that information will cost ya. Dumb ass, nothing is ever free.

"I'll text you the location. No rough stuff. Figured you want her really bad and won't fuck this up. Horny fuckers. A really pretty young girl.

"Bring the cash. Three large."

Chapter Forty-Two: WhatsApp Kris

San Francisco/The Big Island, Hawai'i
Nick Sechi's Journal (with Kris Sorenson)

"I sent you the video. You get it?

"Yes. Kris, you OK?"

"Fine, Uncle Nick. Pretty much all over. I had the phone on my bookshelf recording when the police took him away. I'm thinking of a 'fans only' site."

Holy Mother, like no other. Spare us.

Kayne rolled over, looked at his Fitbit, and mumbled, "Crikey, my love, three AM."

Rubbing sleep from his ice-blues, he eased into my laptop's camera range and said, "Start at the beginning, lad. Leave nothing out."

Kris started to speak, but Kayne interrupted.

"Wait, wait, son. I am truly glad you are not hurt. Now, please proceed."

I nodded at his "fatherly" expression and patted his thigh.

"Thanks, Uncle Kayne. So I was learning to surf, and I met this guy, and we, ahhh... taught each other some important stuff and...."

He was grinning like a jackass eating new-mown hay.

I interjected, "Yeah, yeah, so you were sexin' up this guy. Get to the salient points, kiddo. Why the arrest? I am sure the police will be back to finish taking your statement."

"Yeah, so here's the thing. Lemme write this little escapade out for you, and you can put it in your blog. Give it one of those sick titles like you're so good at, and I'll call you back. Some other stuff I gotta do. Cool?"

"Wait, Kris...."

A knock and Trasker walked into Kris' room.

"Mr. Sorenson, the police are downstairs wanting to speak to you. I suggest you put on a shirt."

Kris waved goodbye, handed Trasker his mobile, pulled on a hoodie, and left his room.

"Trasker, is everything OK there?"

"Fine, Mr. Sechi. Just business as usual."

***

American Stud Boy

By The Kris

"You taste of salt, sweat, and sun. Turn that way a bit more."

My mouth knew the contours of the male torso like a pro. My strong hands caressed, invaded, and stroked the naked Hawai'ian sharing the bed. At 18, I was a cocky soccer jock with a body both men and women drooled over and a non-stop libido in overdrive.

"Your boyfriend, what's his name...."

I growled, "Ohhh, damn, Danny boy... you are so fuckin'... huh? Oh, yeah, that... all good, bro. Matt and I are not exclusive. Lift your arm... yeah, so good...."

The beach boy shuddered as I made love with precision and extreme concentration, far surpassing any dude my age. Daniel Kumkahi, at 22, actually preferred older men. He told me that after he asked me to show him pictures of my hunky uncles. (Don't go getting a big head on this one, Uncle Nick.)

Dude called me his "*Haolie* Boy" when we met at Mavericks Beach on Half Moon Bay, just south of San Francisco. Danny offered to teach me to surf– better, anyway. Our hook-up was epic– no brag, just fact. That first day, peeling off my wet suit, I could see the "island fever" in his eyes. He's pretty hot himself. I learned to surf, and he learned to please The Kris, ya know?

So, tonight, here I am, wet-mouthed, descending his naked back. He reached over and applied pressure to the back of my head.

And he goes, "Damn, that is so good, dude. Umm… yeah."

So, The Kris, the sexing champion that he is, continued with this totally sick make-out, purposely bringing my bud to the brink of intense passion and then softening the play to create the sexual excitement and anticipation that would intensify the closing acts of the hot game. My instincts for my partner's body and how to increase his stimulation and erotic response were becoming famous. Danny Boy was a mass of erotic yearning. My boy was desperately wanting more, relentless and never-ending.

As I pushed him face down, he said, "Jesus. Who the fuck are you, *Kāne*? … ahhh, shit… how'd you learn such depraved artistry?"

He yelled, "Do it, *haole*. Fuckin' go for it."

But The Kris stopped and sat back on his heels between Daniel's legs. This drove the dude crazy.

I changed up the play. I slid down over the beach beauty, spread his arms to lock down Daniel's wrists, and hoarsely whispered in his ear.

"Yes?"

My Danny was surprised by the primal sound of my voice as he responded, "Yeah, brah. I want it all, *tau'ā'ī*."

I stuffed my jock in the dude's mouth and said, "Grab hold of something, nasty boy. This is gonna hurt, and I am not going to stop."

***

"No fuckin' way, man. Get your naked, white *aio* back over here. Whaddya sex up and split? I want some sweet pillow talk, or tomorrow, I throw you off the board and feed you to the sharks."

He hooked an arm around the waist of the attempting-to-depart Kris and yanked me back onto the bed. Our bodies still glistened with sweat as we combined into a body lock/hug-up on the wet sheets, both of us again in the refreshing flush of sexual release.

My hand touched something just under his side of the bed, his gym bag. I went for his sweaty gear, but something was wrong-- heavy at one end.

So here's where I was smooth as fuck, guys. I just laughed and tied him to the bed like we were going for another, even more rougher round.

Backing up, I opened the satchel– bingo, a Glock (I think it was, anyway).

I didn't touch it like you taught me, Nick.

I asked him, "Why would you bring a handgun into my house?"

I was pissed off, and he struggled to explain.

"Talk to the hand, bro."

I reached for my phone and called 911.

***

"You sleep?"

"Definitely not, my love. What do you have?"

"My contact at SFPD, Boss. Ready for this?"

"Go."

"Daniel Kumkahi. Aka 'Lil D' Definitely The Company, Kayne... a young assassin usually contracted for surgical strikes. But why Kris? I thought we were dealing with Church big bads."

I could tell that Kayne was trying to control the fear and anger in his mind.

"Our 18-year-old is literally getting in bed with the mob, my love. We are finding that this case has many dangerous implications as the veil is pulled back, and we see what the Shadow of the Lord is doing."

He continued, "While I was outside, I contacted some of our unofficial security resources. The homefront and its members will have doubled-up security. I will notify Trasker, Andi, and Kris. This will need to be SOP as we take on more cases away from home. Our family is exceedingly at risk."

"I have a few favors I can pull in with SFPD, Boss. Kris will not like it, but too bad. Kayne, we should also alert our families in New York, Colorado, and Inala and make sure they are watchful."

He responded, "I haven't called Mitch yet, but I will. I spoke to Darana in Australia, and she has assured me that she will put specific safety measures in place. Ace is Ace, and he sends his love."

"Great, I will call Viola and... hey, wait. Kris' report just dropped."

We paused to read it-- 600 or so words, filling in the story.

"Boss, I am baffled. Our nephew, you know, the one who, about two months ago, was ready to take the tonsure and apply to be accepted for Holy Orders... This kiddo cavorts like a porn star and writes about it like he is the newest headliner at Club Bijou. To use one of your favorite phrases, 'I am appalled.'"

"My observations are these, my love: The salaciousness of his account is no more titillating than your own reports of our ahhh... exploits. It seems that we are a family that enjoys intense libidinous interests. Next, he is cocky as a bantam— typical Sorenson. It's in our convict genes. Finally, he is quite intelligent and resourceful. For one so young, he can take care of himself in even the most dangerous situations. That is somewhat reassuring.

"If we consider this carefully, there is the merest glimpse at his psyche, Nick."

"What do you mean, Boss?"

"We have reprimanded our nephew several times for his heartbreaking sexual acrobats, emphasizing the dangers, emotional and otherwise."

"Yeah, and he shows no signs of slowing down. Proud of his prowess in the sack."

"Exactly, his account, embellished or not..."

"And terribly written. Our boy changes voice a few times in his writing."

My laptop's ringtones sounded.

WhatsApp – Kris was checking in.

***

"You get my blog entry? Cool, huh?"

"What did the police say, Kris?"

"Well, for one thing, they recognized me from the recent altercation in the Castro, but one guy said he knew us-- the Sorenson-Sechis. Then he said it was OK, what I told them."

"Cops told me ole Danny Boy was a hired killer. The Kris is bedding the Big Bads, Uncle Nick. What a studly, hell yeah. You dudes in some trouble out there?"

"Nothing we can't handle. Working with some local law enforcers, getting closer to finding the girl. Just be careful, son."

"OK, Uncle Kayne. Like you say a lot, 'No worries.'"

It looked like Kris had stepped off public transport and was on his way to class at the University of San Francisco.

He stopped and took something from his backpack.

"Check it out. I accidentally, on purpose, forgot to give this to the police. It was in Danny's bag. I thought it might be important for you to see it first."

Kris held up a gold and solid glass object containing something dark inside.

Immediately, Kayne got excited.

"Kris, hold it closer. Nick, screenshot, please. Lad, please turn the object. There. Hold it. Again, Nick."

"Got it, Boss."

"What is it, Uncle Kayne?"

He seemed to ignore the question for the moment.

"Kristof, please listen carefully and do exactly what I tell you. You are to take this to the archivist at the Gleeson Library at USF. Give it only to

Father Miguel Cardenas, SJ, the Archivist. Explain that he is to keep it secure at my request until I notify him personally. He will do as you ask.

"Under no circumstances are you to allow anyone else to have this object, including the police. It will not be safe with them. Do you understand?"

"Got it, Unc."

"What is it, Boss?"

Kayne exhaled and said, "It is undoubtedly a reliquary of the French Saint, Peter de Montfort, containing three square millimeters of his skull bone, encased in rock crystal and gold filigree."

"Why is this of concern?"

"St. Peter died in 1351...

"... of the Black Death."

The Shadow of Evil

Chapter Forty-Three: The MacGuffin

Aston Kona by the Sea, Kailua-Kona, The Big Island, Hawai'i
Nick Sechi's Journal

"I gave Father Grey the contact information for the archivist at the USF library, my love. The recovery of the relic is up to him as it is property belonging to the Notre Dame Museum. I suggested it be destroyed by incineration. Its theft is indicative of an attempt to weaponize the spores of *Yersinia pestis. This bacterium* causes Bubonic Plague, which the remains of St. Peter most assuredly contain."

Kayne gestured to my laptop.

"Please bring up the photos of the holy object, Nick."

I clicked.

"There. Observe. Tell me what you see."

"The dingus... glass or quartz and the metalwork surround-- makes it dazzle."

"Anything else?"

"It looks like the metal has suffered some decay or something. The gold is tarnished, there on the little cross and there."

"Gold is one of the least reactive chemical elements. It does not interact easily with oxygen and moisture. Gold by itself stays shiny. Because the reliquaries of the saints were considered to bring about the intercession of the holy dead, they were made with the purest gold. That is, provided the church of the deceased was wealthy. Poorer communities used other metals in their metalwork. The tarnished pieces you observe are...."

"Copper. Boss, in the pics-- Kris' fingers are green."

"Capital, my love. The exact shade of the right hand of...."

"Generoso Cataldi. The murdered Brother at Notre Dame."

I thought for a moment and continued.

"The umbrella thingo and the bell were just a distraction. Brother Generoso most likely handed off this deadly item the night he was killed. It's the MacGuffin.

"To one Daniel Kumkahi."

He paused, "Nick, what exactly is a MacGuffin?

"Kidding, right?"

My husband slowly shook his head.

"Hitchcock? Just about all his films... I think, in fact, he invented the term. So, a MacGuffin is an object, device, or event that is necessary to the plot and the motivation of the characters but insignificant, unimportant, or irrelevant in itself. How do you not know this, genius man?"

Kayne shrugged.

"In 'Psycho,' it was the $40,000 Marion Crane steals from the realtor's office at the beginning of the thriller. In this case, the relic is the unknown plot objective. We are challenged to discover what it all means."

It was hard to tell if my cinematic trivia made an impression. Kayne continued.

"We have all the pieces-- the Church of the Shadow of the Lord, the genetic research company EnVitro Tec, the 16th-century biological bomb, the dead religious with the green hand stain, an international crime organization, and the girl with the secret.

"Time to visit the Big Bads."

Chapter Forty-Four: A Man of Wax

The Headquarters of the Church of the Shadow of the Lord, Waikoloa Estates,
The Big Island, Hawai'i
Nick Sechi's Journal

"God bless you, my friends. It is such a joy to meet each of you, gentlemen."

One word on this guy – "fake charisma out the ass."

Kayne would say, "That's more than one word, my love."

Anyway, the Reverend Nathan Lahaye was just so damn appealing. At 51 years old and standing 6 feet, he rocked a dark blue suit, a crisp white shirt, and a lavender paisley tie. The only thing more dazzling than his button-down Oxford was his gleaming smile.

His movie-star good looks were crowned by an impeccably styled mane of wavy, golden blond locks with a touch of grey at the temples. Light brown eyes under long dark lashes completed the look. Pastor Nathan, as he preferred to be called, seemed to be continually smiling. A wide-eyed expression with raised eyebrows and his killer grin produced a very practiced open countenance as he spoke.

As I looked at the CEO and world-famous evangelist, my mind went back to a play I saw in San Francisco earlier this year.

Lady Capulet: The valiant Paris seeks you for his love.

Nurse: A man, young lady! Lady, such a man as all the world– why, he's a man of wax.[19]

The Nurse could have told her charge that the guy was a hunk, but she did not. The old family retainer was telling Juliet that the dude looks good on paper. Still, in fact, he was a colossal phony-- not really what you're looking for, Julie Babe.

---

[19] Romeo and Juliet, Act 1, Scene iii

"I am afraid that you have come a long way for nothing, Dr. Sorenson. There is no knowledge of the whereabouts of Chlöe Alden among our church members. This includes the staff of the retreat center. Administrators and staff have been interviewed by the police more than once."

The minister directed that last comment to Detective Makoa Lopaka as if expecting him to confirm, but Mako's expression remained enigmatic.

"There was even an attempt to question our young people at the Daybreak Retreat Center. Unfortunately, without parental consent, there is little we can do."

I kept thinking Kayne was going to jump in with his famous accusatory tone and righteous bombast, a tactic he often used with those we considered perpetrators of evil. I had seen him unleash the wrath of the intellectual, moral, and legal conclusions that caused many of our Big Bads to sputter and dodge at the irrefutable evidence of their crimes.

Alas, he did not, remaining stoic and seemingly under the spell of the magnetic leader and author of seventeen books on living in the light of divine grace, all of which were best sellers.

As I said, my husband had a strange look, as if he were dazzled. The preacher was a beauty, with the ginger coloring and jock's bearing that Kayne found so attractive, but, come on, no way our hero is getting sucked in by this fake.

"If you will indulge me, please allow me to tell you about our building."

Without waiting for permission, the leader of the fastest-growing Pentecostal church in the country uplifted an arm to heaven and brought it down in an arc encompassing the space in which we were standing.

"The headquarters of the Church of the Shadow of the Lord Ministries was completed in 2002. It was designed by a Hong Kong firm famous for receiving the Pritzker Architecture Prize three years in a row.

"It was conceived as six floors of free-formed, vaulted wings surmounted by the tower of Divine Light. Each level contains World Ministry Office spaces, a church school-- Pre-K to grade twelve, and a

232

series of moderate worship spaces. Our large services take place outside in God's glorious handiwork, these paradise islands."

I looked around. Kayne gazed at the scintillating Nathan Lahaye. Mako seemed to be totally out of it, staring at nothing in particular.

Here, we are standing in the Good News Atrium."

He pointed up.

"You can see that the structure of the building is a metal and concrete open frame covered by a skin of broken, twisted, scarred, and damaged brass plates, representing those who are farthest from the Lord. Packed close down here, they are raised as you go up the building, peeled away. First by a corner, then by half, then as if they are only attached by a mere sliver until you get to the tower whose highest reaches are entirely made of glass, coated with a golden finish. The effect is that the light of divine forgiveness descends to all who dwell in the darkness of sin."

I remarked, "So we are standing in hell, as it were."

"Artistically speaking, Mr. Sechi, yes. Let's go up to my office."

"In heaven?"

He didn't bite. Ignoring my remark, he led the way up.

***

The suite was filled with light. The view through all six floor-to-ceiling walls encompassed the west side of the Big Island, a modest ten stories above the ground.

"The church owns ninety-two acres stretching from the slopes of the volcano in the east and over to the ocean on the west. I love to come here and pray at dawn and at sunset. The presence of the Lord fills the space and radiates downward."

Kayne remarked, "And that love light pours out through you, no doubt. Tell me, Pastor, what are these structures we see, there to the south?"

"The most imposing structure is the sculpture titled 'The Hand of the Lord,' by the local artist Ker'i Otala Winston. To the east, you can see the outdoor worship amphitheater that seats eight hundred, with overflow on the lawns and drive-up services available along that side. The arena is actually carved into the sloping lava rock."

As we watched, a red sports car entered the long drive from the highway. It raced the twists and turns of the entrance road and streaked to a stop below us. A staff member ran from the entrance to hold open the door and assist the driver.

From where we stood, we could see the operator step out of the car and remove her black helmet. As she shook loose tumbling cascades of raven black hair, the woman unzipped her red racing suit and stepped out of it while leaning on the staffer's arm. She tossed her racing gear into the open car. Saying a few words to the security man, she pointed beyond the building, reached for her shoulder bag, and walked to the building below us. Before she entered, she stopped, looked up, shielded her eyes, and waved.

"Our home is back through the Acacia trees in that direction."

"Is that an air strip?"

"Yes, Dr. Sorenson. We have grown from a rural Bakersfield drive-in church to a worldwide ministry. Alas, it is the Lord's will that I travel to do his work in the many places where people are touched by the hand of the Lord."

"Is that the Church's building along the horizon, over those hills near the shore?"

"No, I believe that is some biological research company. Fortunately, our neighbors keep to themselves, but there is room for us all in the Lord's paradise of the Big Island, as large as his grace and love."

I remember the smile slipped just a bit, and the Reverend Lahaye looked away when he answered.

A dazzlingly beautiful woman stepped off the elevator from the lobby. She paused, stepped into an adjacent office, and then entered the Pastor's suite without her designer bag. Her smile was a bookend to the Reverend's, and, appearing to be in her thirties, she epitomized health, beauty, and style.

A former real estate developer, Arvella Copelan Lahaye, was from a long line of American evangelists. Often mistaken for a model, she was also a best-selling author and experienced preacher. "God's Power Couple" had graced the cover of *Time* last year and were touted by the broadcast and entertainment elite. Politicos got onto the Nathan and Arvella Train when businessman Seth Lahaye surprised the world by becoming president of the United States. They were often tagged with their famous cousin.

After brushing lips to cheeks, the Pastor introduced us. Ms. Lahaye sparkled but slipped over a mask of concern, saying, "That poor girl. Oh my, our prayers are with her and her family. How devastating to lose a child."

A mere nod and Kayne turned to watch the car in the driveway travel toward the family residence.

Arvella stepped forward, looked in that direction, and almost chuckled.

"I apologize for my rather showy entrance, but…."

"The Pininfarina Concept Car, named in memory of long-standing Ferrari chairman Sergio Pininfarina, is a modern interpretation of the 2-seater Barchetta-- it has no roof or windscreen. Usually, it comes with two matching helmets provided for the driver and passenger. The vehicle is built upon Ferrari's 458 Spider's mechanicals."

He turned to the Pastor.

"You purchased that car at the March 2018 Geneva Motor Show. Four were produced that year. One went to an Arab treasury minister, one to an African head of state, and the third to South Korean businessman Colin Lei Piaoyang. This last vehicle was involved in a fatal crash in Shanghai last December, attributed to extremely high speed and the car's targa or removable roof section-- unsafe at any speed. As one of Ferrari's handpicked customers, you bought the fourth."

Kayne now hit his accusatory tone.

"Yes, yes, you, Pastor Lahaye, for your wife's golden sports car, paid…."

He paused for effect.

"Three point five million in US dollars."

It was as if a bomb had gone off.

I said, "Holy fuck!"

The Lahayes began to speak rapidly over each other. They sputtered through the usual bullshit rationalizations about gifts to the ministry and the need to showcase the richness of the blessings of the Lord. Kayne leveled his stare at the couple and clasped one fist in the other hand before his mouth as if listening to a medical diagnosis.

"The plane."

"To what are you referring?"

"The Gulfstream G650. $72.5 million. When asked why you do not fly commercially, you once said, 'Why would I climb into a tube full of demons to fly from one place to another?'"

"These are old criticisms. I see no reason to...."

I jumped in with, "The idols of the heathen are silver and gold."

Why? Dunno. Just seemed the right thing to say, given the state the Lahayes were in. As they raised their voices, continuing to rant over each other, five somewhat distinguished men entered the Executive's Suite. I heard snatches of their speaking over each other.

"... thought the Board Meeting was ...."

"... heard shouting all the way to my office."

"Is there a problem, Pastor?"

"... calling security because of this...."

"Who are these three men?"

In an instant, Mako raised his voice and pointed out to the far end of the campus.

"There, the old buildings... right there."

One of the Church Board members attempted to shake off his confusion. He stepped to the glass wall and acknowledged, "Yes, it was the original church on this property and our youth camp, which has since moved to... but I don't see what this has to do with... Who exactly are you?"

Mako remained looking out at the ruins, dilapidated and falling down. His voice was filled with sorrow.

"I was in that place as a camp inmate in 2001. I remember watching the new building in which we are standing rise up from the ground. I thought of climbing up here one night when no one was watching and..."

The elder spoke softly, "Hold on, son. It could not have been that bad."

The big cop uttered a sickening laugh. I watched his shoulders heave as he continued, "It's funny. I still can't go to a basketball game. There in the gym, right there. They would blindfold us and make us stand together while they surrounded us. They yelled insults while bouncing basketballs close to us--'DIRTY LITTLE FAGGOT!... FAGGOT! ... FAGGOT!'"

His cry was loud and savage. As he yelled, one more elderly churchman, different from the rest, older and a bit less tailored, stepped into the room.

Mako's trance narrative continued. He breathed deeply, trying to go on.

"Weird, weird shit to do on a kid, ya know. Then there was the cuddling, group cuddling... something about a pair of oranges that were supposed to represent testicles."

He shook his head as if trying to come out of a dream.

"Ya had to talk about your sins with guys' bodies in detail and ask to be fixed. Fixed.

Mako threw his head back and wailed, 'Fix me, God. I want to be fixed!'

He came back with rage in his entire body.

"We fix dogs... why not queers?

"Those of us who resisted or failed to be repaired were given drugs. One of my buds developed seizures because of what they gave him."

Kayne said, "Metrazol, found to cause seizures in young people."

"Another boy who kept having to come back for more treatment – 'cause it didn't work, it never fuckin' worked. He had this electric thing attached to..."

He covered his face.

"I saw how they burned him, man. He was just a kid."

Most of the Board gasped or turned away. One old gentleman sat down.

"Sometimes, they made us take off our clothes...."

Arvella broke in, "Stop. You have to stop talking now. This is not true. What you are saying never happened, and you cannot expect...."

The tortured man leveled his gaze at the woman as he continued, "...for the lap-sitting exercise."

Detective Makoa Lopaka, the Royal Hawai'ian warrior of shining fame, now turned to face the Reverent Nathan Layahe. The man, who was once a very broken boy, spoke softly.

"You don't remember, do you, Pastor? The young pastor who kept asking for me, time and again, over and over, on that old broken couch.... your hands... moving over and around... until you...."

Now, Ms. Lahaye raised a hand and screamed, "I will not listen to this!"

She turned to walk quickly out of the room, screeching, "Nathan, get rid of them!"

The leader of the Church of the Shadow of the Lord looked as if he saw death itself. He was frozen stock still and unable to respond. The Reverend had turned bird shit white and slowly moved only his eyes to look at his fellow Christians in the room.

Kayne stepped forward, as did I. We took the police officer into a hug-up, his powerful arms hanging limply at his side. The preacher nearest us mumbled what I thought were soft words of apology. The old gentleman reached out as if to touch the former camp inmate but drew back his hand at the last minute in a furtive gesture.

I stepped back to assess the expression of the man in our arms. His body seemed to be unmovable. I looked at his stony face and saw that he was not crying.

Mako was staring at the Pastor of the Church of the Shadow of the Lord.

Chapter Forty-Five: The Almost

The Kailua Bay Fishing Pier, Palani Road and HI-19, The Big Island, Hawai'i
Nick Sechi's Journal

"You OK, Big Dude?"

"Yes."

Mako stepped with us into the sunshine as we left the Church Headquarters

I held up my phone.

"Uber or walk?"

"The latter, my love."

Mako remained silent.

Kayne changed the subject somewhat as we left the compound.

"I was fascinated with the psychology of the celebrity of the Lahayes, particularly the smiling pastor."

"I wanted to ask you why you didn't do the usual Sorenson Bomb thingo. You know where you read them their filth as you cross the threshold with that Voice of God cadence you get from your Father. But you got us there, Boss."

I was doing my best to lighten the mood on behalf of the devastated Hawai'ian. He seemed unchanged as we wandered through paths rich in biodiversity-- bleak lava deserts, lush patches of rainforest, and the garden-like landscapes of the northwestern stretches of the island.

"I was observing and verifying theory, my love. The Pastor and Ms. Arvella add up to be textbook examples of the sociological condition known as 'narcissistic charisma.' Interesting specimens, I will say."

I glanced at the stoic face of our friend but said, "Go, Boss."

"His personal gifts-- attributed to a divine power? The 20th-century scholar Max Weber, who coined the term, defines 'charisma' as a quality that sets an individual apart from ordinary humanity-- a superbeing endowed with exceptional powers."

"Able to leap tall buildings in a single bound?" I mocked.

"Let's go to science, lads. Brain-scan technologies and modern statistical techniques help us to analyze the birth of legendary leadership. Many believe it is even possible not just to reverse-engineer charisma but that it's something, at least in part, we might learn.

"I refer to the work of John Antonakis, a professor of Organizational Behavior and Director of the Ph.D. program in management at the University of Lausanne. But a word of caution, while we can create charismatic leaders, there are dangerous consequences of their power."

Kayne gestured to a row of shops near the coast road and a somewhat ragged-edged restaurant. Quinn's Almost by the Sea was just off Palani Road and Highway 19, on a fishing pier.

Fish Tacos, Mahi for Nick Boy. Kayne ordered grilled Ono with pineapple slaw, double on the onion rings-- to share, and Mako passed, watching the sea turtles bobbing in the smooth waters off the pier.

Worried about this guy. Gotta be traumatic to relive all that abuse. He did not want to talk about it.

As we ate, Kayne kept eying our brooding Hawai'ian but continued doing what he does best-- he taught.

"I conclude it is a masterpiece in the phony, to tell the truth. Pastor Nathan is a charlatan. His rhetorical style is what captures the people. Please indulge me for a second.

"His sermon broadcasts always open with cascading photographs of the grinning Lahaye with his famous incisors, standing with his family— sons, daughters, and the ubiquitous Arvella looking as if they are carved from cream cheese. More family at play snapshots, dogs, and children. The fashion model wife with gently blowing raven locks. Next, we see the folks who seek these members of God's anointed. It's white people at worship and in prayerful ecstasy. Then, we see enormous crowds of ethnically diverse and age-representative people. There he is on stage, extending a hand of welcome. And now, the impeccably coiffed and dressed smiling minister starts to speak.

Mako shifted uncomfortably but did not check-in.

"Antonakis delineates nine charismatic verbal strategies in addition to an animated voice, open facial expressions, and passionate gestures. These are metaphors and comparisons, stories, rhetorical questions, contrasts, lists, and repetitions, moral convictions, expressing the sentiments of the collective, setting high and ambitious goals, and creating confidence that dreams can be achieved. The subliminal message is that his flock is on safe territory-- there is no need to fear, and Lahaye speaks for God.

"It is important to note that Lahaye and his star pupil, Arvella Copelan Lahaye, both embody the message. In fact, they *are* the message. 'God is doing something salvific here. How could we possibly be wrong? Sure, we are rich, but that is because we are faithful.' This combination of faith and glory captivates the audience."

Mako slammed the table with unexpected force. Diners turned.

"Shove that crap down the throat of a kid who wonders why he doesn't fit in, and you have death and disaster."

Somewhat bewildered, Kayne began to reach for the man's hand.

"Stop talking about that fuck. Stop!"

Kayne locked eyes with the distraught police officer, saying, *E ku'u hoaaloha, pono 'oe e alo i ka mea i ho'oweliweli e luku ai iā 'oe. 'A'ole 'oe wale nō. Aloha 'oe me 'oe."*

He had very tenderly said, "My friend, you must face that which threatens to destroy you. But not alone. You have friends here with you."

Mako stood and walked out onto the pier. He stripped and dove into the sparkling blue waters and began to swim directly to the far horizon.

The Shadow of Evil

Chapter Forty-Six: Namaka

The Kailua Bay Fishing Pier, Palani Road and HI-19, The Big Island, Hawai'i
Nick Sechi's journal

"Wait, Kayne. He's coming back."

The swimmer turned and glided back to the dock with powerful strokes and forceful kicks. The studly Hawai'ian's freestyle was framed by the setting sun and the cries of circling sea birds. He sluiced through the water like a dolphin, the seawater sluicing off his dark muscles and sleek black hair.

We had run down the access, and Kayne began to disrobe in anticipation of a daring suicide intervention. I was looking to hijack a fishing boat. Now, we both watched Mako return from his frantic aquatic workout.

Kayne stooped to gather our friend's clothes and pull on his own shirt and shoes. A knot of onlookers, tourists, fishers, and diners cruised up behind us. Onlookers had one hand up with cell phones to... well, you know, no moment is private in the 21st century.

Behind us, the bump of the boats rocking against the pier and the screech of the gulls combined with overlapping human squawks. More of the locals and visitors came to see what was going on.

"Yo, no skinny dipping here. What's going on?

"Is that guy drunk?"

"You see the body on that guy. Get out of my way, Henry."

"Got any spare change?"

I did my cop thing, saying, "Step back, folks. Nothing to see here, people."

Which wasn't quite correct as 225 pounds of wet, naked man-muscle pulled himself up onto the dock. Kayne handed Mako his pants. I watched with concern for our friend.

"Hey, any spare change? Mister?"

The wet man was grinning as he pulled on his jeans and leaned against a pylon to slip on his socks and running shoes.

"Hey, gunz up, dude. Hawai'ian muscle for my Insta."

Mako ignored the cries for beefcake and said, "I apologize, you guys. I needed to feel the embrace of my sister Namaka. Since I was a boy, whenever I felt like shit on a shingle, I would go to the goddess of the ocean, and we would fall into each other's arms.

"The situation with the church folks is cool, really. Leaving my head for now. A few years in therapy, my people's and yours-- yeah, I'm OK."

"C'mon, lady. I'm really hungry. Anything is good."

Sometimes, things just smash into a person. Yeah, like my mother was fond of saying, "Nick Baby, it's as plain as the nose on your face." In my defense, the dude I was talking to was naked, and you all know how I am.

It hit us instantly, all three of us at once, like a jolt of electricity. We stood stock-still as if, at any moment, a rare butterfly would be frightened away.

Mako dropped a running shoe and looked up open-mouthed. I almost let go of my backpack as I turned. Kayne stepped forward, went down on one knee, and said softly, "Hey, Chlöe. How about having something to eat with us?"

***

"I sent the files to Scott in Colorado, Boss. He's on it. Chlöe, can I hold onto this?"

I held up the flash drive.

The girl munched down on a Monsta Burger and fries, the *spécialité de la maison,* as Kayne would say.

"Yeah, but how do I know you are the good guys? I was so hungry I forgot to think. Pass the ketchup, please."

I flipped the laptop so that she could see the splash page for The Kayne Sorenson Mysteries blog.

She scrolled, read, and said, "Cool. Yeah, you guys are like the Power Rangers. I have a friend who loves the Avengers. He goes to school in California."

Mako said, "Why don't I take that, Nick? Evidence."

He held out a hand and, with the other hand, took a bite of his own Monsta and onion rings.

"All good, man."

I handed him the drive.

Kayne said, "What's the story on this, Chlöe? Specifically, how did you get the device? It did not come from the Retreat Center, of that, I am sure."

The girl reached into her cargoes and extracted a small black book with a leather cover– The ESV Vest Pocket New Testament with Psalms and Proverbs. Kayne flipped the book open, and we saw the indentation. Someone has cut the stack of small pages to fit the drive inside the small book.

She finished chewing and slurped a drink. She said. "So, when I got to this island, I was supposed to stay with some Hawai'ian people, but I got scared again and hit the streets. Ended up somewhere like wilderness and rocks and stuff. I found this abandoned truck, and I searched for anything that looked valuable that I could sell, ya know? I grabbed that little Bible."

She went in for another pocket emptying.

"I was looking for anything, food, mostly. Guy in the truck had a pretty expensive piece of jewelry, and so I thought I could get some cash for it. Can I get another shake?"

She looked guiltily at the police officer.

Kayne looked the carved stone medallion over. As Mako was two-fisting the last of his sandwich and rings, Kayne slipped it into the breast pocket of our friend's Hawai'ian shirt. It settled against the cop's chest next to the mini New Testament.

"My girl, we need you to send a message to your family...

He never finished.

The intruders were four sizeable guys in T-shirts and shorts. One would have mistaken them for local fishermen stopping at the grill for a bite in the early evening.

They drew handguns and told us to leave with them. We started to follow. As we hit the outdoor seating area, Mako pushed Chlöe to the ground and was about to toss a chair.

One of the thugs fired, and Mako went down.

The earth shook.

Chapter Forty-Seven: Cain

EnVitro Tec, Inc., Waikoloa Reserve, The Big Island, Hawai'i
Nick Sechi's Journal

"Might as well know, you will not be telling anyone, that's for sure."

The white-haired man took a drink of his Johnny Walker Blue Label Scotch Whisky.

He continued while pointing with one finger at Kayne, "Furthermore, if you are who you say you are, you pretty much know what we have cooking here at EnVitroTec, literally."

Kayne said, "The girl."

The Reverend Simeon Matthison winked and said, "Forget about her. You see, if I can figure out how to do it, I am gonna leverage that kid into an appreciation gift – a Golden State prize."

"The land in Orange County, you and your minions will never pull it off."

The maniac pulled close to me. Matthison lifted my t-shirt and lightly touched my abs.

"Fit little ex-police officer. Fired for unnatural acts on the force, no doubt. Heard you and your butt-buddy over there are quite a pair of fighters. Martial arts fairies. Well, how about that?"

I strained at the ropes and hawked a huge drool in the preacher's face, only to be rewarded by a backhand to the face. Kayne unsuccessfully wrestled with his bindings. Armed members of the Company, our abductors from the restaurant, looked on, somewhat amused.

Matthison wiped his face on my shirt and said, "Something like this. No, tell me how this sounds, Ex-Officer. You came out and found the girl, a runaway, but decided she was of interest to some godless flesh peddlers. We can make them Asian, hard to track, and not popular with conservative white Americans right now.

"So, the Church mustered its resources to save the child, albeit after she sustained a head injury. The two consulting detectives were killed in the process."

He turned to Kayne.

"A rough draft, I will admit, but it has possibilities."

There was another earth shift and a rumbling sound from far off. The disruption was accompanied by screeching. This time, the guards showed discomfort.

"Our test animals are behind that wall. EnVitroTec is built into the lava rock, the flanks of the volcano, gentlemen. Mauna Kea is dormant. Has been for almost 5,000 years. She is due to erupt again but at her higher elevations. We get rumbles now and again, which disturb the mammals and the birds, especially the bonobos-- our test subjects. But have no fear. The Lord protects all believers."

The old man of God tossed back his drink and set the glass down.

"We actually could use a couple of healthy human subjects. How about a little plague, gentlemen?"

Kayne asked, "How did you do it, Sir? My husband would say you completely came over to the Dark Side of the Force. You founded a Church and now run a covert, illegal, special operations project to develop biological weapons. That is indeed a fall from grace, is it not?"

"No, no, no, Doctor Sorenson. Weapons? Hardly. We have the data to show that EnVitro Tec helps infertile Christian couples conceive. We are in the business of helping the Lord to build the Family."

The corrupt churchman went on.

"Nathan Lahaye's father and I... seems like a century ago. Malachi was the one with the glory in his looks and in his preaching. People loved him. I used to call him the Heart of the Church. Beautiful man and angelic preacher to tell the truth."

He gestured dramatically and said, "The power of the Lord flowed through him, and the people came, and they donated substantially.

"I was not similarly blessed, you see, and so I became the secularist-- the intellect and guts of the organization. I never attracted the affection of the congregation. There was no room in their hearts for me. So, I became the genius behind the business of our evangelism. And the one who would end up doing the dirty work."

He spread his arms wide and went on.

"The Church of the Shadow of the Lord— worldwide ministries in less than a generation. Astounding. And Malachi and his princeling were God's anointed. So, the money kept rolling in from all corners. I invested. I created our public image. I found the son a trophy wife – not an easy thing to do. Arvella, you see, has a past, and fast cars do not seem to keep her as occupied as we would like. She often strays. In fact, they both do.

"I also take care of their indiscretions— make them go away. No one cares these days if their heroes are committing sins of the flesh, except for a walk on the gay side— always a marketing challenge. It seems my fellow preacher, Fred Phelps, was right. God Hates Fags."

In an attempt to buy time, I said, "You and Malachi Lahaye were like Cain and Abel. Check it out. The Bible never really explains why God withdrew from Cain-- never says he was sinful, disrespectful, gay, or anything like that. God just turns his back on that kid.

"The Big Dude in the sky plays favorites, I guess, huh? What do you think, Pastor? Is God just fickle or creating some drama of his own? Man, it ended up with Abel getting killed. Sounds a little like divine complicity. How about it, Rev? 'Cause I want to fuckin' know."

I received no reply. The insane Jesus guy spoke on, steering back to his own talking points.

"I believe we were speaking of the son. Yes, the Son of the Light. Nathan was difficult. A lot of work. Also, a beautiful man, a gifted preacher, believed in all of it. Stubborn as the day is long. Not a big believer in satisfying his woman. Something you two might understand."

Kayne said, "Under your direction, experiments in the name of the church have produced biological weapons capable of destroying millions."

"Of non-believers, atheists, followers of false religions, sinners, and deviants, like you and your partner in sin. In the name of all that is holy, conversion therapy doesn't work. Why is that not understood by my co-religionists? The Devil will not release his degenerate children. You and your kind must be eliminated from the face of the earth. Then will the shadows be pierced by the divine and holy light."

As if he were hearing himself for the first time, Simeon Matthison paused and stared into space.

"Sometimes, you must take a step away from God to do his work."

He poured another glass of the dark amber liquor.

Kayne said, "The Feldenstine case. You framed Rosa Feldenstine after orchestrating the death of Abraham Feldenstine. Had she been found guilty of murder, she would not have inherited, and the Feldenstine fortune would have defaulted to your church. It is not too much of a stretch to see that it was also you who ordered the death of the defense attorneys, and that plan resulted in the crippling of John Hrynsyshyn."

"In the words of my good friend, Seth Lahaye, the best American President we have ever had, 'You are fake.' None of that is true."

Kayne would not stop.

"Prions."

"Yet somehow, you do impress, Doctor."

"Prions-- misfolded proteins with the ability to infect and cause the destruction associated with several fatal and transmissible neurodegenerative diseases in humans and many other animals. Degenerative brain disorders... prion-infected proteins are defective and extremely useful. EVT has developed a menagerie of them. Not lethal viruses, bacteria, fungi, or parasites. Prions have no DNA or RNA and, therefore, can be engineered into much more dangerous weapons.

"At this time, we are preparing for the distribution phase, and by the time of Pastor Nathan's World-Wide Outreach Campaign, where believers will be energized all over the globe, our deployers will begin with a few very strategic strikes on the heathen world capitals. Very high casualty counts..."

The insane minister held up his right hand and flexed it at Kayn.

"How about a little Black Death, Professor? And how is your family?"

His maniacal laugh filled the chamber, drowning out the animal cries. Kayne struggled to hold his temper.

Throughout this diatribe, Kayne was talking and drawing attention to himself, and I was attempting to wiggle out of my restraints. When he spoke, it was with the assurance of science-based observations.

"Matthison, allow me to make a few important observations. The redness of your countenance indicates you are in the throes of acute alcoholism. I will wager you have had a cirrhotic liver for some time. Further evidence of your condition can be seen in the severe jaundice of your skin and eyes. Acute liver failure is not far off. You will be meeting your maker very soon, I wager.

"Reverend Matthison, because of your biological weapons project, millions of innocents will die. How will that justify your soul with your God?"

The man raised his arms to the ceiling and quoted Exodus 7:19, like a deranged Old Testament Prophet.

"And the LORD said to Moses, 'Tell Aaron to take his staff and stretch out his hand over the waters of Egypt-- over their rivers and canals and ponds and reservoirs--that they may become blood. And behold, there will be blood throughout the land of Egypt, even in the vessels of wood and stone.'

He became florid as he went on with the madness of one who was already damned.

"Sometimes, you leave the light and embrace the darkness. It matters not that many will suffer and die."

The Shadow of Evil

Chapter Forty-Eight: Girl Unleashed

EnVitro Tec, Inc., Waikoloa Reserve, The Big Island, Hawai'i
Nick Sechi's Journal

"Looks like we got a couple of queer-assed bastards here, fellas. What are we gonna do about that?"

The speaker behaved like a sketchy Nicholas Cage character in a bad, direct-to-video movie-- crazy as shit and ready to raise hell. He drew close and prodded his captors with a nightstick.

"Ya know it was these homos turned your brother, "Bam Bam" Danny Kumkahi gay over in Frisco. I heard about that."

Kayne said, "Pardon me, Sir. Please allow me to disagree. No one can change a person's sexual orientation. It is innate, inborn. And I hasten to add, no one refers to the sublime City by the Bay as 'Frisco.' It is always and will ever be San Francisco."

For his Miss Manners-like lesson, Kayne received a gut punch which would have doubled him over had he not been tied to a post as I was.

OK, so let's mind fuck with these assholes before we kick their asses.

I called out. "You fuckups remind me of *The Gang That Couldn't Shoot Straight*. But that would presume you read on grade level. Jimmy Breslin? Queens?"

I tensed my abdominals and took one in the gut and one in the face.

"Who you callin' a queen, you faggot? Maybe we should see how much of a homo each of these girls is."

Stupid-assed bastards.

There was another rumble in the facility. This time, it shook the building with significant seismic force. The fire alarm went off, and the rolling door at the back of the chamber exploded, rocking open and to the right. A flock of enraged raptors soared through the opening in the semi-darkness, coming for anything moving.

Baboons, chimpanzees, and dogs raced into the space, overturning equipment and chairs and tossing every loose thing at their human captors. Two taloned fliers, frightened and screeching, landed on the heads of our torturers, making quick work of their scalps and eyes. As I watched, a punishing bird of prey tore the face off one of the men, shrieking as it raked the doomed assassin's bloody features.

Owls, falcons, and turkey vultures swirled in a rampage, seeking an escape route. Panicked dogs and rabbits raced in circles toward the opposite end of the room. A large white dog emerged from the smoke and commanded the center of the room, barking, snarling, and baring its teeth at the thugs. Cornered at first, the gangsters scrambled in separate directions, trying to escape.

Our prison space was filled with booming and shaking as smoke began to fill the room. There was tension on our bindings and a slicing sensation. The ropes dropped, and we were freed.

Chlöe Austin was on the run. She screamed, "Girl Power!" like she was leading a full-court press amid her team of beasts. Any remaining members of the terrorized Company knocked each other over as they sought to make their escape in front of the army of panicked wild things. Kayne, the girl, and I ran around with the menagerie, waving our arms and shouting. We followed the animals to the front exit as the rear of the building burst forth in flames. More noxious smoke and rumbling explosions erupted closely behind us.

It was all so surreal, as if nature herself were rebelling against the evil darkness that had fallen on the land. I saw the creatures racing towards the light pouring through an opening in the building where part of an exterior wall had disintegrated. Kayne, Chlöe, dozens of critters, the last of the Big Bads, and I, who was grasping the hand of a frightened chimp in each of my hands, scrambled towards the exit as pieces of the ceiling broke free.

And the owl… oh yes, the big grey owl, circling and swooping over everything. It flew at the front of the pack, leading us out to safety.

The last thing I saw was the white dog bringing up the rear, howling like a denizen from the fires of hell and leaving no beast behind.

Chapter Forty-Nine: I'm Melting, Melting

EnVitroTec, Inc., Waikoloa Reserve, The Big Island, Hawai'i
Nick Sechi's Journal

"Dog! What's your name, Daddy?"

Kayne gave me the usual your-libido-is-showing-again-my-love look. *Maintain propriety at all times, please.* As the hot-daddy EMT guy began to examine my bruises and cuts, I forgot my injuries. Both Kayne and I were sitting on side-by-side stretchers being inspected and patched up.

In defense of my frisky behavior, my blood was up from the capture and escape, and I was acting the fool, I admit, but still....

Ignoring my diminutive expression, "Dr. Pretty" gave a bored, I-get-this-a-lot expression and tapped a name tag on a sturdy pec. He shined a light into each of my eyes. The metal plate said, "Williams."

"Try to concentrate, Mr. Sechi. Any shortness of breath? Double vision? Pain in your ribs, abdomen, or groin? I will check for any fractures or sprains."

He raised his fingers.

"How many?"

"Three."

"Good. Follow the light, please."

And I thought Kayne had the eyelashes of a drag queen, man. I think I may require some special treatment.

Dr. Williams pressed my ribs and palpated my soft organs. He bent and rotated my ankles.

"Put your legs up, and please open your jeans. Thank you."

He checked my lower abs, ignoring my commando condition. I looked directly into his dark eyes-- no wincing equals not broken or bruised. I realized I was fascinated by the silky skin tones, high cheekbones, and muscled-up frame I find so attractive in African American men and anyone else, for that matter.

Keep it up, beauty, and we are in big trouble.

"You took some shots to the gut, indicated by these bruises, but nothing seems to be broken or torn. When we get you to the hospital, we will check more thoroughly for internal bleeding and sepsis."

I most likely batted my eyes and smiled like a damned fool.

Thanks, Doctor Dreamboat.

So yeah, as I said, I took a head pounding, and I am acting all sexy-assed, so sue me. I am usually not like this. Well, sorta not.

"Your face took some shots. There is edema in the lips and around both eyes. No teeth or facial bones were compromised. You're going to be prize-fighter ugly for a while. No contusions to the skull."

"Doc, my people are *testa dura* – hard-headed."

"I gave you a mild sedative. Let's get you stretched out here."

"Explains it, thanks."

He turned me and reclined the stretcher, placing my backpack next to my right thigh.

Kayne's medic, a much younger jock type, was flexing Kayne's shoulder.

"Looks like an old injury, Dr. Sorenson. Ever give you trouble?"

"No, Doctor. I just need to warm up a bit more when I exercise."

"Yes. As we get older..."

"Oh, please stop talking, Dr. Chan. Thank you. You may proceed."

The kid chuckled and continued tapping Kayne's upper body.

I heard him also run the pain questionnaire as I signed a form. Kayne's response was always negative.

"You'll be getting sleepy soon, also, Doctor. It should last until we get to Queen's North Hawai'i Community Hospital. Just up the highway a bit."

Dr. Chan called over his colleague. "Sam, check it out. Like on the blog, dude, the Mark of Cain and that famous black forelock." He started to sweep it up, but Kayne reached up and did his signature brush away.

My guy said, "Seriously, Rick? Kindly maintain professionalism."

"I apologize, Dr. Sorenson. I am a huge fan. You may put on your shirt and lie back.

He handed Kayne the medical form.

"Just my signature, Dr. Chan? There is no space for a mobile number. Perhaps…"

From my gurney, I busted, "Dude, you're married, and you don't own a phone."

I wiggled my wedding band. The four of us laughed.

A firefighter came up to check on us. He said, "The counties issued a call for the eruption protocols, but… strange, Sam, the lava just stopped."

We looked from our hillside perch, watching the dying eruption. And I'll be fucked. It *did* stop; it just sat there like a hellish lake of fire.

"Look!"

I yelled and pointed at a lone figure trying to find a way down from an obliterated roof in the darkness. He attempted to fight the blaze as the structure caved in around him. No way the rescuers could get to him.

Shadows and radiance seemed to intertwine above the flowing rock and boiling smoke. A layer of thin gray ash coated the landscape and the roadway.

Finally, the building was swallowed like Marion Crane's 1957 Ford in the swamp in Psycho. Only this lake was red, not green. First, you thought it was going under. Then, there was a pause followed by a complete envelopment with explosions hurling brimstone high into the air.

"Pele devours Matthison and his evilness."

It was Rachel Takeda.

Yeah, we found out it was she who brought up the reserves, police cars, fire trucks, first responders, state children's services workers, and forest rangers. A tangle of tourists was being held back by the highway, wanting to know what had burned down.

Rachel summarized, "The Rangers seem to have corralled the animals. Most of the birds seemed to have gotten away. The lab did not have a lot of employees since it was after business hours. We are detaining the suspected members of the Company. Chlöe is with Children's Services. I believe they are calling her family."

Kayne said, "Lahaye?"

"Most of his Board has resigned. Your visit to the Church's headquarters and the accusations created the rift. Matthison's rant and interrogation, which went out over the web, was incrimination out the ass and will be the basis for litigation against the Church."

Kayne turned to me with a questioning expression. I shrugged and wiggled my fingers in a keyboard-typing meme. I said, "Never even saw what I was up to posting that jerkwad. Total fuckups, Boss. Jimmy Breslin could have written a sequel to his mob book based on these numb nuts bastards."

Kayne reflected, "They had an instrument of great destruction right out of the Apocalypse, but the combined intelligence of a gnat coupled with the compassion of a narcissistic politician. Perhaps, one day, that combination will mean the end of us all."

No one said anything for a bit. In the night, lights whirled against the rocks and hills. Somewhere, a chimpanzee barked. An owl, *Pueo,* called from a nearby tree.

We both looked at the police officer, mindful of his fallen colleague.

Neither of us dared to ask....

Chapter Fifty: No Wobble

Queen's North Community Hospital, Waimea, The Big Island, Hawai'i
Nick Sechi's Journal

OK, so this is where I tell you the bullet hit the owl medallion or was embedded in the mini New Testament in Mako's breast pocket. The Royal Hawai'ian sustained minor injuries, and he'll be dancing the fire dance at the next *lū'au* over in Lahaina or smooching up his Dani with savage passion.

No.

I am afraid we upset the ER staff at Queen's North Hawai'i Community Hospital when we both jumped off the stretchers-- drugs or no drugs and headed for the ICU.

Kayne tossed over his shoulder, "Tell them who we are, please, Officer Tanaka."

Dani was holding his man's hand, the one without the IV drip. Machines made ICU noises and numbers, and green graphs bounced and scrolled across the screens. Tubes and cords hung from stands with keyboards at the ready.

"*Aloha, e ku'u mau hoa.*"[20]

Before Kayne could answer, I jumped in.

"What's Hawai'ian for, 'How is it possible to look hottern fuck after being shot in the head?'"

All four of us enjoyed a laugh.

Mako reached for Kayne and pulled his face close. He said, "'*O 'oe ka 'ānela o Pele, Kayne. Aia nā 'uhane a puni 'oe.*"[21]

---

[20] Hello, my friends.
[21] You are Pele's owl, Kayne. There are good spirits all around you.

Dani whispered, "Mako called him Pele's owl. An tole him dat he sees da spirits of old Hawai'i in the air all round him."

"Yo, gimme some of that, studly."

I leaned in for my own nose rub.

I blushed bright red from forehead to toes.

"Bollocks, ya mug. Save some of that heat for me, you old married husband. Some fine man stud right here, sport."

We all laughed again.

I pointed to the head bandage, more on Mako's left side than on the right.

From the patient, we heard, "It is a matter of physics, *ko'u Ni'ko*. The bullet was high velocity, and thus, there was no side-to-side wobble of the brain. That is what causes irreversible harm. The bullet thingo passed through noncritical parts of my brain, causing little damage. Consequently, with my robust Polynesian constitution, I am on the mend... Bob's yer uncle, mate."

I roared... laughing and pointing.

"No, seriously, Mako dude, you got him down. Kayne J. Sorenson, Ph.D. he knows his shit-- Aussie brogan to the max."

Kayne did a pretend sneer at our teasing.

"Imitation is the highest form of flattery. But in all honesty, Nick and I are grateful you've survived."

A nurse stepped into the unit, closing the sliding glass door behind her. She pulled a very stern face.

"Way too many people in here. Don't care who you all are. Everybody out."

Then she smiled and cocked her head to one side. She pointed to me.

"Damn, soldier, you run face-first into a meat grinder? Bet you were handsome once. Ouch."

She looked closer and said, "Naw, your gorgeous is coming back, plain to see."

Pointing to the patient, she went on.

"Has this one been telling you all about the bullet to the head thing? Hanging onto life by a thread? Hell, muscle boy here took a crease to his skull, is all."

She tapped up the computer display.

"Yep. No brain involvement at all. The Officer was out there for a bit, calling for his...."

She waved a hand at Dani.

"All of that... and all this...."

She waved around the unit.

"... is just for making sure of that fracture. We are taking Officer Lopaka for more X-rays and then to a private room. Whoa, the King Kalakaua Suite. Who's your daddy, handsome? Not HPD, that's for damn sure."

The ICU nurse nodded to a colleague on the other side of the glass partition. It seems Kayne and I were wanted.

Nurse Realness continued with one hand on her hip and up in Kayne's face.

"Now, you two listen to me. You get out of here and sit your asses down in those wheelchairs. Those two orderlies are taking you to the ER for the rest of your tests."

Dani chuckled, "You bes listen to dis *wahine*."

Now, she flashed her eyes and did a fierce snap, almost touching Kayne.

"And don't you go giving me those crystal-blue eyes that get the boys all moist. You both look like hammered shit. Get your asses in those chairs and follow orders."

***

They ended up keeping us overnight, replacing fluids, checking lungs for smoke inhalation complications, and all that. We shared a room. Neither of us accepted the pain meds-- a couple of macho bad-asses.

No poisons in this body.

"How are you handling the elevators, my love?"

I held up a face mask and lifted it up to my eyes.

"Or just shut my eyes. Amazing, really. I can handle it. Are you doing OK, Boss?"

We received a report that Kayne's spleen needed watching and figured we'd get it looked at in San Francisco.

"Anxious to get home, Nick. I miss Kris quite a bit."

"Same here, Big Man. Won't be long, now."

He scrolled through his phone.

"Hey, Boss, I never did find out. How did Chlöe get free at EnVitro Tec?"

"According to Rachel, one of our captors decided he was going to mess with the young woman. That little shelia put some moves on that bugger straight off the basketball court. Illegal in sport but highly effective. She actually lobbed a metal trash basket at his head, and Snarky went down."

"Tough little kid. Musta checked him good."

"The media is all over the happenings with the Church of the Shadow of the Lord. The Lahayes are in seclusion, and there has been no comment from the White House. Recognize her?"

He gave me his phone.

"Holy shit, Boss. The woman who was dogging us at the South Bend Airport."

I scrolled.

The headline read, "Woman Connected with Reborn Hawai'ian Mafia Held for Questioning in Indianapolis."

Chapter Fifty-One: Garland

Queen's North Community Hospital, Waimea, The Big Island, Hawai'i
Nick Sechi's Journal

"I wanted to say thank you for helping me."

Kayne took the hug up and said, "If I remember correctly, Ms. Austin. You and your animals kicked some gangster arse and rescued us."

I joined in and said, "Like Captain Marvel, girl."

Chlöe said with a smile, "Yeah, I get that a lot."

She took a lei for each of us and put it around our necks.

"*Aloha,* and thank you."

The King Kalakaua Suite of the Queen's Medical Center was plush. Police Officers coming to see Detective Makoa Lopaka smiled as they exited the bedroom, moving past us into the suite's living room. A tall gentleman, talking to Rachel, motioned Chlöe in. We could see the girl talking to the patient and presenting him with a necklace of flowers as a thank you.

Charles Vance came over to us, motioning us to a sitting area in the VIP suite.

"You have my utmost esteem and gratitude and that of my family. To say that we are delighted to have my granddaughter returned to us safe and sound would be a profound understatement.

"I have indicated that the sale of the Orange County land is to be divided three ways: The True Colors Fund, Covenant House, and the Historic Hawai'i Foundation will be the recipients. In addition to compensating you for your work, I wanted to do something for your nephew in accord with my gratitude and in consideration of the danger he was able to escape. However, I understand from your blog, Mr. Sechi, that Kristof Sorenson has a full scholarship at the University of San Francisco."

Kayne said, "Truly generous of you, Mr. Vance. I will provide you with Kris' contact information and let him know that you will be contacting him. Young Kristof will advise you as to your kind stewardship on his behalf. I will also text you our office contact information. Our administrative assistant is Ms. Andi Rodriguez. If you should ever need us, Sir..."

"Thank you, Doctor."

I said, "Chlöe?"

"I must say, Mr. Sechi, I am at a loss. For now, she will be staying with Jack and Risë in Santa Barbara until Nancy and Rolf decide how that family will do what's best for my granddaughter. I must say that her father is feeling very guilty right now. Nancy is a whole other story.

"When you talk to Kris, Sir. Ask him about Jamison Welton and the Silverman Academy in Marin County."

"Welton? Any relation to Beatrice Welton?"

"Yes. Jamie is her grandson. He is a student at Silverman."

"I have known Bea for quite a long time now.

We were interrupted by a man in a chauffeur's livery.

"I beg your pardon, gentlemen. Could any of you direct me to Dr. Kayne Sorenson?"

"Found him, Bro."

Kayne nodded.

"Dr. Sorenson?"

"Yes?"

"I am here to take you to your aircraft, Sir."

We both turned, but Charles Vance smiled, shrugged, and said, "Don't look at me, fellas."

Kayne asked the chauffeur, "Tell me, young man, is it the 'Firehawk?'"

"Of course, Dr. Sorenson."

Chapter Fifty-Two: Succession

Kona International Airport to Melbourne, Australia
Port Melbourne, Australia
Nick Sechi's Journal

I asked rather groggily as the Xanax wore off, "So, who's flying the plane, dude?"

The pilot in the seat on the opposite side of the Cessna Citation X pushed his hat back off his face and blinked sleepy eyes.

"Your husband, Sir."

"Oh, that's just nifty."

I conked out for another seven-hour nap.

***

As the limousine pulled out of the Melbourne Airport, Kayne pulled me closer. He started to carefully nuzzle me up but whispered very close to my ear.

"Observe the chauffeur, my love."

"Oh fuck. What now? I don't do multiple kidnap victims this close, Bossman."

"Relax, just make a note. I am going to snooze."

Nada. The smoked glass partition between the driver and us never went down. He never spoke to us or acknowledged us at the pickup. The Red Cap did the luggage, and the stretch was parked curbside with the back door open.

My laptop pinged.

A familiar and handsome Sorenson filled the screen.

"You guys giving each other road head in that esky ute,[22] Nick, ma brotha?"

Damn, I need my Aussie Slang dictionary for this trip, big time.

"Kick, holy shit! No, no, I need to get ready for this mashup. When did you guys get in? And what are you doing with clothes on?"

"Yesterday, with my incestuous husband, Mitch. The house in Port Melbourne, Victoria... Da and Darana-- so this bad boy gotta be good... which is not to say that, given the circumstances, the four of us couldn't..."

A growl and a sleep drool wipe from the world-class consulting detective sleeping against my shoulder. "Turn that bloody little wanker off, please."

I tipped the screen

"There's my big brother."

"Cheers, ya bloody little pissa. Now get stuffed." He went back to sleep.

"Grouchy bastard."

The was gonna be some fun time.

***

Number Fourteen Beacon Vista was a modest house near the water. The Sorenson triplets were born in this house and spent their first 18 months here with their mother and an Aboriginal amah. Ace would come from Inala with baby Mitch when he could. Eventually, they all went west to the ranch.

Mitch, Kick, and Darana welcomed us up the steps to the big porch. I fished in my pocket for a few Australian Dollars for the driver. We rounded up in the living room when the explosion happened.

"Push this fuckin' thing, ya bleeding wuss. It ain't a pram. It's a wheelchair."

---

[22] The Australian slang combines terms for utility vehicle with small ice cooler, hence – a pickup truck for partying.

An orderly rolled the Lord of Inala into the room like the entrance of Zeus himself. Kick stepped behind Mitch. As fearless as the champion jock was, Thomas Michael Sorenson, Sr., whom everyone called "Ace" and for whom Kick was named, scared the piss out of the young jock.

"Da, how delightful to see you and in your usual good humor."

"Send that bluey husband of yours over to me, Kayne. Needs to give the Captain a pash.

"What the bloody Hell happened to ya face, boyo? I hope ya gave as good as ya got."

I bent in for a kiss up and said, "Do not grab my 'arse,' Ace."

He did anyway, doing his signature roaring laugh as I stood back up. We both greeted Darana. She is as refined as Ace is rawboned.

"Thomas Michael, get these mugs a drink, and I'll have…."

Darana said, "The Capi, Captain. Restocked this morning. Your father prefers the lemon and basil, Master Thomas."

The *pater familias* grunted and pouted, looking ever so much like his junior namesake, caught with his hand in the cookie jar.

I walked back to the entranceway to tip the driver bending over, back to us, arranging the luggage.

I heard Kayne say, "Upstairs, third bedroom on the right, young Kristof, unless Darana has arranged us differently."

The young man in black livery spun around and shouted.

"How did you know, Uncle Kayne? You never saw me until now."

Astonished, I opened my hand, dropping the bills which floated to the floor. Kayne walked over and pulled the three of us together.

"Just before I fell asleep, I observed that each time you approached a rotary, Kristof, you attempted to go to the right-- American driving. That first one out of the airport, you went around twice. How could that circumstance come to be, considering the wry sense of humor of this family? Also, my young ward, your hairline, under the back of your cap. I memorized it quite a long time ago. Like a fingerprint…"

***

"St. Vincent's Hospital, Melbourne. Where the three of you mugs were born. This thingo is usually a simple procedure, but given my whatever the fuck is goin' on, it may be more. Gonna be open and shut, seein' as how... any fuckin' way."

Ace waved away all concern for his health.

Dinner was on the back lawn in the beautiful Fall evening. Our catching-up conversations dovetailed with tomorrow's operation. Kris sat at the feet of his grandfather as we all enjoyed some after-dinner drinks. Every so often, Ace lovingly touched his grandson's head.

Kayne whispered to me.

"You'd better hang on, my love. This is gearing up to be the Sorenson version of "King Lear," Act 1, Scene 1, Nick, and it is going to get just as tragic-- the Division of the Kingdom, or who loves Da the most."

He looked over the assembly before continuing.

"An alternative scenario would be Kris having to stay here and run Inala, and I will fight the two of them on it. I do not care that it makes all the sense in the world to my father. It will absolutely ruin the lad."

"I got your back, Bossman."

I poured us another glass of red wine.

"... which is a way of sayin' I have made some decisions regarding who is to run Inala now that yer old man is gotta take 'er easy."

Ace reached down and took Kris' hand and kissed it.

"One of yas know this aw ready. An it's gonna be aw right, I can assure you. The experience is in no way on the lean side, and the intelligence and the courage is there-- has always been there. Ya just need balls and brains to run the place."

I could feel Kayne tense beside me.

"Three weeks ago, just after you left 'stralya, Mitch, one of the best things that ever happened to this old bastard came about."

Ace looked at his three sons and the others who surrounded him.

"Darana said 'yes.'"

Holy crap!

The place went wild. Cheering and congratulating in two languages, hugging and kissing like loonies... Kick and Kris went off the rails, trying to outdo each other in handless summersaults and scrappin' until Mitch and Kayne pulled them off.

"I raised me a bunch a hoolies, for fuck sake. Two generations of 'em. Na more– this one's gonna be refined, ya blokes."

Darana looked so beautiful as she said, "It's too early to tell, but we are hoping for a girl."

"You lads need a sister, and the bloodline needs some color-- you all are so fuckin' white. You need to promise me that... should anything... well."

The Captain was interrupted by an altercation at the back gate. The argument seemed to be between a servant and what appeared to be a delivery person. There was shouting.

"Says, 'Sorenson,' mate. Whadda mean no one ordered a pizza? Bloody Oath! Have a lookit that. Waz it say? Cargo Pizza, New Quay– S-O-R-E-N-S-O-N."

The man was pointing to the receipt taped to the box. The houseman shook his head and tried to turn the man out. But the blue-collar stepped into the yard. I felt a physical alert hit all of us.

Fuck me dead!

"You, ya old rat bastard, who's gonna pay for this pizza? Bugger me. It ain't gonna be me, mate."

The angry scowl died on the deliveryman's face as Kris ran into his arms.

I took the handles and wheeled my father-in-law over to his black-sheep son.

"Bleeding Jesus, Mary, and Joseph, Eric Sorenson. Only you would do this to a man with a bad heart." He reached up.

The captain and the secret agent were crying.

Epilogue: Silverman Texts

Hey, Jamie. You busy?

> Sup girl? Getting used to the place?

Yes. I really like it. Nobody teases.

> Wait a bit. Some of that. Silverman is just kids, and kids do stuff. You know?

I guess. But not like my other school.

> I'm running for student government in the fall. Gonna vote for me? I'll send you some cool games.

I was on your web page. I liked it.

> Thanks.

You need a lower-school campaign manager. Got someone in mind?
(Hint, hint)

> Get this boy the female vote?

Guaranteeing it. Wanna be friends?

> Def, girl. I like jocks a lot.

Thanks for coming to my basketball game, Jay.

> Silverladies rock! You were great!

Thanks, it was good.
Delphine Iverson rocks.

> Crush?

Probably. But I think she has

a girlfriend.

You like anyone?   ...

Hey Jay, you there?

                                        Sorry. Was thinking.

                                          Never, never, never tell, OK, Chlöe? Seriously.

Friends never tell, Jay.

                                          So, he's a college guy-- goes to USF. Sophomore in the fall. Emailed you a pic.

***

Wow, very hot. Wait. That's Chris Sorenson. His family got me outta some trouble recently. Nick and Kayne. They are married.

                                          He spells his name with a "K." He's like my best friend 'cept he doesn't know it. We haven't done stuff and all that. Just like him, a lot. He has a boyfriend, and I've been seeing some guys too. Sort of. Hung out with N & K in LA before enrolling here. Nick taught me MMA.

That's way cool, Jay.

                                          Heard Kris lost a grandpa. (sad emoji) He has two. I just have a grandma.

I have one grandfather.

...

Hey, here's something. Guess where
Nick and Kayne are headed now, bud.
Wanna know?

                                Sure.

Kayne surprised Nick with a vaycay.

                                Cool. Where'd they go?

Australia. How cool is that?

                                Hope they don't run into
trouble.

The End

The Shadow of Evil

Thomas Paul Severino

Acknowledgments and Reader's Notes

My father's voice can be heard in my writings, for I carry him in my memory still. He served in World War II with his brothers and friends. He was stationed in Hawai'i and often spoke and sang of the island paradise. I remember, as a boy, climbing the stairs to our attic and finding a grass skirt and some other curiosities that would be an invitation for his stories about Hawai'i. This tale, in many ways, is our heart's return.

I have attempted to use the most authentic style for the Hawai'ian language. I love its musical sound, replete with glottal stops. You pronounce every vowel. I hope my story conveys honor and value to the people, the wildlife, and the culture of that beautiful and mystical land. Except where Anglicized proper names are used (e.g., The Royal Hawaiian Hotel), I have deferred to the accepted native spellings (e.g., *Hawai'ian, lū'au, Hawai'i, etc.*). Non-English words and dialogue are italicized.

Dani Kale' Okapa, Mama Uluani, and the High Chieftess, Aila'au, speak English with beautiful Polynesian accents. I regret if I have not presented them well. I truly believe accents remind us of the treasures of human diversity.

There are others whose contributions I must acknowledge. Many thanks to my husband, Anton S. Wallner, Ph.D., for his help with encouragement and perceptive plot suggestions.

Also, to my friend, Keith Hickman, for expert advice and incisive copy editing, I extend a huge thank you.

To my friend Gerry Iacullo, who offered encouragement and plot analysis, I appreciate your support.

During the Pandemic of 2020, the country and the world are grateful to healthcare workers, sanitation workers, custodial workers, farmers, donors (both large and small), and volunteers for their self-sacrifice for their families and the world community. Selflessness is the best expression of the human spirit. Thank you for leading us closer to a day of hope.

Note to readers:

End Conversion Therapy in your state.

Know the facts. Advocate.

http://www.nclrights.org/our-work/bornperfect/

Help a Runaway.

Important information:

The National Runaway Safeline

https://www.1800runaway.org/

Call 1-800-RUNAWAY or Text 66008

Afterword:

Thank you for reading <u>The Kayne Sorenson Mysteries: The Shadow of Evil.</u> I hope you enjoyed the tale. Look for the continuing stories of Kayne Sorenson and Nick Sechi in <u>The Kayne Sorenson Mysteries: The Pearl of Great Evil.</u>

An excerpt from this, their latest case, follows.

The Shadow of Evil

The Pearl of Great Evil

A Kayne Sorenson Mystery

Thomas Paul Severino

Prologue: Nihonmachi

San Francisco, California
Nick Sechi's Journal

The body lay on the steps of the Japantown Peace Pagoda in the plaza of the same name, between Geary and Post, in San Francisco's Western Addition. April's early morning mist gave the cherry trees, blushing with pink blooms, an impressionistically smudged look – smeared color, suggesting flowers, trees, sky, and buildings. We pulled up from our jog to interrupt a ragged vagrant's stooped-over investigation.

Kayne spoke loudly, "Please do not disturb that man, Sir."

He jumped in to intercept. I dialed 911.

"OK, OK. The guy's dead. Pretty sure. Hasn't moved. I've been watching him since they dumped him there. I wasn't gonna steal nothing, Mister."

He stepped back. Some two more homeless folks lumbered out of the fog to see what was going on. One woman was pushing a Walgreens shopping cart heaped with the last of her worldly possessions.

I asked the first man, "What did they look like– the men who left this body here?

"Too foggy. Can't see shit in this mess. Got the cataracts. You guys cops?"

"No pulse, Nick."

I did a few close shots with my mobile.

"Sure act like cops, but don't look like any cops I ever saw. Disguised."

She pointed at Kayne, in running shorts and shoes, bending over the corpse and examining the ground around.

"Please keep them back, my love."

The former police officer that I was, waving my arms and saying, "Move along, people. There's nothing here to see," seemed automatic. There weren't many spectators at that early hour, anyway.

Kayne said to the first ragged guy. "Do not move from where you are standing, and don't let anyone come over to the dead man. OK, mate?"

The man nodded, and Kayne began to walk slowly in circles around the corpse. A few times, he stopped and got his nose to the ground. Three times, he picked something up only to toss it away.

A young woman in business casual came up to me as Kayne returned to the body.

"I'm Nancy Morikawa. I am the Japantown Commerce Association Coordinator for the Northern California Cherry Blossom Festival. The parade kicks off at 11 AM, four hours from now. Considering we have a dead body smack in the middle of the festival route, what do we need to do?"

I answered, "Hello. The police have been called. Have your set-up folks move those barricades to here. That's just far enough away. The police will be coming in from Geary Street. Should be quick, but have your volunteers stand by in case we get a crowd."

As we spoke, the EMT truck and a squad car came off the thoroughfare and onto the plaza. A quartet of professionals hopped out of the vehicles and began to take over the area.

"I want two other units coming in from Osaka Boulevard. Need to cordon off the area. Hello, Nick. Who'd ya kill this time?"

"Always with the mocking, Captain. What's the deal, Marty?"

"Sorry, bud. Too many long shifts kicking my fine Black ass... I need this festival like I need a hole in the head. Heard you were on the call-in, and so I thought I'd head up the look-see. You guys on your way home from a night at the gay bars? Pair of party boys...."

I said, "We were running, Marty."

"Just figured, shirtless, wet, and making trouble..."

I harumphed. We made our way over to Kayne.

"Knew this was gonna be big if our two neighborhood private eyes were on the scene. So, what do we got, Sam Spade?"

Kayne said, "Good morning, Officer Simmons. Permission to touch the body."

My husband already had his hand out.

"Not without these, Dr. Sorenson."

Captain Martin Simmons of the San Francisco police snapped his fingers, and his partner tossed each of us a pair of nitrile gloves.

"Dex, Andy, keep back for just about five minutes and let these two semi-clad superstars do their thing. Thank you."

I repeated, "We were running, Marty."

"Umm, humm."

Kayne's movements over the dead man were as soft and gentle as a violinist playing an adagio. He inspected shoes, fingernails, hair follicles, and major muscle groups. He pushed up the pant legs and the sleeves. Removing a shoe, he rotated the ankle, then moved up and did the same with the wrist. No dirt under the nails or bruises on his knuckles to suggest he fought off his assailant. Kayne gently began to turn the dead man.

I recorded the details of the corpse with my phone and made a few notes in the app.

The face was contorted in a hideous death scream. The left side of the head was battered, from forehead to cheekbone, but there was little blood. The right eye was opened in a blank stare, whereas the left was closed with significant bruising around the socket and the side of the nose. That side of the face, all the way back to the ear, was a deep purple. The coloration resembled a port-wine stain. The flesh under the bruise had sagged as if one-half of the man's visage had melted.

Our colleagues with SFPD bent closer to hear what Kayne had to say.

"The man was assaulted elsewhere and moved here. The dirt on the clothing is different from anything in the immediate vicinity of the Pagoda. Lividity and rigor would suggest he has been dead for no less than five to six hours. He was knocked to the ground and dragged on his backside.

"Please observe the traces of dirt and plant material on the seat of his pants as well as on the back of the shirt. The pine needles on his athletic socks, cuffs, and other areas of his dorsal side, along with the clay deposits on the body, may suggest he was murdered within the precincts of the Presidio, specifically near Fort Winfield Scott. Another option is Golden Gate Park."

With an index finger, he moved the pine needles in the palm of his hand. Kayne looked up at the police captain.

"Both of those conclusions would be false."

"So tell me, Doc. Explain it to me like I am in the second grade."

"It is not what is here, but it is what is *not* here. The dominant conifers in both places I mentioned are Monterey Pines. It is important to note that Monterey Pines grow side by side with one of our non-native species, *Eucalyptus obliqua*. The clothes and dirt on the corpse contain no odor of eucalyptus oil. Likewise, there is no litter associated with that species, cones, leaves, etc., found on the body. If indeed the deceased was dragged on a forest floor, even for a short distance, you would see a biological imprint together with a soil sample in the collected detritus that contains evidence of that very deciduous species. A chemical analysis of such will confirm my conclusion.

"No. These are the needles of a Bishop Pine, a rather rare species. It is found mostly in Northern California but definitely not in San Francisco, Captain."

Kayne turned out the deceased's right pants pocket to reveal seven folded bills and an assortment of change. No wallet was found on the body.

"This man attacked at home or in or near his vehicle. You will find his wallet and ID there."

Kayne held out the cash.

"Robbery was not the motive."

He inserted his hand into the left pocket and opened his hand. In his palm was a folded piece of green and white paper, about three and a half inches square.

"What is it, Boss?

Kayne carefully turned the object in his hand. It seemed to be a small sculpted object. The mottled green and tan, fan-like structure was clipped flat at the bottom. The ridges of the fan undulated across the crescent. There was a tiny green twisting form on the top of the object.

"It's a lily pad, and that little guy is a frog."

"Made from paper, my love."

The amphibian glistened with an opalescent sheen.

 Kayne turned his attention back to the dead man's face. He delicately opened the eyelid. Inside, the socket was black, red, and purple. Turning to one of the EMT officers, Kayne asked for forceps or tweezers and a cotton swab.

From the orifice, he extracted a hard stone-like object covered in gore.

I handed him my water bottle. Kayne swabbed the gooey extraction and gave the big, wet Q-tip to the EMT.

After its impromptu bath, the cleansed object was lustrously white and slightly pear-shaped. Martin Simmons held out his hand for a closer look.

Behind us, Nancy Morikawa screamed and fainted on the stone pavers of the Peace Plaza amid the blowing cherry blossoms.

www.ingramcontent.com/pod-product-compliance
Lightning Source LLC
Chambersburg PA
CBHW060303260626
47160CB00007B/2493